HEALING KISS

Without thinking, Trixianna grabbed the pie pan, and it burned her fingers. The steaming pie clattered to the floor. Trixianna pursed her lips tight to hold back a screech from the searing pain. She certainly didn't feel like the hardened criminal that Sheriff Chance Magrane thought she was.

"My God, woman," Chance exploded. Rushing to her side, he grabbed her arm and hurried her over to the pump. With several jerky motions, he pumped cool water onto her stinging fingers.

With her lower lip caught beneath her teeth, she watched as he capably soothed the burn with a gentle touch.

Black hair curled along the backs of his wrists and up his arms. Mesmerized by the sheriff's strong hands, she forced her gaze away.

She shivered as he rubbed small circles into her palm with his thumb and then turned her hand over, pulled it to his face and pressed a kiss into her palm. The touch of his mouth branded Trixianna. Before she could catch her breath, he bestowed a feather-light kiss to the tip of each finger with a velvety, tender warmth. His clear blue eyes smoldered with fire and never once left her face.

She trembled, wrapped in his invisible warmth.

"Better?" he questioned in a hoarse whisper.

She nodded without thinking.

He dipped his head, his eyes closed. He brushed his lips against hers with a sweet tenderness that buckled her knees.

BAD COMPANY

CAROL CARSON

LEISURE BOOKS   NEW YORK CITY

Dedicated to my husband, Darl, who never stopped believing.

A LEISURE BOOK®

November 1998

Published by

Dorchester Publishing Co., Inc.
276 Fifth Avenue
New York, NY 10001

ISBN 0-8439-4448-X

> *What is woman?*
> *—only one of Nature's agreeable blunders.*
> *—Hannah Cowley*

Chapter One

Grand Fork, Kansas, 1888

Trixianna Lawless had never shot a man before, but a stranger with a drawn gun stood motionless in the shadowed opening of her front door. She knew she might not have another chance to save herself. As the sun nudged its head above the eastern horizon, she forced the hammer back on her dear departed papa's Colt revolver. She squeezed her eyes shut and pulled the trigger.

The percussion reverberated in her ears. Nearly paralyzed with fear, she cracked one eye open. Her breath came in heart-stopping gasps. She could see by the bloodstain on his dusty shirt, she'd hit him high in the right shoulder. She watched, horror-struck, as the man's eyes widened in surprise.

He opened his mouth, muttered, "Well, hell—" and

pitched forward at her feet like a felled oak tree. His long body lay over the threshold, one half in her front parlor and the other half on the covered porch.

She slapped a hand over her mouth to hold back a scream of downright terror. She'd killed him.

Gingerly placing her weapon on the damask-covered foyer table, she crouched beside him and pressed shaking fingers against his neck. Finding a steady pulse beneath the warm skin, she thanked God he still drew breath. She scanned the deserted street outside, then grabbed his arms and hauled the lanky trespasser into her parlor, where he proceeded to bleed all over her best braided rug. She turned him over to examine his wound. It was then that Trixianna noticed the star pinned to his shirtfront.

In all of her twenty-five years, had she ever done anything right? The victim of her latest blunder—*the sheriff, of all people*—lay unconscious on the floor.

The bullet had torn through the side of his shoulder and, by some miracle, without seeming to inflict much damage—except indirectly now to the parlor rug. He bore a knot on his temple the size of a walnut, too. He was sure to wake with a pounding headache and a bad temper.

She ran to the kitchen, grabbed several clean towels and dashed back to the unconscious man. She knelt beside him, and her hands trembled as she folded the towels. She placed one beneath his shoulder, and the other she tucked inside his shirt. Pressing down, she prayed it would staunch the bleeding, scanning his pale face in hopes of seeing signs of life. She loosened the tight grip he held on his gun, and replaced it in the holster strapped around his thigh.

Groaning aloud, Trixianna sank onto the nearest

chair. She'd lived here only two weeks, trying not to draw undue attention to herself.

She figured shooting the sheriff would draw undue attention.

Sitting, fretful, she rationalized that there had been prowlers around, Peeping Toms even. Their whispers had echoed outside her window for the past two nights and made her a mite skittish.

Even so, she could hardly believe she'd actually pulled the trigger. She reminded herself that he had trespassed into her home with a drawn gun. And it was not even a reasonable hour of the morning! What could the man possibly have wanted? Even if he was a lawman, the man's intent might have been to murder her in her bed. Or worse. She shuddered at the thought.

Her mouth went dry. With her head propped in her hands, Trixianna fixed both eyes on her houseguest. Under different circumstances, she might have found him handsome. His face, bronzed and weathered from the sun, struck her as possessing a particular strength, and tiny laugh lines around his eyes hinted at a sense of humor. Thick, black brows almost met above the bridge of his straight nose. He needed a shave; black whiskers darkened his jaw. His body, long and lean, stretched almost the length of her parlor, and . . . oh, my stars. Her stomach fluttered and heat stole through her body, making her quiver from head to toe.

Lord above! Was she actually thinking romantically about a man whom she had shot—who'd wanted to shoot *her*?

The sheriff moaned, startling her. She bent over to peer close, her face mere inches from his. His eyes fluttered open, then blinked rapidly. They were a vivid blue and filled with bewilderment.

She jumped to her feet and backed away.

He lifted his head. Fine lines bracketed his mouth and eyes. "You're under arrest," he said, his voice raspy, "for attempted murder of an officer of the law, bank robbery and . . . ruining a perfectly good morning." His head fell back to the floor with a thud. He uttered a muffled curse.

"Sir, I have never robbed a bank," Trixianna protested. Imagine, accusing her of such a thing!

He staggered to his feet, his left hand clutching his injured shoulder. "But it was you that shot me?" he asked, his voice thick and unsteady.

"I did, sir, but you were breaking into my home with your pistol drawn." She tried to look calm and betray nothing of her annoyance . . . or her fear.

"I *am* the sheriff."

"That doesn't give you the right to trespass."

He rose to his full height, his feet spread wide. He appeared a bit unstable, but he filled her parlor with a tall, imposing presence.

Trixianna refused to cower. Even though her nose came only to the middle of his chest, she tilted her head up and scowled at him.

He gave her a tight smile. "As the sheriff I can pretty much do as I damn well please."

"There's no reason to use profanity, sir."

He continued as if she hadn't spoken. "Why shouldn't I just lock you up and throw away the key, Miss West?"

"My name isn't West."

"Oh?"

"No, sir, it's Lawless."

He smiled again. "That's for sure."

Honest to Pete! Attempting to curb her temper with such an exasperating, impolite man proved almost more than she could manage. She took a deep breath. Between clenched teeth, she said, "It's Trixianna Lawless."

Still chuckling, he clamped a hand around her upper arm. "That's a good one, Mad Maggie, but you're coming with me."

He moved toward the door, tugging on her arm. Trixianna tugged back and dug in her heels.

"My name isn't Maggie, I haven't robbed any bank, and anyway, I can't go out without a bonnet." She wrenched her arm free, sidestepping him.

"Good Lord," he groaned. His face paled as he grasped the door frame.

Guilt assailed her when she saw his pain. After all, she had caused it. She stood a minute, thinking about what she should do, then plucked her bonnet off the peg by the door. She would accompany him, but only to see a doctor, and to get these ridiculous charges straightened out. She glanced at him. He glared back.

"I'll come, but not because I have done anything wrong. I see you're having difficulty, and I wouldn't want you to faint again."

He gritted his teeth, his expression implacable. "I never fainted."

"You most certainly did." She propped her hands on her hips, defying him to disagree with her.

"Humph." Grumbling a mild oath, he sank to his knees. Blood seeped through his fingers.

She bent over him, placing the back of her hand against his forehead. "You need a doctor, sir."

He slapped her hand away. "Quit calling me sir. It

makes you sound like a lady and you're no lady."

Trixianna straightened and cleared her throat indignantly. "I *am* a lady and I *don't* rob banks. What would you have me call you, then?"

"Sheriff will do right fine."

For a man squatting on his knees, he seemed very sure of himself, thought Trixianna. His confidence hadn't flagged a bit. She supposed a man in his occupation needed all the confidence he could muster. "Well, all right, then, Sheriff, you do need to see a doctor."

Pulling himself to his feet, he yanked a handkerchief from a pocket, unbuttoned his shirt and placed the scrap of cloth against his wound. He pulled the bloody towel away and handed it to her. Grimacing, he glared at her. "It hurts like hell."

"I would imagine," she commiserated, "although, of course, I've never been shot." He seemed extremely rational for an injured man, but he must be confused in his head to think she could rob innocent people of their hard-earned money. Why, she was as honest as . . . well, surely as honest as he was.

Sheriff Chance Magrane cursed the day he'd decided to arrest Mad Maggie West alone. One woman? How much trouble could one be? Now he stared at her, dumbfounded. About as much trouble as sporting a wooden leg in a roomfull of termites.

Even coated in Kansas prairie dust, she couldn't weigh more than a hundred pounds, and she was at least a foot shorter than he was. But in the blink of an eye she'd managed to bring him to his knees. In fact, he'd been knocked senseless on the fool woman's front stoop. He hadn't fainted, however. How could he ever explain how a woman had gotten the drop on him? He'd be the laughingstock of Grand Fork, for God's sake.

What was she up to anyway? Already dressed in a prim—if not downright dowdy—gray dress, with her hair pulled up tighter than a banker's purse, she looked like his spinster aunt, Tildy O'Hara. Hell, it wasn't even six o'clock yet. Where was she going so early in the morning?

She wore a worried look on her heart-shaped face, and rightly so. Her pink lips were puckered in an expression of concern. For his well-being? He doubted it. More likely, concern for her own hide.

Two weeks ago Monday, Mad Maggie West had robbed the Dena Valley Bank twenty miles due east of Grand Fork. The telegram had described her the same way the wanted poster in his office did: red hair, green eyes, short of stature. The telegram failed to mention the freckles dusting her stubborn nose. There was little doubt in Chance's mind, though, that he had the right woman. She was a dead ringer for the gal in the poster. Her circumstances were right, too—a stranger in town with money in her pocket who kept pretty much to herself.

According to B.J. Johannsen, the mercantile owner, she'd bought all his canned and jarred fruit. Then, his face as red as store-bought flannel, B.J. had explained how she'd purchased all the fancy ladies' unmentionables in his store. Poor B.J. thought he'd be stuck with those "frilly, gol-darned frew-fraws" till Kingdom Come. There weren't many women in Grand Fork, and the few that lived there bought sturdy, durable and, in Chance's mind, boring underpinnings.

Personally, Chance liked to unwrap a woman and

13

discover a little pink lace or red satin and silk. He hoped he'd never see Mad Maggie in those new drawers; that woman was already more trouble than she was worth. He hated to admit that he found himself attracted to her, especially those darn freckles.

She startled Chance by reaching out a hand to him, coming dangerously close to his gun belt. He grabbed her wrist. Surprised by the delicacy of her bones, he loosened his grip but kept a firm hold.

"Honey, don't you ever reach for my gun if you know what's good for you."

"Sheriff, I know your shoulder is paining you, but don't be such a silly goose. I wasn't reaching for your gun. I was merely trying to assist you."

"Silly goose?" Chance would have been insulted if it weren't so damned funny. "Silly goose?"

"It's just an expression," she insisted. She brushed a hand over her hair as if a strand had come loose. He doubted a strand, much less a single hair, could budge loose even in a spring twister. That bun was tight enough to make his already aching head pound harder.

"I'm arresting you, Mad Maggie, so let's just mosey on down to my office where I can lock you up. Then I'll look up the doc so you can stop worrying about me."

She stomped a foot in a peevish show of temper. "Stop calling me Mad Maggie. I can't go to jail. I'm innocent, and besides, I have things to do, you know. I'm telling you I've never robbed a bank."

"Never?"

"Never!"

"We'll see about that." He motioned her out the door.

She started around him, albeit with no small amount of reluctance, her head high, her freckled nose twitching in obvious irritation. Chance figured she hadn't put up more of a fuss because she *had* shot him. Of that she was definitely guilty. Though she did seem more agreeable than he'd expected.

The walk between her home and the jail seemed about as long as an Easter sunrise service, particularly in light of the woman's continual grumbling. *Mistaken identity, never robbed a bank, upstanding citizen, and on and on.* She talked all the way to the jail. He released a sigh of supreme satisfaction when he had her safely behind bars.

Mad Maggie West. And Sheriff Chance Magrane had made the arrest and incarcerated her. Now all he needed to do was find her accomplice, and someone to verify the charges. Humming, he locked up his prisoner with a twist of the key and went in search of the doctor.

Locked up. In a jail cell. Trixianna grimaced as the stale scent of unwashed bodies and what smelled like moldy cheese assailed her nose. There was another scent she didn't recognize and, in all honesty, preferred not to know.

She wasn't frightened, even though her heart beat fast and her palms were damp. No. She was more perturbed than anything else. She knew she was guilty of nothing more than defending herself.

Still, the fact that Grand Fork even had its own jail disconcerted her. How much crime could go on in one small town anyway?

She recalled with irritation why she had moved to Grand Fork, Kansas, in the first place. Because she'd needed to escape Abilene and hadn't wanted to leave Kansas, she'd disembarked from the train at its first stop. What a stupid way to pick a place to live.

For better or worse, though, Grand Fork was now her new home. A curious thing about the town—it didn't have a fork, grand or otherwise. It was a typical small Kansas town, with one main street that was muddy when it rained and dusty when it didn't. It boasted two mercantiles, a bank, a hotel, one restaurant, a hardware store, a livery stable and more than enough saloons. And a jail with two cells.

"This is the most disgusting thing I've ever laid eyes on," Trixianna muttered. She grimaced as she arranged her skirt about her so as little as possible touched the lumpy straw-filled mattress. She looked around, assessing her surroundings.

Aside from the bed, her tiny cell held only a chamber pot, a tin bucket and a three-legged stool. A loud snore brought her attention to the identical cell next to hers. Trixianna couldn't tell the gender of the person inside since all she could see was a back, but because of his dress, she guessed it was a man. She did think she recognized the odor emanating from the body. "Phew!"

He was sleeping off a drunk. Even in sleep he wore a hat, a moth-eaten, stained, ten-gallon hat of indeterminate color. Aside from the hat, however, he wore nothing but red-flannel underwear with a rip in the buttocks that displayed one lean, pale hip. The sight brought heat to Trixianna's cheeks. She averted her gaze to take in the rest of her temporary abode.

The sheriff's office and jail had one small window covered in greased paper that allowed in very little light. The single room, though small, held a scarred, flat-topped maple desk, surprisingly neat, and a swivel chair behind it. On the desk was a tintype of a young woman with her arms around . . . a goat? How odd. Beyond that was a potbellied stove, two wooden chairs, and a locked gun cabinet. Behind the desk the sheriff had nailed auction notices and wanted posters.

Trixianna gasped.

Someone had put her image on a wanted poster!

Below the sketch of her face were these words:

WANTED
DEAD OR ALIVE
MARGARET (MAD MAGGIE) WEST
RED HAIR, GREEN EYES, SHORT STATURE
FOR BANK ROBBERY, GENERAL THIEVERY AND HORSE STEALING
$500 REWARD
CONTACT SHERIFF IN DENA VALLEY OR ABILENE

That indifferent lout of a sheriff had left Trixianna alone for over two hours, and according to the timepiece pinned to the breast of her dress, it was approaching nine in the morning. Where was the man?

Although Granny had always told her it was unladylike to squirm, Trixianna found herself doing so. Beneath her posterior, the mattress complained. She grimaced in distaste and stood up. She stomped her feet once to bring a little warmth into them, causing them to ache worse. They felt like blocks of ice. The cold cell was damp, and no fire burned in the stove to warm the room.

Making sure her snoring cell mate was still turned away from her, she arched her back. She released a sigh of relief. If only she could relieve the chill in the jail as easily. She paced the wooden floor, hoping to bring feeling into her frigid toes.

Her stomach growled, and she realized that the sheriff had hauled her away not only without a word of apology, but also before she'd had the chance to eat. Hot oatmeal with cinnamon and raisins. A cup of steaming chamomile tea. Her mouth watered, reminding her that her pies weren't getting baked by themselves either.

Sinclair's Fine Restaurant's patrons would be going without pies this dinner hour. Mr. Sinclair himself had informed Trixianna only Friday that business had improved considerably since he had begun serving her "delicious, home-baked pastries." What would he say when she didn't come round?

Trixianna tugged on the ribbons of her bonnet, and in a fit of pique tossed it to the floor. Remorse pricked her conscience. An image of her granny shaking a finger at her and scolding like an outraged blue jay sent her scurrying over to pick it up and place it upon the cot. She smoothed the fabric with chilled fingers, and contented herself by imagining berating the sheriff when he returned . . . if he returned.

How long did it take to get a little wound like the one she'd given him bandaged anyway? He should be finished and releasing her from this ridiculous situation . . . now.

"Argh."

Trixianna whirled at the sound. Her companion rose from his bed and stretched his arms above his head. His eyes widened when he caught her staring, but otherwise he showed no other reaction. He simply removed his over-large hat and sketched her a bow. A smile played upon his lips. He seemed not at all embarrassed about his casual state of undress—that is, his red-flannel drawers and drooping gray socks. His silver hair stood up in spiked clumps all over his head. She was so astonished by his appearance and demeanor, she stared openmouthed at the man.

He looked at the hat in his hands and held it away from his body, a look of utter disgust on his face. With a flick of his wrist, he tossed it up on his cot.

He cleared his throat. "Madam, what brings you to our humble abode?" He spoke in an eloquent baritone, a sharp contrast to his bedraggled appearance. His very proper British accent tickled Trixianna no end. She'd heard that the English were interesting people and often infectiously eccentric.

"I shot the sheriff," she admitted.

"You killed him?" His tone of voice betrayed obvious astonishment.

"Oh, n-no," Trixianna stammered, taken aback. She pressed a hand to her heart. "I just wounded him. It was a near thing. Actually, I didn't want to hurt him, just scare him away."

He coughed, covering his mouth with one hand. Although it was an obvious ploy to cover his laughter, she found the attempt endearing.

He stepped forward, gripping the bars that separated them. A mischievous gleam came into his eyes. "And what did our fine sheriff do then, my dear?"

"He fainted."

This was apparently more than the man could stand. He backed up, roaring with laughter. He fell onto the cot, pounding the mattress with his fists as tears coursed down his face. "He fainted," he repeated, gasping for air. "Sheriff Magrane fainted. Oh, that's delicious. Simply delicious."

He suddenly jumped to his feet, then crossed the expanse between them. He gripped the bars once more. "Then what happened?"

"He arrested me."

"What for?" His avid gaze never left her face.

"For robbing a bank . . . b-but I didn't do it."

"You jolly well did not."

Astonished, she asked, "But how would you know that, sir?"

He tossed his head with a flourish, pomposity discernible in his every move. His eyes flashed with outrage on her behalf. "Why, you are obviously a woman of breeding and refinement. Why, that galoose—no, what is that word you people use over here?"

"Galoot?" she suggested. Several others, none as complimentary, came to mind.

"That isn't what I was looking for, but it will do. That galoot wouldn't know a fox's brush from a hairbrush."

Trixianna wasn't sure she knew the difference either, but she knew that it wasn't complimentary to the sheriff. She liked that.

The man's expressive face changed, turning somber. "I have been somewhat remiss, madam."

"Oh?"

"We haven't been properly introduced." He bowed again. Reaching through the bars, he took her hand in his. "May I?"

Taking her silence for acquiescence, he continued. "Alistair Burns, the sixth Viscount of Huxford."

"Oh, my, are you a lord then?"

"Yes, well . . ." he mumbled, shrugging his shoulders. "I know you Americans hate titles, and when you try to use them you muddle them ever so badly. Although I'm sure you are that rare exception, madam."

She grinned at the compliment.

"Forget the lordship nonsense. My friends call me Burnsey."

"How nice to meet you, Burnsey. These circumstances aren't what I would prefer, however."

"I fully agree."

"I'm Trixianna Lawless."

He still held her fingers through the bars. He brought them to his lips and gave her a whisper of a kiss across the back of her chilled hand. "Charmed."

Trixianna felt an unwelcome blush creep into her cheeks. "So why are you in here, Burnsey?"

He leaned her way, his face mere inches from hers, and whispered, "I have been known to indulge a bit."

"Oh?"

"Yes, it's a fact. When I drink, I get this urge to gamble, and when I gamble, I always lose my shirt." He shrugged his shoulders. "And my trousers, and my waistcoat, and my boots apparently." He frowned at his stockinged feet. "Whatever I'm wearing. It's all so terribly dull, you see. Someone usually informs Sheriff Magrane when I go on one of my benders, so before I bare myself to the whole of Grand Fork, he escorts me here, where I get the chance to sober up without embarrassing myself further. This time, somewhere along the way, I misplaced my bowler and ended up with that monstrosity." He gestured at the cowboy hat on the cot. "I'm sure that is some cowpoke's idea of a joke."

"The sheriff locks you up just for drinking too much?"

"Oh, I'm not locked in." He pushed open the door and, to her astonishment, strolled out of the cell. Then he sauntered back in, pulling the door shut behind him. He gave her a benign smile.

"You mean, I'm freezing to death and all this time, you could have started a fire in the stove?" She instantly felt appalled at her bad manners, but he didn't even seem to notice.

His smile disappeared, and his face reddened. "I beg your pardon, Miss Lawless. I wasn't aware of your condition. Let me remedy that straightaway."

He hustled out of the cell, seemingly unconcerned that she could see his bare skin. He had the stove going in no time.

He walked around the desk, opened the middle drawer and removed a set of keys. As if he'd done it on several occasions before, he returned to her cell and unlocked the door. He gestured her out. "Come stand by the stove and warm up."

Trixianna felt her jaw drop . . . for the second time since she'd arrived in the Grand Fork jail. She took an abrupt step, unsure if she should leave the cell.

"Come, come, Miss Lawless, I accept full responsibility." He leaned over to whisper in her ear. "Maybe we'll even plan your escape."

He took her elbow and escorted her across the room. Like a gentleman, he pulled both chairs near the stove and waited until she seated herself. The warmth of the stove helped dissipate the chill in her body.

He hustled around and started the coffee. When it bubbled, he rose to pour each of them a cup.

"It's not tea, but you Americans seem to adore this stuff even when it's thick enough to float a boat." After handing a cup to Trixianna, he sat down and crossed one knee over the other in a casual pose. She tried to keep her eyes on his kind face instead of the gaps between the buttons of his drawers.

She nodded in agreement. "That's true enough, Burnsey, but I myself drink a cup of chamomile tea every morning. I feel it's good for ill humors."

He nodded. "I just knew you were a woman of refinement. Now tell me, Miss Lawless, how did the sheriff think you of all people could rob a bank?"

She turned, pointing to the picture on the wall behind the desk.

Burnsey's head swung around, and his eyes widened. Coffee sloshed out of his cup and onto the wooden floor, where it left a widening brown stain. "God's teeth," he muttered as a strained expression spread across his face. His head swiveled back to her. "Why, it's the spitting image of you."

"I know." The coffee churned in her empty stomach as the truth hit her. The drawing *did* look like her. What chance did she have of defending herself? No one in Grand Fork knew her. No one would come to her aid. She was alone.

Burnsey reached over and patted her hand in a fatherly fashion. "It may look like you, but I know it's not."

"Thank you, Burnsey, but the sheriff thinks it's me. What can I possibly do?"

As if conjured up by their conversation, the door swung open and in he strolled. He'd washed up and changed into a clean shirt of forest green. He was still unshaven, but the shadow of his beard didn't mask the pale, strained expression. He walked with a stiff gait, the arm beneath his injured shoulder held close to his side.

His thick brows drew together in a frown as his gaze

passed first over her, then over Burnsey. To her amazement, a flush started above his shirt collar and worked its way up his face, forming two crimson splotches on his cheeks. Trixianna watched in fascination as he waggled a finger between the collar of his shirt and his neck.

"Dammit, Burnsey, you could at least cover yourself with a blanket."

"Good morning to you, too, Sheriff Magrane," Burnsey replied. "Where's your hat? I never realized you even had hair, but a fine head of hair it is."

The sheriff rolled his eyes heavenward. "I lost it," he grumbled. He slanted a grim look at Burnsey. "Just who the hell said you could release my prisoner?"

"How's your shoulder, Sheriff?" Trixianna asked, worried about the drawn look on his features. She was afraid he might faint again.

"I'll live," he muttered.

He cleared his throat. She glanced up to find him staring hard at her. A muscle quivered at his darkened jaw. She had been rubbing her free hand up and down her arm to get warmth into it. Under his intense stare, she self-consciously stopped the motion.

He contemplated her a moment, his eyes widening. He swiveled his head around, then grimaced at the sudden movement. He cast a brief look at the stove. His left hand absently clasped his right arm close to his side.

"Well, hell." He strode over and awkwardly poured himself a cup of coffee from the pot warming on the stove. "Thanks for getting the fire and the coffee started, Burnsey, but you still haven't answered my question."

He moved around his desk, his footsteps slow and

deliberate. He sat down, placed the cup on the desk in front of him and crossed his legs at the ankles. With a grimace on his face, he laced his hands across his flat stomach. His gaze stayed riveted on Trixianna, and he seemed to be studying her, his expression one of cynical amusement.

"God's teeth, Sheriff, she's not going anywhere."

"Huh," he said.

She noted his clenched jaw, and watched his narrow gaze fix on her. "When will I get out of here?" Trixianna asked. Her voice came out sounding shakier than she would have liked. The wanted poster had her more than a little worried. Terrified was more like it.

"When the federal marshal gets to town."

"When will that be?"

"Well, let's see," he said. He leaned back and closed his eyes. "I sent a telegram to the sheriff over in Dena Valley and to the one in Abilene."

"Abilene?" Trixianna asked in a choked voice.

His eyes opened, the pale blue orbs searching her face. One corner of his mouth twisted upward. "I expect we'll see him when he gets here."

"I can't stay here," wailed Trixianna. Her voice broke with uncertainty.

"You should have thought of that before you robbed the bank over in Dena Valley. Folks just can't abide bank robbers. Why, I remember back when I was just a boy, I heard tell that some rascal tried to rob the bank right here in Grand Fork. He was caught red-handed, and hauled off to jail. This very one, in fact.

"The sheriff—it was ole fiery-tempered Red Eubanks then—he didn't put up with much of anything. He just took that fella out and hanged him from a tree right at the end of Main Street. There's a big old cottonwood near the river just the right size for a hanging. By God, the criminal element stayed away from Grand Fork for quite a spell after that."

Trixianna swallowed a lump in her throat that felt the size of a watermelon. "Oh, my stars," she whispered.

"Quit trying to scare her, Chance. You know she didn't rob any bank," said Burnsey, coming to her defense. He stood up and placed a comforting hand on her shoulder.

"Besides, I want to hear about your fainting spell." He winked at Trixianna.

They both turned their heads in time to see Sheriff Chance Magrane blush like a schoolboy.

"Well, hell," he muttered.

*What one beholds of a woman
is the least part of her.*
—Ovid

Chapter Two

Chance found his hat.

He picked the black Stetson up off the porch where it had fallen off his head at the time of his *incident*. He pulled it low on his forehead and released a sigh of contentment. All morning he'd felt half-naked without it.

His shoulder ached like a kick in the . . . well, it hurt bad. He was hungry, tired and feeling downright surly. He rubbed his chin in thought as he debated the wisdom of crossing the threshold into Mad Maggie's house. The scratchy growth beneath his fingertips reminded him why he'd risen early and left home before he'd shaved or eaten. He'd wanted to get the jump on her. Instead, she'd gotten the jump on him.

Just yesterday he'd seen her as she walked ahead of him down Main Street pulling a child's wagon behind her. A red-checked tablecloth had covered the contents, so he'd been unable to tell what she'd carted around town. Dressed the same as any other Grand Fork woman, in a plain dress and poke bonnet of dove gray, she wouldn't have drawn his attention except for one thing. Well, maybe two, he admitted to himself. The dress had done little to disguise the shapely curves beneath the fabric, and he was after all a man. He couldn't help but notice a young, good-looking woman.

In addition, she had stopped outside Sinclair's Restaurant to speak with Sinclair himself, who'd stood on the stoop frowning into the street. Bertram Sinclair was known as an incorrigible rascal, and he was known to speak only under duress. What had startled Chance into eavesdropping was hearing Bert actually chuckle when she stopped to chat.

"Why, ma'am, I can't begin to tell you how happy I am to see you this morning." His jowly cheeks had crinkled in an honest-to-goodness smile.

That hadn't sounded like the Bert Sinclair that Chance knew. Chance had leaned against a storefront and lowered the brim of his Stetson to hide a grin. He had never before seen anything on the man's face besides a scowl.

"Mr. Sinclair, it's a pleasure to see you, too." Her husky voice had frozen Chance in place. She had looked a bit familiar, but she had to be new to Grand Fork. He could never have forgotten that sultry voice. Although her bonnet had concealed the upper half of her face, he'd detected a button nose and a decidedly determined chin.

The two had entered the restaurant together. Chance had been debating whether to follow when the woman suddenly exited, her wagon empty except for the folded table covering. She'd dropped several coins in her reticule and looked up. She'd caught him watching her, and had given him a tentative smile.

It was then that he had recognized her from the wanted poster in his office. Shocked, he'd belatedly remembered to tip his hat. She'd given him a bewildered nod, and had taken off down the boardwalk, her skirts swishing. The wheels of her empty wagon had screeched until they had become a faint echo as she had turned the corner and disappeared. His head reeling with excitement, he'd sprinted after her, and watched her enter the Miller parsonage next to the Methodist church.

Pastor Miller had taken a six-month missionary assignment at the Kansas Indian reservation. Chance had thought his house was empty. Obviously not. He'd wondered who had gone and rented it to a wanted criminal.

Now, a day later, he'd found himself standing on the porch—the same one where she'd shot him.

He stepped inside. As his eyes adjusted to the dim interior, a stain on the braided rag rug caught his attention. It was his own blood. His shoulder throbbed in recognition.

The Millers had left their own furnishings, and from what he could tell, the room wasn't much changed. He stepped through the parlor and into the adjoining kitchen. He stopped, scanning the scene he found there.

All the available space overflowed with cooking equipment. Bowls, spices, measuring utensils and a sifter with bits of flour still clinging to its metallic sides covered the round oilcloth-covered table. A half-dozen tin pie plates lined the sideboard. A bowl of

29

drying, brown apple slices stood in the sink. Chance grabbed a slice and tossed it in his mouth. His mouth puckered with the tart taste.

With a single finger, he pushed his hat to the crown of his head. He stuck his hands in his back pockets, his thoughts jumbled with possibilities.

She liked to bake?

She appeared to have a considerable sweet tooth . . . or a lover with one? Her accomplice? And if so, where was he?

"Where the hell are my pies?"

Chance spun at the angry voice and the sound of stomping boots on the front porch and across the parlor. His hand went to the gun at his hip. When he saw Bertram Sinclair enter the kitchen, he lowered his arm.

"Look at this!" Bert gestured wildly around the kitchen, his arms spinning like a child's tops. His squat body quivered with apparent indignation. "My pies aren't even in the oven yet."

Chance spoke calmly, even though his heart beat a strong tattoo against his chest. "Bert, what are you doing here?" He stared at the red-faced man, who looked mad enough to kick his own dog.

Bert shook his fist in Chance's face and thundered, "What are *you* doing here and where the hell is that Lawless woman?"

"She's not your concern." Chance hung onto his temper by a slim thread. He stared at Bert until the man lowered his arm.

"The hell you say." Bert scowled. His eyes scanned the kitchen. "What about my pies?"

"They aren't going to get made today, so take yourself on back to the diner and save your misery for someone else."

"Sheriff, I got a business to run." His eyes burned still, but he'd dropped his threatening demeanor, maybe realizing that Chance's tolerance was exceedingly low.

"Then do it, Sinclair," he barked.

The sound of Bert's retreating footsteps echoed in Chance's ear as he took one last look around the kitchen. Other than the kitchen fixings, nothing looked out of place. He even checked inside every cupboard and container, be it a sack of potatoes or a tin of coffee. But there was no indication in this room that the woman incarcerated in the Grand Fork jail was a bank robber.

Well, what had he thought he'd find?—sacks of money stashed under the sink, or maybe her accomplice hiding behind the stove? Annoyed with himself, he moved down the hall to the bedroom.

The door stood ajar. He gave it a push, his gun hand ready. The door creaked as it swung open. Hesitant to step inside, he stood beneath the lintel scanning the empty room. Even under the most ordinary circumstances, a woman's bedroom made Chance uneasy. He suddenly had a nightmarish vision of an irate father toting a shotgun and an unwilling groom and a weeping bride standing before a preacher. He gave an involuntary shiver.

Inside, the bed was unmade. A white coverlet had been haphazardly thrown over its head and the sheets lay tangled at the foot. Her pink night rail lay puddled on the floor near his booted feet. Chance knelt down to pick it up, then stopped, his thumb just brushing the satin fabric. He yanked his hand back. He sucked in his breath as warmth curled deep in his groin and his head spun with unbidden thoughts. He released a slow breath. A breeze floated through the open window, fluttering the curtain and sheets. Her scent lingered in the room, surrounding him, exciting him. He turned to leave.

As he spun, his boot struck something soft and unfamiliar and a screech not unlike a pig squealing pierced his ears. He looked down. A white cat, the long fur along his back erect and his tail twitching, stared back with furious yellow eyes. Chance quickly lifted his foot and reached down to soothe the angry feline. The cat hissed, scratched his outstretched palm, then skittered away.

"What are you doing to that poor kitty, Sheriff?" The silky voice of Annie V. startled Chance. His face burned, but he didn't dare turn around quite yet. His half-aroused body was slow to quiet.

She sidled around him to stare up into his face. "Ah, honey, did I surprise you?"

"Well, hell." He shoved his Stetson lower on his brow.

She stood beside him, peeking into the room. "Ooh," she crooned. Her avid gaze took in the rumpled bed. She turned her animated face upward and looked, good and long, at his face before she whispered, "Honey, you haven't visited us in a while, have you?"

"I've been busy, Annie V.," he grumbled.

"Sure you have, honey. I heard. How's the shoulder?" She kept her avid gaze on his face, but one of her hands rested lightly on his arm.

He shook his head and smiled as he steered her outside and onto the porch. He would catch hell with the busybodies in town if he had to explain how he and the owner of the Annie V. Saloon had come to be alone in the bedroom of the minister's home.

"I hear you fainted." Her tone was conversational; her eyes twinkled with amusement.

He swore aloud. "I didn't faint."

Annie V. chuckled. She bestowed a kiss on his heated cheek. "Whatever you say, honey."

"What the hell are you doing here anyway, Annie?" He crossed his arms over his chest and leaned against the porch rail, doing his best to look unperturbed.

She was dressed as if she were on her way to a fancy shindig, in an unladylike, but easy-on-the-eyes, low-cut dress. The thing was striped in two shades of god-awful purple, and she wore pink stockings and pink shoes. Her full breasts looked plumb ready to burst out of the damned dress. She looked about as out of place on the streets of Grand Fork as that Mad Maggie woman did in his jail. Startled by that thought, he wondered where it had come from.

"I always pick up Trixianna's apple pandowdy at noon," she said.

"Trixianna?"

"You know, Trixianna Lawless? That nice lady whose bed you were just slobbering over. The lady who shot you and made you swoon. The very same lady you're holding in your jail. The—"

"All right," he interrupted. "All right."

"I was just hoping she made my pandowdy before you hauled her away. Do you honestly think that sweet, innocent Trixianna could do something like rob a bank? Really, Chance, I thought you were smarter than that."

"Innocent?"

"As an angel in heaven."

He stared at her.

"As a newborn lamb."

His lips twisted as he tried to hold back a smile.

"As a June bride."

A laugh worked its way up his throat.

"And as pure as the driven snow."

"Her?" Chance threw back his head and roared with laughter. "So am I, Annie V., and so are you."

Trixianna had watched Sheriff Magrane leisurely finish his coffee before he'd locked her away in the jail cell. Before leaving, he'd handed her a dried-out biscuit that he'd pulled from his top desk drawer. It looked as tasty as baled hay, but she took it and, because she had been brought up with good manners, had thanked him all the same. He'd informed her in no uncertain terms that it would have to do until supper. Next, he'd warned Burnsey to keep his hands off the keys and to start minding his own business.

He'd left then, backing out the door, his eyes staring daggers at the both of them. Burnsey had found his clothes in a bundle on the floor, and had also left, with a promise to return with his eminently respected attorney, who, he'd promised, would waste no time in releasing Trixianna from the horrid cell she now occupied.

By late afternoon, the eminently respected attorney had yet to arrive. Trixianna found herself bored and anxious and staring at the wanted poster that had begun this whole mess. Under scrutiny, she and the woman depicted there really looked nothing alike. That woman's nose was bigger, much bigger, and her eyes were as cold as snow.

34

She admitted to herself that she could see the similarities and how the sheriff might mistake her for this Mad Maggie person. . . . though her own face wasn't nearly as round and her eyes weren't quite as squinty. She could certainly understand how the sheriff could misconstrue her reasons for shooting him. What she couldn't comprehend was how, after talking with her and hearing her explanations, he still thought she was a criminal. How could he *still* think she was Mad Maggie West?

She, Trixianna Lawless, who had never done anything remiss in her entire life? She was honest, open-minded and optimistic. She considered herself a forward-thinking woman. For twenty-five years she had been a dutiful daughter, a considerate sister, a generous and faithful churchgoer. She had been her papa's willing cook and housekeeper in Abilene until his death a year ago.

After her papa had died, she and Georgette, her twin sister, had continued living in the house that had been their family home. When Georgette had married four months ago, her husband, Jonathan, had naturally moved in with them. Papa had left the house to the girls equally, and both sisters had agreed that the only thing to do was to continue to share the dwelling.

But now Trixianna was alone, estranged from Georgette because of a misunderstanding that started out so simply . . . and ended so wretchedly. She remembered the day vividly.

"Why, Jonathan, it's a dove. Georgette will love it." Trixianna had held the delicate porcelain figurine up to the sun shining in the bedroom window. She turned it this way and that so that its tiny features caught the

light. She smiled at the fragile simplicity of its design.

Jonathan's eyes glowed with pleasure. "I sure hope so. Our three-month anniversary is tomorrow and I wanted to get her something special."

"You're celebrating your three-month anniversary?"

Jonathan blushed. "We celebrate every month."

"I never knew you were such a romantic, Jonathan." She kissed his heated cheek in an attempt to ease his embarrassment. "I'm sure she'll be pleased." Trixianna carefully rewrapped the statuette in brown paper and placed it back in the box from which Jonathan had removed it.

She got down on her knees to put it back beneath the bed, where it would stay hidden until tomorrow. As she pushed, the box snagged on a wooden floorboard. Trixianna thrust her head under the bed. She slid the package farther back. Although the box was now concealed from view, in the process the front hem of her skirt got stuck on a nail sticking out of the floor.

"Is something wrong, Trixianna?" Jonathan lowered his head and peered at her.

"Yes, I'm stuck." From where she was, half under the bed, she yanked, but the fabric refused to budge. "Could you pull my dress to the side? I've caught it on a nail and I really don't want to rip it."

Jonathan leaned over her back, pushing her skirt aside and partially baring her legs.

"That's good, dear," she stated. "I've almost got it."

"Can I do anything more to help?" he asked. "Perhaps if I get under the bed, I could free it."

"No, no. No sense you getting stuck under here, too. I just need to scoot to the side a bit." Trixianna wiggled sideways, tangling her skirts even more.

Unfortunately Jonathan discovered he was standing

on her skirt at the same time she wiggled. He lost his balance and fell forward onto Trixianna's bottom. He clutched at the coverlet to keep from falling. She cried out as his weight toppled over her. "Jonathan!"

It was at this unfortunate moment that Georgette walked into the room. Her screech resounded against the four walls, sounding like a cat with his whiskers caught in a milk separator.

Jonathan scrambled to his feet, pivoting to face his wife. His hands still clutching the coverlet, he pulled it completely off the bed when he turned. Trixianna ripped her dress free and backed out from under the bed as fast as she could, but as she did, the quilt caught her skirt and effectively raised it up almost to her waist. She flushed miserably as she stood and tried to straighten out her skirt with one hand while holding onto the box with the other. She glanced at Jonathan, who also wore a pained expression. As she watched, his face turned from crimson to white as fresh milk. His mouth opened and closed, but no words came forth.

Georgette had a hand pressed over her mouth, and she was visibly trembling. She gulped hard, tears streaming down her face.

"How c-could you?" she choked out, her watery eyes on Jonathan but her words aimed at Trixianna. "With my own h-husband."

Georgette spun toward Trixianna, turning hurt-filled eyes on her. "I despise you."

A violent shiver ran down Trixianna's spine. She had never seen such wrath on her sister's face. In desperation, she spoke. "You've misunderstood what's going on here, Georgette. Nothing! Nothing is going on. Honestly."

Georgette snatched the box from her hands. Roughly,

she unwrapped the package. "So now you're getting presents, too." She threw the lovely figurine across the room, where it hit the wall with a resounding crash. Crystalline shards rained to the floor like hot teardrops.

Georgette burst into deep, tortured sobs and ran from the room.

Jonathan gave Trixianna an apologetic look. She shooed him away with a wave of her hand. Her voice shaking with apprehension, she said, "Take care of your wife."

There was no consoling Georgette that day or the next. She blamed Trixianna. She would not accept their explanations, so Trixianna had left Abilene, feeling disgraced and humiliated for something she hadn't even done. As she'd boarded the train for Grand Fork, Kansas, an unknown town chosen simply because it was the train's first stop, she'd hoped Georgette would come to her senses soon and allow her to return home. . . .

Trixianna's stomach grumbled with nausea as she recalled that dreadful day.

But nausea wasn't the only reason her stomach grumbled. She'd eaten only that one stale biscuit all day. Hunger gnawed at her as well.

When the door swung inward, she breathed a sigh of relief. She hoped Burnsey's lawyer was here to release her.

No such luck.

Sheriff Magrane sauntered inside, tipped his hat, then tossed it onto a chair. He folded his arms across his chest and leaned back against the desk. As he studied her with something akin to satisfaction, his clear blue eyes glittered.

"So, *Miss West*, how are we doing?" he drawled.

His emphasis on the name didn't go unnoticed by Trixianna. From her perch on the cot, she raised her eyes to his, and bestowed upon him what she hoped was a withering glance.

He gave an amused chuckle.

So much for withering glances. She stood up suddenly, and as she did, her heavy chignon finally slipped its pins and tumbled down her back. She grimaced, then stepped close to the bars of her cell, her hands clasped together, her head held high. Much to her chagrin, her unruly hair tickled her neck and fell into her eyes. With a quick shake of her head, she tossed the burnished mass over her shoulder. She kept her hair tightly bound on purpose. When she wore it loose she felt it made her look girlish, and apparently so did the sheriff, for he gaped at her, his eyes wide with shocked surprise.

My God, she's beautiful.

Chance stared, tongue-tied. With her rich, glowing russet hair loose, she managed to look downright erotic even dressed in her prim, high-necked gown. Her hair caught the scant afternoon light and surrounded her with a luminous halo of red-gold. The mist of her hair framed an oval face of near perfection—smoldering green eyes, ivory and rose complexion and a full mouth that begged to be kissed. And a handful of kissable cinnamon freckles. His lips tingled at the thought of doing just that while he ran his fingers through the heavy mass of her hair. While lying on that mussed iron bed back in her—

What the hell was he thinking?

Chance straightened and turned his back on his prisoner. His blood pounded, his face grew hot. His trousers became uncomfortably snug. With painstaking care, he moved around his desk and gingerly sat down. He kept his gaze on his desk, pretending to read the opened newspaper that lay there, until he felt he could look at her again without making a fool of himself.

He glanced up and gulped. She stood with her hands still clasped together in front of her, her delicate brows slanted in a frown. Her unwieldy hair spilled about her like a shimmering russet waterfall. He gulped again, glad of the desk in front of him and the bars that separated them.

"Are you all right, Sheriff? You look a little pale."

"Huh," he muttered, keeping his eyes down. He drummed his fingers on the wooden desktop, feigning disinterest, when all his thoughts were centered on the lady bank robber in his jail and all the indecent things he wanted to do to her. She had rattled him so badly his hands shook.

"Sheriff, I know you'd like to go home and rest, so why don't you just release me under my own recognizance? I promise to stay put."

"Huh." *Jesus, Mary and Joseph.* He sounded like the town idiot. He *felt* like the town idiot. He glanced up and blinked. She was observing him with an intensity he found unnerving. She was obviously trying to catch his eye.

"Recognizance," she repeated. "You know, you release me, I stay put until I have to appear before the judge or the marshal or whomever."

His gaze on the newspaper, he answered, "I know what the damn word means, but my answer is no."

"Why not?"

"Because I don't trust you, that's why not."

"Look at me, Sheriff."

She had no idea how sensuous her voice was. He looked at her, drinking in her beauty. How could he have not noticed her before?

"I'm hungry, you're tired and we both just want to go home and forget this day ever happened."

"Amen," he muttered. He concentrated on his aching shoulder, and the heaviness in his groin slowly eased. If he kept his gaze below her eyes and above her breasts, he could do fine. That stubborn nose of hers reminded him that she was a criminal and not one of Annie V.'s good-time girls.

Suddenly, the door banged open and in burst Burnsey, followed by a well-dressed man, who looked somewhat familiar to Chance, and Annie V. Following close on her heels came Bertram Sinclair and, God save him from interfering relatives, Chance's own aunt, Tildy O'Hara.

They all bore dinner trays in their hands.

Chance moaned aloud.

"Well," Tildy asked, her voice like sour milk, "were you planning on starving her to death?"

"Lord, Tildy, she robbed a bank. She shot me."

"So, that means you can't feed the poor child?"

"Well, hell. It kind of slipped my mind what with all the confusion."

Tildy scowled at him. He remembered the look from his youth. He was now treading on extremely thin ice.

"She's not a child, and I was gonna feed her—eventually."

Tildy snorted before giving Chance an unpleasant glance. Uh-oh. He was in for it now.

"Well, I was." Christ, now he sounded like a kid, defending himself. He forced himself to settle down.

Glancing at the group crowded into his small office, he murmured, "Do you think she needs four meals?"

"I just brought her a little something from the diner," admitted the store owner with a scowl. "You know, for all the pies she's brought me and all." He dropped the tray on the desk and scuttled out the door, glowering at anyone who might dare to comment.

For a moment, all was silent until Annie V. spoke. "And I consider Trixianna a friend—"

"Thank you, Annie."

Chance had almost forgotten his prisoner. He looked over at her now. Her deep green eyes glittered with what looked like genuine tears of gratitude. He almost choked on his disbelief. How could a cold-blooded criminal be grateful about such a little thing?

"—so I was going to share my supper with her."

Burnsey spoke last. "I was coming with my lawyer anyway, and I thought she might be hungry." The short, submissive man with Burnsey looked none too thrilled to be in the jailhouse. In fact, Chance thought he seemed likely to faint, and he looked about as law-yerly as Chance's gelding down at the livery.

"Now, wait a doggone minute," Chance bellowed. Everyone but Tildy jumped. "Who is *this* fella? I don't recall seeing his shingle hanging anywhere in Grand Fork."

"I'm not from Grand Fork." The deep bass that sprung from the lawyer surprised Chance. He'd been expecting more in the way of a squeaky outhouse door, not the somber tones of an English aristocrat.

"And you are?"

"James," he replied. "I'm originally from London.

42

And no, I haven't put out a *shingle* as you so quaintly put it. I don't need to."

"Why's that?"

"Chance," said Tildy. "That is neither here nor there. This woman needs to be fed. Open up this cell immediately."

"Aunt Tildy," he remonstrated. "This is none of—"

"Don't you take that tone with me, young man." She placed her hands on her hips. The icy glare she threw at Chance quelled his retort. Tildy was a tyrant when riled. "Furthermore, have you let her out at all today?"

"Hell, no."

"Did you even think of her needs?"

"What needs?" he demanded. Christ, the woman was a criminal. Didn't anyone realize that but him?

Tildy turned her head and pointed a plump finger at the chamber pot in the corner of Trixianna's cell.

Burnsey snickered. Annie V. just simply guffawed. Heat worked its way up Chance's neck and tightened his collar. He unbuttoned the top button on his shirt, shrugging his shoulders. His head throbbed, his gunshot wound ached, and now this. He shook his head, waiting for Tildy to ruin what was left of this day. What he wouldn't give for a hot bath and a bottle of cheap whiskey.

"Do you expect a woman to use that *thing* in front of you and God and all creation?"

"She's a wanted criminal, Tildy. She might escape. Do you expect me to escort her out to the privy every time she needs to . . . um, you know . . ." Damn! He was blushing.

"Yes, I do. You were brought up to be a gentleman and you're not acting like one. What's more—"

Annie V. interrupted. "I guess it's time to be leaving." She set the tray on the desk beside Bert Sinclair's. "I'll come back tomorrow, Trixianna."

"Thank you, Annie." Her soft voice held a slight tinge of wonder. Chance glanced at her, surprised by the delicate hue of pink glowing in her cheeks.

"I do believe we'll take our leave now also, dear," Burnsey said. "I think Miss O'Hara has things well in hand." He bowed to Tildy, who quirked a brow at his noble gesture.

"Why, thank you, Mr. Burns. I believe I do."

"I'm sure of it," he replied, backing out the door and taking the superfluous tray with him. The so-called lawyer followed him out.

"And furthermore, Chance Magrane," Tildy said, "I will not allow this young woman to sleep on that—" With a disgusted look on her face, she waved her hand at the cot in Trixianna's cell. "—Filthy, bug-infested thing that you men actually call a bed."

"If she doesn't sleep there, then where would you have her sleep? In my own bed at home?"

"Exactly."

"What!"

"Have you ever had a woman in jail before?"

"Well, no."

"My point exactly." She patted Chance's cheek. "I've spoken to the mayor and he agrees with me. Miss Lawless will be sleeping in your house tonight."

Woman is man's confusion.
—Vincent of Beauvais

Chapter Three

"No way in hell am I letting her out of this jail."

Fascinated, Trixianna watched Chance's brows draw together in a frown.

"And no way in hell will she sleep in my bed."

"You will let her out." Tildy's face looked as red as an expensive ruby.

"Over—my—dead—body," Chance ground out. His pale blue eyes flickered with irritation.

From her vantage point behind bars, Trixianna listened, mesmerized. She stared at the fierce byplay between Chance and his aunt. Chance exuded a vitality she envied and yet found deeply disturbing. Her heart thundered in her ears with . . . excitement? She didn't know why, but as she watched Chance's tense, hard body, an intense tickling started in her stomach and inched lower. She swallowed hard against a lump that had lodged in her throat.

Trixianna was rather glad Tildy was on her side in this matter. Already she could see that the woman had the upper hand with the sheriff. Nearly as tall as Chance, Tildy stood toe to toe with him, her eyes as cold and icy blue as the sea. As she ranted, her bountiful chest rose and fell like a ship rolling over the waves. Like a train, too fast and too large to stop, she ran roughshod over her nephew.

"You listen here, Chance, no lady is going to sleep in this jail, not tonight nor any other night." She poked a finger into his chest, not once but three separate times. His eyes narrowed, and obvious annoyance hovered there.

Tildy continued, apparently unconcerned about his furious demeanor, although it scared Trixianna half to death. "Since you have an extra room in your house, then Trixianna can—"

The line of his mouth tightened. "Her name is Maggie West."

Tildy screwed her mouth up in a frown. "*Trixianna* can stay in your home where you can keep an eye on her if you think that's necessary."

"Tildy, maybe you've forgotten, but I am the sheriff. I can keep anyone I want in jail, whenever I want, be it man or woman."

"No, you can't. I simply won't allow it."

"Allow it?" Chance backed away and leaned against his desk. He folded his arms over his chest and winced. He turned his head toward Trixianna and glared at her as if the pain in his shoulder were all her fault. She guessed it was. She kept her peace, however, since his anger was now directed at her and she had no wish to be the object of his verbal fury.

"If I was to let her stay in my house, wouldn't that cause a ruckus?" he said. "You, of all people, should

46

know that, since you're one of the town's gossiping busybodies. I may have lived in Grand Fork only five years, but even I know that much."

"I don't believe you were raised to be a rude jackass, Chance."

Chance rolled his eyes.

"Besides, we trust you, dear. What scandal could possibly go on between our good sheriff and a good-hearted bank robber like Trixianna here, who, by the way, I don't believe robbed any bank."

"Oh?" His eyebrows rose in amusement. "Who made you the expert?"

"I don't much like your tone, young man."

He shrugged his shoulders as if to say he didn't *much* care what she thought either.

"I know an honest face when I see one," Tildy said, "and that is an honest face—and a very pretty one, in case you hadn't noticed. Much prettier than someone else we know." She tilted her head in Trixianna's direction with a significant lifting of her brows.

"Tildy, for God's sake." He gave his aunt a scowl, then looked Trixianna over, first up and then down, taking his time doing it, until she thought she'd die of humiliation. Though uneasy beneath his scrutiny, she boldly met his gaze. Those intense blue eyes of his assessed her every feature. She had no idea what he thought, for his expression revealed nothing.

Her stomach chose that unfortunate moment to growl. Both Tildy's and Chance's brows rose.

"Good Lord, open that door before the woman expires right there on the floor."

With a look of exasperation, Chance turned to get the keys out of his desk drawer. Under his breath, he mumbled, "We should be so lucky."

Tildy patted Trixianna's hand through the bars. "We heard that, young man."

He rolled his eyes heavenward again, then strode over to the cell and unlocked the door. He stared at Trixianna. "If you so much as blink an eyelash at that outside door, I'll shoot you," he warned.

Trixianna glanced at the revolver holstered on his thigh, then at the derisive expression on his face. She didn't doubt for a minute that he meant every word he said.

"I won't," she promised.

"Do you need to use the necessary, dearie?" Tildy asked.

"Thank you, no." Trixianna ducked her head to keep Chance from seeing the blush blossoming on her face. Earlier in the day, when she'd been alone and in desperate need, she'd taken advantage of the chamber pot. She hated to admit to its use now, though, in front of the sheriff and his aunt.

Tildy went about rearranging Chance's desk to her satisfaction. She patted her iron-gray hair, which she wore pulled up tight in a bun. Spectacles, seemingly forgotten, were pushed up on top of her head. She cast a quick glance at Chance, then turned the tintype of the girl with the goat face-down and folded the newspaper. She placed the paper over the tintype. Chance scowled at his aunt, but said nothing about her actions.

With both plates of food set out, she brushed her hands together in a dismissive gesture. She then pulled an extra chair over to the desk for Trixianna. "That should do it." She smiled at Trixianna. "Eat, both of you. I'll be off now."

As Trixianna rearranged her skirts to sit down, Tildy

leaned over and whispered in her ear. "Ask Chance about Fanny."

With that, she kissed Chance on the cheek.

He mumbled his good-byes.

She reeled out of the office, her brown sateen skirts swishing behind her like a schooner in full sail. "You youngsters have a nice evening."

"Youngsters? A nice evening? That's about as likely as getting milk from a bull," Chance muttered.

"What are you going to do now?" Trixianna asked, curious about his intention now that his aunt was gone.

"What the hell can I do?" The fork he'd just picked up clattered to the table. He placed both hands palms down on either side of his plate and stared at her. "You've seen this town. You can't take a pi—That is, you can't take a pony down the street without everybody commenting on it. If I keep you jailed, there'll be hell to pay. Tildy will get her sewing circle to talk to their husbands, meaning the mayor, the barber, the . . . well, dammit, every man in town, and they'll be after me night and day to release you and make you stay at my place. She's plain got me over a barrel."

"I'm sorry if I've caused you any problems, and I certainly don't want to go to your house either, but this is your own fault."

"My fault?" He jumped to his feet, causing the dishes on the desk to rattle against each other and threaten to overturn. "How could this possibly be my fault?"

"You've arrested the wrong woman," she replied in her most sensible tone. With a sense of conviction, she continued. "I'm not this Mad Maggie person. I keep telling you, but you aren't listening. I have never

49

robbed a bank. Not ever. Period. End of discussion."

"I'm listening now, all right, and this is not the end of the discussion. Either you're lying through your pretty white teeth, or I'm no lawman."

Trixianna resumed eating, refusing to look into his angry face.

"And another thing, Miss West."

"Miss Lawless," she said between bites.

"Miss West," he repeated. "I don't reckon you'll be going anywhere soon because this blamed town and its busybodies will know what you're up to every single minute of every single day." He resumed chewing on a biscuit, his elbows on the table.

"Oh?"

"You won't be able to use the outhouse without someone telling me how long you were in there. You and I will be the talk of the town. And that's for damn sure, or I don't know Grand Fork."

"I don't believe it for a minute, Sheriff. Surely the good people of Grand Fork have better things to do with their time than watch what I'm up to."

He rolled his eyes, then stuffed the last of his biscuit in his mouth. He picked up his fork and pointed it at her. "Shows what you know."

"Tell me about Fanny, Sheriff."

He stopped with the fork above his plate, then took a deep breath. He resumed eating his supper, his eyes on his plate. "She's my intended."

"Oh, you're going to be married?" She didn't know why she found the news so disconcerting. The sheriff meant nothing to her, but for some reason a sense of loss swept over her. She, too, wanted to get married someday, but so far she hadn't had so much as a male caller. Most men found her too forward. She didn't think they much liked freckles and red hair either.

"Yeah, in less than two weeks."

"That soon?" She chose her words cautiously, veiling her inner feelings from his shrewd, discerning stare. "Would that be her in the tintype on your desk then?"

He answered with a nod. He looked up, and their eyes met and clashed. Trixianna bit her lower lip in confusion. The expression on his face disoriented her, and set her pulse pounding. Chance glanced away first, his face coloring slightly. He drummed the fingers of his left hand against the tabletop and stared at his half-empty plate of food.

She endeavored to bring her overwrought sensibilities into order and to remember what they had been discussing. "You've had a long engagement?"

He reached across the table and cupped her chin to get her to look at him. Although his touch was surprisingly gentle, her heart skittered in her chest. "I don't talk about my personal life . . . with prisoners. Got that?"

Trixianna gulped. "Yes, of course."

He pushed his plate aside and stood up. He straightened, grimacing, as he stretched his back and shoulders. "It's been a long day. I'm dog-tired and my shoulder hurts like hell. Let's say you and me get on out of here and go to bed."

His choice of words embarrassed Trixianna, but she refrained from commenting. She ducked her head and went in search of her bonnet. She pushed her hair out of her eyes, and with the few pins she found scattered on the cell floor, managed to pin it up and get her bonnet on over the heavy mass.

She turned to find Chance watching, his pale eyes

shimmering with some indefinable emotion as he stared at her. He quickly averted his gaze, grabbed his dusty black Stetson and shoved it low on his forehead. He ambled toward the doorway, checking to make sure the fire in the stove was out as he passed.

"The dishes?" she questioned.

"Let 'em be." He grabbed her arm. "Tildy wanted you to eat. By God, she can clean up. Let's get going."

Of all the blamed fool, downright idiotic ideas Tildy had ever concocted, this was the worst one yet. Chance grumbled under his breath as he moved unsteadily down the boardwalk, pulling Mad Maggie behind him. The woman must have the shortest legs this side of the Mississippi. He slowed his step only because if she fell he wasn't certain he could help her up again, much less drag her to her feet. His shoulder burned as if it were on fire, and his head ached. He felt like he'd been ridden hard and put up wet.

Without a doubt, this had been the longest day of his life.

And it wasn't over yet.

He still had to put Mad Maggie to bed, make sure she couldn't escape his home, *and* try to sleep with her under his roof.

Just the thought of her in his bed gave him all sorts of notions. None of them sheriff-like.

"I need to go to my home first."

He pulled up short and stared down at her. Her face betrayed nothing, except quiet expectation. He considered himself pretty shrewd when it came to reading people, but he was having a helluva time understanding this one. He decided she must have had some time on the stage. When he looked at her, he saw a stunning face and a stubborn tilt to the chin, but no deception and no guilt whatsoever. He sighed deeply. "What for?"

She looked directly at him. He stared into her compelling green eyes, feeling as though she were putting a crazy curse on him or something. He shook his head and moved his gaze to the tip of her nose. "I need to pack some clothes and pick up Angel," she said.

"That wouldn't be your accomplice, by any chance, would it?"

"Angel is my cat," she said, a hint of exasperation in her tone.

He chuckled. "That cantankerous fluff of fur?"

She stepped back from him, her eyes wide, her cheeks blooming with color. "Were you in my house today without my permission?"

"You bet, Mad Maggie. I was searching high and low for a stash of money. Didn't find it, though."

"You went through my things?" She lifted one hand to her mouth. Her fingers trembled. He couldn't say why, but the actress's mask was gone. Anxiety shone in her eyes as clear as the tiny freckles peppering her nose.

"What's the matter? Afraid I'll find something?"

"No," she countered. "I have nothing to hide. It's just that I find it disconcerting to know someone has gone through my belongings."

"That someone being me?" He shoved his hat to the back of his head and leaned down to look straight into those sharp, emerald eyes of hers. He hoped she'd give something away. Instead she gazed at him, her cheeks rosy and her chin tilted at a stubborn angle. What he got was a frank, unblinking stare.

"Yes, exactly."

Her straightforward answer amused him. "You're afraid I might muss up those sexy new underclothes of yours. Eh, Maggie?"

He didn't think her cheeks could become any redder, but they did.

"My stars, is nothing private? And it's Trixianna, Sheriff, Trixianna Lawless."

He shook his head and took her arm, pulling her along with him down the walkway. Her feet tapped a quick pitter-patter alongside his in an attempt to keep up. He smiled to himself. "Nothing's private in Grand Fork. Let's get your clothes and your mouser and get going. I understand that besides your ability to rob banks, you cook, too, Mad Maggie. This arrangement might turn out all right after all. I really cotton to a hot breakfast of ham and eggs in the morning. How about you?"

"You expect me to cook for you?"

"Why not? You should earn your keep."

She stumbled up beside him and clasped his arm, jerking him to a stop. She'd grabbed his right arm, wrenching his shoulder at the same time. He clenched his jaw to keep from yelling out loud. Holding his arm tight against his stomach, he bent over and took several deep breaths.

Trixianna could have kicked herself. She'd hurt him . . . again. Her eyes welled with tears. She was such an unthinking ninny. "Oh, what have I done to your poor shoulder?" Fine lines of pain were etched around his lips, tightened in a thin line. His face was pale and coated with a sheen of perspiration. "You're not going to faint again, are you, Sheriff?"

"Go ahead, pile on the agony," Chance gritted out, frowning at her from beneath the brim of his hat. "Are you trying to unman me in the entirety, or is this your usual manner of chasing off men?"

"I beg your pardon?" Heat blossomed in her cheeks. My stars. Wasn't that something someone did to a horse's private parts? "I didn't mean to—that is, I—"

"Never mind." He straightened and started down the boardwalk.

She hurried to catch up to him.

They finished the walk to her home in awkward silence. When they got there, Chance stood in the doorway. "I'll be listening to every sound, especially the back door swinging shut. Don't you try anything. Go on now and get your things."

Trixianna rushed past him. She hurriedly packed a bag with clothes and a few other essentials, then put a yowling Angel in a covered basket. She was just walking back into the parlor when she heard a female voice calling to Chance. She came to stand in the doorway. He'd stepped off the porch and stood waiting.

"Chance, I've been looking all over town for you," the panting female voice continued. "You are certainly hard to keep track of."

He stood up, removed his hat and held it in his hand. He ran his fingers through his thick hair and cleared his throat. As soon as his hand left his head, a raven lock of unruly hair fell forward across his forehead. "Fanny."

The woman from the tintype stood before him trying to catch her breath. Young and abundantly wholesome, with big dew-kissed brown eyes, enormous buck teeth and round cheeks, she reminded Trixianna of a beaver. *What a dreadful thing to think,* but it was true. She was pleasantly plump; some might even say fat. Trixianna thought she would bear the sheriff many fine, pink-cheeked children. She wanted to detest the woman on sight, but the earnest smile she gave Trixianna was contagiously friendly.

"Why, you must be Trixianna. I'm Fanny Fairfax. My, but you're the talk of the town today." She bestowed a toothy grin upon Trixianna as she patted a lace handkerchief against her cheeks, then began waving it at her face. "You shot my Chance here, but it was all a mistake, Tildy told me. Thank the Lord he's going to be all right. They say he insists you robbed the Dena Valley bank, but I just don't think you look like a bank robber."

She gave Trixianna an assessing gaze, then turned her stout body toward Chance and tapped him on the forearm with a pudgy hand. The lace hanky flapped between her short fingers.

Chance had yet to speak. Actually, he looked overwhelmed.

"Thank you, Miss Fairfax," Trixianna said. "That's kind of you to say." Why couldn't Fanny be stupid or mean? She so wanted to dislike her.

"Oh, call me Fanny. Everyone does. My father—he's the mayor of Grand Fork—he says I've never met a stranger."

Of course he would marry the mayor's daughter, thought Trixianna. If it weren't for bad luck, Trixianna would have no luck whatsoever. She suppressed a sigh of resignation.

"Why, you can say that twice and mean it," a male voice said.

A gray-haired, older gentleman dressed in a suit of fine broadcloth approached from the direction of town. He stepped up beside Fanny. His face was

56

round and red, and he wore a bucktoothed, bucolic grin. Spectacles were perched precariously on the end of his nose.

Of course this had to be Fanny's father. She was his spitting image. And he was the mayor of Grand Fork.

"Frank." Chance acknowledged the mayor with a nod of his head.

"Hear you're having a houseguest, Sheriff."

"How'd you find out already?" He shook his head. "No, don't tell me. Tildy."

The mayor laughed.

So the man knew Trixianna would be spending her nights beneath the roof of his affianced daughter's beloved. He was certainly understanding, or at the very least, very accommodating.

Trixianna wondered why Chance hadn't spoken to Fanny. Not even a kiss hello. Perhaps he was shy around her, although he didn't seem self-conscious about much of anything else, particularly where Trixianna was concerned.

"I understand you fainted, son." A jovial chuckle leapt from the mayor's lips. His belly, pushed tight against his plaid waistcoat, quivered with laughter.

A shadow of annoyance crossed Chance's face. He glowered at Trixianna before turning back to the man. "I did not faint."

Trixianna ducked her head to hide the grin that threatened to become all-out laughter. If she ever got out of this pickle, what good stories she would be able to tell Jonathan and Georgette back in Abilene. If Georgette ever forgave her. She swallowed hard against the pain of remembrance.

She looked up to find Chance, the mayor and his daughter watching her with expectant faces. She realized with a start that they were waiting for a reply from her. "I'm sorry, my mind drifted. Did you ask me something?"

"Were you figuring out how you could escape from my evil clutches?" Chance asked.

"Chance!" cried Fanny. "That is no way to speak to a lady."

"Fanny, that is no lady," he replied, his voice thick with frustration.

"Now, son, we don't know for certain." The mayor rocked back on his heels. He studied Trixianna with a speculative gaze.

"That she's a lady or that she's a bank robber?" Chance asked.

The mayor flushed as he offered Trixianna an apologetic look.

"Good Lord, Frank." Chance's voice was tight with anger. "Have you seen the wanted poster in my office? It looks just like her."

"I may look a bit like that awful woman," Trixianna replied. "But she has squinty eyes and a rather large nose."

They turned as one to inspect her nose. She now knew how a past-its-prime mule felt on auction day.

Chance shrugged his shoulders. "She's the one," he said smoothly. He glanced at the mayor. "And I can't believe you and these meddling townsfolk won't let me leave her in jail where she belongs."

"There's no privacy for a woman in that jail, Chance, and you know it."

Chance frowned, his mouth clenched. Trixianna saw a muscle jump at his jaw. "All right then, let's head over to my place. You got everything you need, *Miss West?*"

Trixianna nodded. "Miss Lawless," she reminded him, though knowing it was futile to do so. He would go on thinking she was Mad Maggie West until the woman herself showed up in Grand Fork.

Fanny must have missed the exchange, for she went on as if nothing were amiss. "I'll be over tomorrow," she gushed. She waved the hanky clutched in her pudgy hand, and tapped Chance on the arm.

"Fine." He shrugged his shoulders, then grimaced as he settled his hat on his head. He nodded in farewell to the mayor and Fanny. He reached for Trixianna's baggage.

"Your shoulder," she reminded him. He frowned, but didn't say anything more when she tucked Angel's basket beneath one arm, and her valise under the other. With his good arm he began pulling her down the street.

As Fanny waddled away, she called over her shoulder. "Bluebeard sends his regards."

Chance flushed a deep red, and released a vivid oath beneath his breath, but he didn't acknowledge her remark about Bluebeard, whoever that might be.

Trixianna's stays pinched her ribs and cut off her air as she attempted to keep up with the sheriff's suddenly aggressive pace. She lengthened her stride, hoping she wouldn't collapse before they arrived at their destination. Her mind kept muddling over his odd demeanor toward his bride-to-be.

Trixianna's mind whirled with myriad possibilities. Why had he never once looked, really looked, at Fanny throughout their entire conversation? Baffled by his peculiar behavior, she wondered how he'd ever worked up the gumption to ask the young lady for her hand in marriage.

His rapid progress through the streets of Grand Fork and her own polite manners kept Trixianna from questioning him although she dearly wanted to. Curiosity killed the cat, she reminded herself.

He stopped suddenly, giving her a chance to catch her breath. For a brief moment he studied the house in front of them. She couldn't see his eyes, hidden beneath the brim of his hat, but she saw the satisfied set to his mouth.

He pushed open a squeaky gate and pulled her up the walk. She got a brief glimpse of the house before being hauled up two steps and onto the wide front porch.

The simple clapboard house was painted white and had another smaller porch on the side. Two tall narrow windows on either side of the door looked out over the dusty street. The yard was neat, the house newly painted, and a wooden swing swayed to and fro on the porch.

Before they went into the house, Trixianna said, "Thank you for putting me up here, Sheriff. I know you didn't want to."

Chance stopped on the threshold and stared down at her. "I don't like being told how to do my job by everyone in town, but I've got little choice."

"I want to thank you anyway."

"Hmmf. I've got an extra room, just a bed and dresser, but you'll have your privacy. I suppose even an unsavory criminal such as yourself deserves as much. There's a kitchen you can use and an outhouse out back. I keep my life simple, so there's nothing fancy such as the minister has in his home."

He leaned down and looked her square in the eye. He gently tapped a finger on the tip of her nose. "Just remember, I sleep light with a cocked pistol at my side, and I'm not the only one watching you. Grand Fork has its eye on you as well, so don't even think about trying to run off."

"I won't." His nearness robbed her of coherent thought. His broad shoulders blocked the doorway; his breath caressed her cheek. His thigh touched one of her legs, and even through layers of cloth a jolt shot through her. She swallowed hard and shook her head.

He straightened up and shoved away from her. "Well, then, come on in. I'm too damned tired to stand here and engage in parlor talk with a wanted criminal."

Chance left her in the extra bedroom and sauntered back to the kitchen. A glass of buttermilk and a slice of cornbread sounded like just the thing before he went to bed. He lit a lamp and set it on the round wooden table. He was surprised when it clattered against a canned jar of peaches. He was even more surprised to see that the kitchen table was covered with more baking supplies, including pie tins, lard, sacks of sugar and flour and more things a bachelor such as himself sure as hell couldn't identify. Chance recognized the hand of Bertram Sinclair in this. Damn this town and their meddling ways! Muttering to himself, he walked back down the hall to tell the woman.

She must have forgotten to close the door, as it stood slightly ajar, allowing him a shameless chance to glance inside and watch her unobserved. She stood by the window brushing her long hair. Bathed in the amber glow of an oil lamp, she looked angelic, as if she were not of this world. She had her back to him as she stared out at the night while tending her hair. With slow strokes, her graceful hands swept the brush down the length of her thick, auburn locks. He watched her intently, his heart in his throat.

When her hand reached the end of her hair, he noticed her apparel. Or lack of it. His stomach joined his heart in the region of his throat.

The light behind her shadowed her slender figure, and made her silk nightgown of palest pink almost transparent to Chance's own personal perusal. He allowed himself to slowly scrutinize every inch of her without her knowing. A narrow waist gave way to gently rounded hips. As he lowered his gaze, he noticed how her hips tapered into long, unending legs. Legs that gave his imagination free rein. Why he'd ever thought her limbs were short and stubby, he couldn't recall. His pulse quickened. He dropped his gaze and saw tiny feet peeking out beneath the hem of her gown.

She whirled, as if she'd sensed him standing there. He lifted his gaze, only to behold more of her. From full high breasts, taut nipples jutted against the pink fabric. He fought for composure, gulping in air.

Their eyes met, hers wide with surprise. He couldn't shake the overwhelming need to take her in his arms and kiss her senseless. He clenched his hands into fists. It was a struggle to remain calm and remind himself just who and what she was.

"I thought you'd gone to bed." Her husky voice rasped against his raw nerve endings.

"I had," he said in a choked voice. He cleared his throat. God, what he wanted to do to her. And didn't dare.

The way to a man's heart is through his stomach.
—19th-century proverb

Chapter Four

"I just came to tell you that—" Chance cleared his throat again. "That Sinclair fella brought over your cooking things. I guess the money-grubbing crook expects you to keep baking pies for his restaurant while you're in my custody."

"All right," she said. "Is that all you wanted?"

No. "Yeah." He turned on his heel and yanked the door closed behind him. He closed his eyes, and leaned his aching head against the wall. He drew in a deep breath, surprised to find his hands shaking, his pulse pounding and his knees as weak as a newborn foal's.

He took himself across the hall to his own room, where he shed his boots, unbuttoned his shirt and lay down on top of the bed, his hands folded across his belly. He stared at the ceiling, longing for what could never be.

He told himself it had been a hellish day; a person

wasn't shot every day. He told himself he was just plain worn out; he'd been up since before sunup. He told himself he just needed a good night's sleep, it was his mother's remedy for whatever ailed you.

He lay awake a long time telling himself that just because a beautiful woman slept beneath his roof, he had no right to her, especially when she was a wanted criminal. And he was an engaged man.

He fell asleep not believing a word of it.

Trixianna put pen to hand before retiring for the night. She'd find a way to mail her missive tomorrow.

Mr. Jonathan Lacina
Abilene, Kansas

Dearest Jonathan,

I sincerely hope you have rectified the situation with Georgette. I know her temper is somewhat fierce, but my sister has a sweet side, which I'm sure you've discovered in your four months of marital bliss.

She is probably not yet over her pique with me, and that breaks my heart. I hated to leave Abilene under such trying circumstances, but I feared for your life as well as mine. Were you able to glue together the lovely dove statuette? I suspect that Georgette isn't ready to accept the gift just yet. Maybe in time.

I'm living in Grand Fork, Kansas, now. My baking enterprise is thriving, although at the moment business is a little slow. I hope that with a few changes, things will pick up.

Grand Fork is a hospitable town and I've made

several new friends. Alistair Burns, Burnsey to his close companions, is from England and has that wonderful accent. Right now he lives quite close and we are able to converse freely. Annie V., another new friend, owns her own thriving establishment, and she and her colleagues love my apple pandowdy.

I've met the sheriff, Chance Magrane, quite by accident. He seems a nice enough fellow, though I believe his health is precarious.

Take care of yourself, Jonathan. I think of you as a brother now. Be patient with Georgette, but until we straighten out this situation, perhaps it would be best that you not mention my letter.

> *Yours truly,*
> *Trixianna Lawless*
> *Grand Fork, Kansas*

When just a smidgen of night still darkened the sky, Trixianna set out with oil lantern in hand to explore the sheriff's home while he slept.

Granny Lawless's warning voice whispered in her ear about intruding upon other people's privacy, but curiosity overcame Trixianna's qualms and common sense. She prayed that unlike the cat, curiosity wouldn't kill her. Before she started baking, she wanted to find out more about the man with whom she found herself sharing quarters. And snooping seemed the only way to go about it.

She put her ear to the sheriff's bedroom door, heard a light snore, then tiptoed down the hall.

Her feline companion, Angel, followed, hissing and jumping at shadowed corners, the hair of his back standing on end. She tried to shoo him away in case he woke Chance, but he had a mind of his own.

She wondered if the rest of the house was like the room the sheriff had given her. It had no curtains at the window, no wallpaper or paint on the walls, no rug on the floor. Four bare pine walls surrounded a single iron bedstead with chipped white paint and a simple four-drawer maple bureau. Rough linen sheets, a moth-eaten blanket and a flat pillow covered the bed. The dresser drawers had been empty. Late last night, she'd put her clothes away in the chest, and placed her tortoise-shell brush and comb and a scrimshaw box of hairpins atop the dresser so the room would look more lived in.

Four rooms, including her own, occupied the simple one-story clapboard home—a parlor, a kitchen and two bedrooms, with a narrow hallway running through the middle of the house. As she wandered, she saw a clean, though sparsely furnished, house with some hint of the sheriff's own indomitable personality. However, as she thought about it, she realized it didn't really reflect him at all; the man wasn't frugal with words, only with furnishings. It was something to mull over when she had the time.

The parlor had no rug to warm it, no knickknacks to decorate it, no womanly frills to enhance it. No mementos. No photographs of Fanny or a family. Not even a single small table.

Two ladder-back pine chairs graced either side of the fireplace. A worn serpentine-back sofa in a floral design of faded green, pink and white faced the fireplace and held one clue as to the manner of man who sat there in the evenings. A book. Trixianna picked it up, and became so startled by the title that she dropped it onto the sofa. She stared at the cover—

Charles Dickens's *A Tale of Two Cities*. She flipped back the flyleaf and found a dedication—*To Chance, No hard feelings, Rider*. Although eaten up with inquisitiveness about Rider's identity, she set the book back as she'd found it. Again the sheriff surprised her—she'd doubted the man knew how to read, much less that he would read a novel by someone like Dickens.

As she turned from the parlor, she caught the glint of a shiny object on the mantel. She crossed the room and picked it up. In her palm, she held a single brass key. She stared at it, wondering if it could possibly be another jail key. Behind her, Angel let out a loud screech that was so startling, she dropped the key in the pocket of her apron. She waited, listening for the sheriff's bellow. Hearing nothing, she heaved a sigh of relief and sauntered across the hall to inspect the kitchen, completely forgetting the key in her pocket.

Yes, thought Trixianna as she prepared to bake her pies, he kept his home simple . . . including the kitchen. *Very simple*. The man apparently didn't know a soup ladle from saddle soap. There weren't enough supplies to put together a simple supper, much less the kind of baking Trixianna routinely did. Although oddly enough, he had a fairly new enclosed range that was quite expensive and more than sufficient for her meager needs. Maybe he'd purchased it with his new wife in mind.

Thank God Bert Sinclair, even with selfish motives, had thought to bring over her own kitchen stores and utensils.

Beside her Angel meowed, having followed Trixianna into the kitchen. He lay on the floor in front of the range, and began grooming himself. She laughed at the feline, who kept both eyes glued on her as if he expected her to disappear at any moment.

Humming, she set to work.

Within a matter of minutes, Trixianna felt right at home. She was comfortable in the kitchen. She kept close to her heart the memories of her and Georgette learning the womanly arts while laughing and gossiping with their mother and Granny Lawless. She missed them all very much.

But she thanked God that for now she wasn't in jail, and that she could cook to her heart's content.

Sometime during the night Chance died and went to heaven. Or so he thought upon awakening. He lay still as delicious home-cooked smells drifted to him from the kitchen. Cinnamon, sugar, apples. His mouth watered and his stomach grumbled, reminding him that he'd never gotten around to drinking that glass of milk and eating any cornbread before bedtime last night.

He sat up, and was immediately sorry. He'd died all right . . . died and gone to Hell. He eased back on the bed, his bandaged shoulder on fire, every muscle in his body aching. A tremor raced down his arm and into his fingers. He rubbed his burning eyes and stubbled face, cursing long and loud.

Hell. He'd been shot by a woman. It stung his pride nearly as badly as it pained his body.

He shouted another string of profanity just for good measure.

And *she* came running.

He heard her tiny booted feet scamper down the hallway. The object of his longing and his dreams . . . and the outlaw woman who could bring him closer to five hundred dollars reward money. His just desserts. He couldn't decide if he wanted to throttle her neck or savor it with his mouth. He groaned and closed his eyes.

The door swung open. "Sheriff Magrane? Chance, are you all right?"

He popped one eye open and glared at her. She stood in the doorway, clad in an ugly gray dress, an apron round her tiny waist. She must favor the color, for every time he'd seen her she'd been dressed in gray. Her hair was pinned up; thank the Lord for small favors. Hair like that should only be let down in a bedroom.

A smudge of flour dusted the end of her freckled nose. He released a deep sigh. She didn't look like a hardened criminal. She looked sweet, innocent and damned beautiful.

He took a deep breath. "I'm right as rain, Maggie. Never better. I—" Just to prove it, he shot out of bed, then tripped over the bed coverings. He grabbed the footboard to recover his balance. "Mother of God, what time is it?"

She pulled up the timepiece pinned to her bodice and squinted at the face. "Eleven-fifteen."

He hadn't disrobed last night, but as he tried to pull his shirt off his shoulder to wash up, he discovered he couldn't raise his arm. "Hellfire." He waited for a reaction to the vulgarity, and was surprised to receive none.

Instead, she stepped forward and helped him remove his shirt. Her gentle touch sent a shiver up his spine. She seemed not to notice. "Near the end of his illness, my papa had difficulty dressing and undressing himself, too," she said matter-of-factly. She took

69

the shirt, folded it and placed it on the bed. "The undershirt?" she questioned.

He nodded, his pride seriously bruised by having to accept her help. Still, he leaned over so she could pull it off. Parts of him trembled, other parts quivered and other, more delicate parts groaned with delight. She had the softest, warmest hands and a considerate touch that belied her no-nonsense demeanor and criminal background. And she smelled delicious—half cinnamon and spice, and the other half all-over womanish.

She blushed when she asked, "Do you need help with the rest?"

He blushed when he answered. "No."

She started out the door, then turned and asked him, "Can I fix you a late breakfast?"

Why did the woman have to be so damnably polite? He shook his head. "If that's pie I'm smelling, I'll just grab a slice on my way out."

"Okay, fine. Is cranberry all right? It's the one I kept for us."

"I've never had cranberry pie, but I'm sure it'll do. I'm so hungry, my stomach thinks my throat's been slit."

She gave him a thin smile, her hands folding and refolding the edge of her apron. "Could you maybe do something for me while you're out today?"

His fingers stilled on the buttons of his trousers. He looked closely at her. Her eyes darted nervously from his hands to his face. "No."

She continued as if he hadn't given her a negative reply. "Would you wire Jonathan Lacina in Abilene? He can verify who I am and that I did not rob the bank in Dena Valley."

"Is he your lover, or maybe your accomplice?"

If possible, she blushed a deeper crimson. "No, Jonathan is my brother-in-law."

She left him alone then, pulling the door shut behind her. He heard the sound of her receding footfalls and wondered why guilt ate at him. He knew before the day was over he would send a telegram to Abilene to verify her story.

The man was a beast.

No, he was worse than that. He was dreadful and unspeakably mean. A tyrant.

And as Granny Lawless used to say when Trixianna's father wasn't around to overhear, he was a prime specimen of masculinity.

When Trixianna had first touched Chance to help him take off his shirt, she could have keeled over from the feel of his body. She'd never laid her hands on a man in such an intimate way. The softness of his skin surprised her. She'd expected it to be rough like sandpaper. Instead, it was as smooth as a baby's. A fine down of black hair covered his broad, powerful chest. The silky-soft hair and supple skin on his chest contrasted deeply with his overall fierce appearance.

And his scent. Oh, my. Trixianna could still smell him, and he'd been gone from the house for an hour. Even after sleeping all night, he'd smelled heavenly, like warm summer sunshine and worn leather and, oddly enough, spearmint. She felt close to swooning when she thought of it.

Without thinking, she stuck her hands in a dishpan of dirty dishes and gasped, yanking her stinging hands out of the scalding water. For God's sake, she'd just poured the water straight from the stove.

"Damn." A wave of guilt shot through her. She glanced over her shoulder, even knowing she was alone. Men swore all the time. Why couldn't women?

"Damn," she repeated. "Damn, damn, damn."

She knew why men swore. It felt pretty damn good.

Chance's stomach churned. He sat up straighter. He scratched his chest. His face broke out in a cold sweat and gooseflesh crept up his arms and back. He shook all over like a palsied old man. He rushed outside to catch a breath of fresh air, but when he stepped out on the boardwalk, his stomach convulsed. He dove around the side of the building, raced toward the rear and reached the outhouse just in time to empty the contents of his agitated stomach.

The woman had poisoned him.

It must be her plan to escape. His stomach heaving, Chance negotiated his way down the street, only once fleeing the walkway to empty what little was left inside his stomach in an alleyway. He sent two young boys playing there off screaming in horror.

Ignoring strange looks from the Widow Pierce and her sister, the Widow Simmons, out doing their shopping, and another questioning glance from the undertaker, he made it home. By that time, he'd also sent a whimpering dog skedaddling with his tail between his legs.

Exhausted and angry, he stomped up onto the porch, his hat in his hand. Every square inch of his body either itched or prickled or burned as if he'd been marked with a cattleman's branding iron. He was going to murder Mad Maggie West.

* * *

Trixianna jumped when Chance burst into the kitchen startling both her and Fanny. She glanced over to see the smile on Fanny's face disappear and her features pale. They had been getting to know each other over coffee and slices of cranberry pie. In mid-sentence they'd stopped talking and looked up in surprise when the sheriff had rushed into the room, a murderous look on his face.

"Why, Chance, what happened to you? You look downright ghastly," cried Fanny. She jumped to her feet, her fingers splayed across her chest.

He waved her away with one hand. She flushed, remaining silent, and retreated to the far side of the table. Trixianna felt sorry for the poor girl. She couldn't imagine why Fanny would be engaged to such an unfeeling brute.

Chance pointed a trembling finger at Trixianna. "You poisoned me."

Fanny gasped aloud as she glanced at Trixianna. A look of uncertainty shaded her round face.

Hives covered Chance's face and neck, and even his hands. Sure as God is in Heaven, Trixianna thought with no small amount of amusement, the ugly red weals must blanket his entire body. Trixianna bit her lip to keep a smile off her face.

"I didn't poison you. As you can see, Fanny and I have been enjoying the cranberry pie ourselves with no ill results."

"Yes, it's quite good, Chance. You should try a piece." Fanny gave him a bright smile.

"I did," he ground out between clenched teeth.

Her smile disappeared.

Suddenly, his face paled and he jerked away, racing out the door. It slammed against the wall with a loud thud, then bounced back, shuddering on its hinges. Fanny exchanged a pained look with Trixianna. The anguished sound of Chance's wretching, followed by a mournful groan, reached their ears.

Fanny's eyebrows rose in amazement, her eyes wide. As she slid onto one of the kitchen chairs, she whispered, "Goodness."

Trixianna nodded in agreement.

When Chance came inside, a slick sheen of perspiration covered his blotchy face, and his eyes were bloodshot.

Trixianna opened her mouth to speak. He shushed her with a shake of his head. "Maybe you didn't poison me, *Miss West.*" He gave her a pointed look. "I can see you're both eating that god-awful stuff, but I feel like I'm about to die."

"You look just like a big, plump strawberry." Fanny giggled, then clapped a hand over her mouth. "I'm so sorry," she whispered.

He gave her a humorless smile. "Now what do I do?"

"Have you got any calamine lotion?" asked Trixianna.

He nodded. One of his hands reached inside his shirt to scratch his belly; the other rubbed his forehead, making it, if possible, more red and irritated. He was a sight, all right. Trixianna agreed with Fanny—he did look like a giant strawberry. It was all she could do to keep from laughing.

"I think—" she said. Her voice sounded unnaturally high to her own ears. She started again. "I think that'll help the itch. For the, uh, stomach upset, I do believe it'll just have to work its way out of your system. That is . . ."

"I think I can figure it out." He spun on his heel,

flinging his shirt aside as his fingers dug furiously into the broad expanse of his back, which was covered with long underwear. The last thing she saw was a blue shirttail flutter to the hall floor.

The bedroom door banged shut, rattling the dishes on the table. Fanny, who had been leaning around the table watching his exit, exclaimed, "He seems a bit perturbed. It's not dangerous to his health, is it?"

"Oh, no," Trixianna promised with a shake of her head. "Aside from a fearsome need to itch, the only thing you'll have to worry about is his temper." Trixianna's lip trembled with the need to grin. She exchanged a look of amusement with Fanny; then they both burst into peals of laughter.

Fanny quieted, the smile slowly fading from her features. Her right brow rose a bit. "What do you mean that all I'll have to worry about is his temper?"

Trixianna shrugged her shoulders. "You'll be caring for him, won't you?" *She* certainly couldn't help the man. Chance would rather have a rattlesnake in his bed than have *Mad Maggie West* in his bedroom.

"Why, I certainly won't," Fanny said matter-of-factly. "That would be scandalous. I'd be the talk of Grand Fork."

"But you're engaged," Trixianna countered. "And besides, *I'm* the talk of Grand Fork."

Fanny stood to leave. She reached for her hat and reticule. She pulled lace gloves from her bag and yanked them over her pudgy fingers. She tugged on the bodice of her lilac gown, the buttons strained over her abundant bosom. "That may be, but I simply could not help him. Why, I get nauseous at the sight of blood."

"Blood?" *What blood?*

A look of supreme discomfort crossed Fanny's placid face. "I'm simply not tending him. Goodness, I'd have to touch his person." She shivered from head to toe, as if she found the mere thought of laying a hand on the sheriff's body repugnant.

Touch his person? What did Fanny mean she couldn't touch him? Caring for Chance while he was under the weather took precedence over propriety, and besides, they were engaged. Indeed, this was a strange relationship. Trixianna's curious nature kicked in again. No, no, no. She gave herself a mental shake. It was none of her business. "What about his aunt?"

"Tildy?" Fanny made her way around the table. She stood at the door and smiled, then patted her hat in place over her simple brown-haired bun. "Why, I do believe Aunt Tildy left on the afternoon train for Wichita. Her sister, Martha, isn't well. She's got the arthritis and sometimes needs a bit of help. Tildy's been planning that trip for a week or so."

"Chance will have to doctor himself then," Trixianna insisted.

"I'm sure he can." Fanny bobbed her head in reply. "That man is perfectly capable of taking care of just about anything."

She stepped over the threshold and looked over her shoulder. "I'll see you later then, Trixianna. Perhaps I'll stop by tomorrow to see if you or Chance need anything. Bye-bye now."

Trixianna stood in the doorway and waved goodbye. She watched as Fanny made her way down the street. The young woman waved at every buggy in the street, patted each child's head she passed. She even stopped to pet a stray dog. She was obviously well loved and admired. But what about her and the sheriff? Did he love her? And more importantly, did she love him? Theirs didn't seem like a love match, certainly not one made in Heaven.

Trixianna shook her head. It was absolutely none of her business, but still, she couldn't help thinking about it. She stepped back inside wondering. . . .

"Hey!" An exasperated male voice echoed down the hallway, shattering her reverie. She refused to answer to *that* insulting call.

"Mad Maggie!"

Or that one either. It wasn't her name and she wouldn't dignify it with a reply.

"Maggie!"

The window panes rattled. Chance's deep voice echoed inside Trixianna's ears.

"Maggie!"

She cringed. She bit her lip.

"Trixianna Lawless! Get your sorry butt in here before I throw you back in jail!"

Trixianna smiled. Sure, he was threatening her, but in his condition she doubted it held much meaning. Besides, it just proved what a little perseverance could accomplish. She hurried down the hall and pushed open the door. "Thank you for finally using my real name. That wasn't so hard, now, was it?"

He gave a disgusted snort. "I figured it was the only way I'd get you in here, *Maggie*." He had the audacity to wink at her. He stood facing her with his hands on his hips, dressed only in short-legged cotton drawers. The unbuttoned shirt-top was bunched down over his narrow hips. The drawers sagged around his lean waist, but hugged his buttocks and the bulge of his masculinity.

Trixianna's face heated. Yet she couldn't tear her gaze away. She found herself staring at his well-proportioned physique with an unladylike fascination.

A physique that was as red as a ripe cherry and as angry-looking as a boiled Boston lobster.

His face was bright crimson, but she figured he wasn't embarrassed, although had she been dressed so scantily she would have been. Since his unclothed body from the tips of his ears to his bare toes was also red, she knew hives covered even those places that were clothed. Such a sight. Bright pink skin even showed through the thin white bandage covering his shoulder wound.

If the look in his eye was any indication, embarrassment was the furthest thing from his mind. His brilliant eyes glowed like bits of blue stone, hard and uncompromising.

Trixianna couldn't find the words to speak.

"I can't reach my back," he grumbled. He turned around and showed her his back. Staring at her over one broad shoulder, he said, "Rub it in." He pointed to the bottle of calamine on the dresser.

She stepped forward on slow, hesitant feet, ignoring the blatant command. He picked up the lotion and handed it to her. She took it in shaking hands. She hated to admit how much his presence disturbed her. He alternately thrilled and frightened her. She wasn't sure which emotion scared her more. "Are you sure you want me to do this?"

"Who else, for God's sake?" he stormed, an annoyed edge to his voice. He looked out of the corner of his eye at her. "After all, you're responsible."

The nerve of the man. She leaned toward him, her fear lessening, replaced by indignation. "How was I to know you were allergic to cranberries? My cranberry pie gets raves from everyone else."

"Well, not me. Now, put it on. The itch is driving me crazy."

She raised up on tiptoes and stared at him.

He angled his head away, his eyes narrowed. "What now?"

"Well, what do you say?"

He shrugged his shoulders in mock resignation, then turned to face her. "Isn't it enough that you've shot me, *and* poisoned me? Now you want me to beg for your damned help? Haven't you about humiliated me enough in the last two days?" He ran his hand through his hair. "My God, woman, I'm standing here all but stark naked, itching like I've got the world's worst case of poison ivy. I still feel like pukin', and there couldn't be one damn cranberry left in my belly."

She stiffened, having been put in her place by his words. "That's not what I wanted, Sheriff."

"Then what is?"

"I just wanted to hear a please." She swallowed the lump in her throat. "I'm sorry for acting like a child." She motioned for him to turn around. He complied. She poured a small amount of the lotion into her palm and rubbed it in small circles on his lower back.

Chance shivered when she first placed her cold hand on his smooth skin, but her fingers soon warmed up and his muscles relaxed. She traced the line of his back. He shivered again. She heard him swallow. With upward strokes, she massaged the medicine into his skin until a thin layer of the lotion coated his back.

He released a long breath as she lifted her hands

79

away. "Dammit, I'm sorry, too," he said. "I shouldn't have yelled at you."

"No, Mr. Magrane, you shouldn't have. It wasn't very polite. Your bad reaction to the cranberry pie wasn't my fault."

He turned around and gave her a slight smile. "Call me Chance. If we're going to live together, you can at least do that."

"All right." She stepped away, the bottle clutched tightly in one hand. Her heart pounded in her chest. Her voice came out shaky as she asked, "Is there anything else I can do for you . . . Chance?"

He gave her a beleaguered grin. "Please don't leave town."

She couldn't help the surprised lift of her brows. "I guess that wouldn't be fair now, would it?"

He gave a short bark of laughter and shook his head. "No, ma'am, it would not. If I have to chase you, let's at least be somewhat evenly matched. Right now, I'm about done in. You could walk away slowly, and I couldn't catch you. I'll bed down in front of the door, though, if I think you'll take off."

"That won't be necessary, Sheriff. Let me prove to you that I can be trusted, that I'm not this Mad Maggie West."

"I won't argue because I'm too done in to care. But know that tomorrow, if you're gone, I'll hunt you down and drag your sorry butt back."

"Fine. You'll see me right here. But for now I'll let you sleep." Trixianna stepped out the door, slowly pulling it closed behind her. She leaned against the door, waiting for her heart to stop thudding. She didn't understand why he made her so uneasy.

The bed ropes groaned as he lay down. "Thanks,

Trixianna," came his deep, masculine voice through the door. He sounded tired, yet there seemed to be a faint trace of humor in his voice as well.

She bit her lip, and as casually as she could manage, walked back to the kitchen. She wondered if Chance could eat a currant pie. She had left one unopened bottle of green preserves, more than enough to bake him one.

Angel curled around her ankles as Trixianna sat at the kitchen table. She stared at the bottle in her hand, rubbing her thumb over the label and remembering the feel of Chance's skin beneath her fingers. Warmth flowed through her and she felt blissfully alive. Even under the sheriff's lock and key, she didn't honestly mind her unusual circumstances. Until he could sort out the mistake in identity, she could still bake and support herself. She had Angel for company, and the sheriff might even need her, just a little bit.

And in the meantime, she had the puzzle of Chance and Fanny to sift over. It was like a dime novel—*The Mystery of the Sheriff and his Betrothed*.

It certainly was better than any dime novel Trixianna had ever read. It also took her mind off the way he made her feel—things she had no right to feel about this man.

> *He that has too much to do*
> *will do something wrong.*
> *—Samuel Johnson*

Chapter Five

Miss Trixianna Lawless
Grand Fork. Kansas

Dear Trixianna,
   I was extremely cheered to receive your letter. I can't begin to tell you how worried I was when you left. I know women today consider themselves quite independent, but a woman traveling alone can be so vulnerable. I worry about you as I would about my Georgette.
   As soon as business allows I shall endeavor to write more frequently. For some unknown reason, Abilene is suffering from a rash of untimely deaths right now. As an undertaker I can't complain, but I do feel sorry for the poor bereaved families. It seems one never knows when the Lord will call you home.
   It sounds, though, as if you're getting along

splendidly in your new community and making friends. I have to wonder why a thriving town such as Grand Fork would have a sheriff with question-able health. They must be very compassionate to keep him on when he has difficulty doing his job.

Although Georgette would never admit it, she misses you dreadfully. She mopes about the house or talks all the time about some of the pickles you and she used to get into when you were children. I think it's a good sign that she can discuss you now without anger.

I'm planning a business trip soon to Grand Fork, and I hope she will agree to accompany me. Don't fret, I have no intention of telling her you are there. I'm hoping that she will be so surprised when she sees you that she will forget why you left in the first place.

You are constantly in my prayers, Trixianna. I know the two of you will work out your problems soon and all will be well again. I'm looking forward to the day when we are a family again. I know you are, too.

> Your brother in heart,
> Jonathan Lacina
> Abilene, Kansas

"Five hundred dollars."

Bounty hunter Sam Smith leaned a tad closer to the table beside him in the restaurant where he sat eating his evening meal. He strained to hear the conversation between an eager young deputy and two other men.

The deputy, his badge shiny and new and pinned to his shirtfront where no one could miss it, went on to tell his cohorts about the arrest of the notorious Mad Maggie West in Grand Fork.

In his wanderings, Sam had heard tell the bounty on the bank robber was five hundred dollars. That could sure buy a whole passel of whiskey and wicked women.

Grand Fork. He puzzled over the town. He thought he knew its location, although his sense of direction was none too accurate. He didn't think he was far from it but he didn't know if it was north or south. He could find out easily enough.

"Howdy, boys."

Three curious faces turned his way.

"I couldn't help hearing you say that Mad Maggie West got herself arrested in Grand Fork."

The deputy swallowed a forkful of stew before replying. "Yep, that's a fact, sir."

"Ain't you that bounty hunter Sam Smith?" one of the others asked.

"That's me." Sam lifted his chin and grinned at the inquiring fellow. He liked the idea that he was well-known.

"Looks like you missed out on a nice bundle this time around, Smith," the deputy said.

"I reckon I'll just mosey on over to Grand Fork and collect that bounty."

"I just said she's already been arrested."

"Uh-huh." Sam nodded in agreement.

The deputy set down his fork. "The sheriff in Grand Fork arrested her, and has her in his jail."

"Just where is Grand Fork?"

"Due south." The man to the deputy's right answered. "I reckon it's about fifty miles."

"Would that be past the livery or past the rail station?" Sam asked.

"South, son, beyond the train yard."

"Good."

"What are you going to do?" asked the deputy.

"Collect that money."

"You can't do that," the deputy insisted.

"You gonna stop me?"

"Well, no."

"Then I'll be seeing you all." Smith threw a couple of dollars on the table, smiled amiably and stood up. He left the three men staring at him like he was as loco as a rabid dog.

Lawmen. They didn't have sense enough to spit downwind. And, by damn, if there was one thing ole Sam Smith knew how to do, it was skirting the law.

Trixianna had just put the last pie of the morning into the oven when she heard a pounding on the front door. She wiped her hands on her apron, then yanked off the scarf she'd tied around her hair. She pushed a straggling strand of hair from her face, then hurried to the door and pulled it open.

She stared a moment in shock before she found her voice. "My stars! I hardly recognized you!"

She openly gaped at the man standing on Chance's threshold, his fist poised to knock again. If not for the twinkle in his eye, she never would have thought this was the same person she'd come to know in the Grand Fork jail.

"I do clean up rather nicely, don't I?" Burnsey stated. With a gloved hand, he brushed at the lapel of his elegant black frock coat. He lifted her flour-dusted fingers and brushed a light kiss across the knuckles.

"Alistair Burns, sixth Viscount of Huxford, at your service, madam."

"My stars."

"You're repeating yourself, my dear."

The epitome of the perfectly dressed English gentleman, Burnsey looked about as out of place in Kansas as a professional gambler did in a church. From the tips of his polished black boots to the elegant white silk ascot tied in an expert knot about his neck, his appearance astounded her. He even clasped a cane in one gloved hand. She stared like a woman turned to stone.

"Aren't you at least going to invite me into your new jail for tea?"

She closed her mouth, then stepped aside. "Forgive me. I'm just . . ."

He strode through the door, whipping off his black felt derby as he entered. Over one shoulder, he called, "Jolly well bowled over? Flabbergasted? Overwhelmed by my exceedingly good taste, charm and devastating looks?"

"Yes, yes, yes." She squeezed his hands in hers. "It's so good to see you, too."

He chuckled, then set her away and peered into her face with a critical gleam in his eye. "How has our big galoot been treating you?"

"Why, just fine, of course."

"What do you mean, 'of course'? The man imprisoned you, first in that horrid cell and now in his own home." He frowned, his eyes level with hers. "Has he been taking advantage of your good nature?"

Trixianna's cheeks flamed. How? she wondered. By asking her to rub lotion into his warm flesh and making her want to touch him in other, more intimate places? By making her wish for something between them that could never be? She turned away, heading for the kitchen. "Let me start the tea."

"Humph." He followed behind her, his walking stick tapping the floor. He seated himself at the oilcloth-covered kitchen table, and then he cleared his throat expectantly. His fingers drummed impatiently on the tabletop. "Something's afoot here, isn't it?"

Trixianna glanced over her shoulder.

He gazed back at her, a look of concern etched on his face.

"No, not at all," she replied, unable to stop the slight tremble in her voice.

Burnsey's mouth twisted in a wry expression of doubt. Trixianna knew she was a dreadful liar.

Abruptly rising to his feet, he said, "I know Chance. He can be a bit, how shall I say, uncivil, almost to the point of rudeness. He's not mistreating you now, is he? Or making advances? Not that I would blame him. If I were a younger man . . ." He tapped the cane against the side of the table.

Trixianna blushed, her heart in her throat. Could the man read her mind?

"I'll speak to him if that's the situation," he said. "He can be surprisingly naive about women."

Trixianna hurried to his side and pushed him gently into his seat. "You're reading much more into this than necessary."

"I doubt it. I consider myself an excellent judge of character. You are a beautiful young lady who has never so much as loitered on the streets, much less robbed a bank. The idea is simply abhorrent." He shivered and made a disgusted face. "But aside from that, the sheriff is a fine-looking man in the prime of his life."

Trixianna's face heated as she thought of the sheriff. Yes, he was handsome. Very handsome indeed. And he'd arrested her falsely, didn't believe her and didn't trust her. He thought she was a heinous criminal. She shook her head.

Burnsey raised one eyebrow. "Aha, I believe I see the problem."

"It's not what you think; he thinks I poisoned him."

"What?" Burnsey asked. His eyes rounded. Obviously, that wasn't what he'd expected her to say.

Chance rolled over in bed, roused from a decent sleep by the sound of voices and an enticing aroma wafting from the kitchen. He lay back, smiling. What was Mad Maggie cooking today? He hoped cranberry pie was not on the menu. Grinning, he shook his head, then stumbled out of bed to awkwardly clean up and dress. He sat back down on the bed, appreciating the fine scents of Maggie's baking, until the throbbing in his shoulder wound lessened. It was a sore reminder of the criminal woman residing in his residence.

Sometime around midnight the itching had stopped and he'd been able to fall asleep. He'd slept like the dead, for the second night in a row. If he wasn't careful, the county would terminate his position as sheriff for allowing his prisoner to escape while he slept. Although arresting the infamous bank robber Mad Maggie West was a feather in his cap, he hadn't exactly been keeping a close eye on her. But she was still here this morning. He'd give her that much.

Chance sneaked down the hall to eavesdrop on the conversation in the kitchen. Maybe his prisoner was

planning her escape . . . or another bank robbery . . .
or more likely still, she was planning how she'd try to
dispose of him the next time.

A knife, maybe?

How about a Gatling gun?

What was it they said? "Third time is the charm"?
He'd be careful, that was for sure.

He stopped at the entry to the kitchen, peered
around the corner and listened.

"He thinks I poisoned him."

She sat across the table from Burnsey. They were
drinking tea as if they were seated in a fancy English
castle and both were upper-crust Britishers. That
Burnsey was a corker. Chance shook his head.

The woman's green eyes sparkled with pleasure as
she listened to Burnsey. Falling about her face in curling ringlets, her russet hair lay mussed. Flour
smudged her freckled nose, but Maggie or Trixianna,
or whatever she called herself, looked like royalty. She
could be a princess. With her head held high, her
shoulders back, she enhanced his plain kitchen.

She sure didn't act like any criminal Chance had
ever encountered. Of course, he'd never encountered
a female desperado. She had him damned confounded.

"He thinks you *what?*"

"Poisoned him."

"Did you?" Burnsey whispered. He leaned across
the table and clasped her hand in his. "If you did, I
promise I won't tell a soul."

"Of course not." She sounded highly offended.
Chance smiled. "All he did was take a slice of my cranberry pie with him when he left yesterday morning.

Then he came home later, sick and covered from head to toe with hives."

Burnsey hooted with laughter.

Unable to hide her own grin, she continued. "Since Fanny and I were in the midst of eating a slice ourselves, he couldn't really accuse me further of trying to harm him. That's really all there is to tell."

"Where is he now?"

"Still sleeping. I imagine he didn't get much rest. A rash like that can be rather tiring."

"Tiring?"

This time she leaned forward and whispered, "It itches something fierce."

"You say he was covered with this rash from head to toe?"

"Why, yes."

"And how would you know that?"

"Well, I helped, I mean, I—" Her cheeks bloomed with fiery color.

Chance thought this would be a good time to make his presence known, but the devil in him kept him silent and still in the hallway. He wanted to see her squirm a while longer. Besides, when rattled, lawbreakers often gave themselves away. And she had yet to give him any real evidence other than the physical resemblance to the woman depicted on the wanted poster.

"It's not what it seems," she said. "He hasn't taken advantage of me or compromised my reputation in any way—"

"God's teeth," Burnsey interrupted. He dropped his cup, rattling the saucer. He paused for a moment, then sighed resignedly. "I will concede this is better than the jail. No woman should have to stay there.

"However, a woman of decent upbringing shouldn't see enough of an undressed gentleman to know that his body is covered with *anything* from head to toe."

"What about you?"

His brows rose. "What about me?"

"I saw you in your long underwear and you didn't seem too upset about that."

"That was quite different," he retorted. "I'd been inebriated."

"Well, I don't see any difference. Besides, I didn't have to see him to know that he was covered from head to toe. My sister, Georgette, is allergic to strawberries, and the same thing happens to her whenever she eats them."

Ah-ha. So there really was a sister. If she was the wife of the man Trixianna had mentioned, Chance needed to find out that woman's maiden name and where she lived.

"But you did see him, didn't you?" insisted Burnsey.

If possible, her face became more rosy. Her voice sounded resigned when she said, "He was sick and hardly capable of doing anything untoward. I merely helped him with the lotion to relieve his itching. He couldn't reach his back."

"And what was he wearing when you *helped* him?"

"Burnsey, this is—"

"What was he wearing?"

Her shoulders stiffened. "His drawers . . . just like you were."

"Well, that's something," Burnsey grumbled. "But hardly appropriate attire to be seen by a single young lady such as yourself. I expect this took place in his bedroom, as well."

"Yes."

91

"Did he try to kiss you?"

"No." Her freckles stood out like drops of maple syrup against her apple red cheeks. Chance found himself wanting to kiss all those enticing freckles . . . one by one.

"No? *I* would have. And by the look on your face, I'd venture to say you wouldn't have minded either."

Her shoulders slumped forward. She looked up at Burnsey through lowered lashes. Chance's stomach dropped to his feet at the soft expression on her face. The smile she gave Burnsey set Chance's pulse racing and his blood pounding in his veins. "Yes, I probably would have liked it," she admitted.

His curiosity aroused . . . as well as other parts of him, Chance listened avidly. And watched with smug delight.

"I believe the sheriff is a strong, yet kind man," she continued. "When he thinks of it he can be considerate, and he's always been fair, even while locking me up. He's determined and decisive and knows just what he wants."

"I'm not so sure," Burnsey said.

"Maybe not . . . but you're right, he is very handsome, as you pointed out to me. He also thinks I'm a liar, a bank robber and a fraud. None of which is true."

"I'm well aware of that. You have an honest face."

"Thank you. But don't forget I shot him. So no matter what I feel for him, he will never give me a second look, except maybe to lock me up in that horrid jail again. Besides all that, he's engaged to Fanny."

"Well, you know what they say, dear. The third time is a charm."

"Third time for what?"

"You've shot him, and given him hives. You should

think of something else to keep him home where he can discover what a precious gem you are. Have you thought of breaking his leg?"

She laughed out loud, then covered her mouth with the palm of her hand.

Chance decided this would be a good time to make his entrance. He'd learned quite a bit in his short spell of eavesdropping. She had a sister, she found him handsome and she wished he'd kissed her. And she didn't seem to be lying about any of it, including the fact that she still insisted she hadn't robbed the bank in Dena Valley, although he guessed she wouldn't admit it if she had. He was mightily confused, and more than a little attracted to the woman, whoever she was.

Trixianna almost jumped from her chair when Chance sauntered into the room. She raised her eyes to find him watching her. She wondered if he'd heard any of their conversation.

Chance glanced at her companion. "A little early in the day for you, isn't it, Burnsey?"

"And I'd say it was a wee bit late for you, Sheriff."

Chance tipped an imaginary hat. "Point taken. My esteemed houseguest can tell you I've been a little under the weather."

"And looking much better also." Trixianna noted that the unsightly blotches had disappeared overnight, revealing taut bronzed skin. Reflected sunlight shining through the windows glimmered on his handsome features and danced in his pale blue eyes.

"Why, thank you," he said.

She felt a new emotion radiating from him—a bold eagerness she didn't understand. His gaze raked over her, and settled on her face. She self-consciously licked her lips.

Burnsey cleared his throat and stood up. "Thank you for the tea, my dear. A delight, as usual. Next time I'll bring James and we can discuss your incarceration." He pulled on his gloves, settled his hat just so and bowed. He tipped his cane over one shoulder. "Sheriff, please be kind to her. She's a rare one."

"Oh, no doubt 'bout that." A thoughtful smile curved his mouth. "I'll try to be nice if you'll promise to stay off the rotgut and keep your fine English clothes on, Burnsey. Half the men in Grand Fork now sport a pair of your Wellingtons and one of those ugly bowler hats. Frankly, I don't see how you can afford to lose another pair of boots."

Burnsey flushed, then looked Chance square in the eye. "No gentleman would ever question another about his finances, but believe me, sir, when I say that I certainly have the means. In the future, however, I will make every attempt to stay clear of the liquor."

"Much obliged." Chance brushed back his hair with the fingers of one hand. He turned to Trixianna just as she noticed droplets of water glistening in his raven-black locks. His hand stopped in midair when he caught her expression.

Without thinking, she reached out and pushed a wayward strand off his forehead.

He stood still, his eyes contemplative.

Up close, she saw he hadn't shaved this morning, for a dark shadow shaded his jaw. She could tell he'd washed up, though, for the smell of lemony soap clung to him.

Trixianna brought her hand self-consciously to her side and peered out the door.

Burnsey had disappeared from the house unnoticed by either of them.

They cleared their throats simultaneously, then glanced at each other.

Chance's eyes narrowed and his head shot up. "Is something burning?"

"Oh, my stars!" She rushed across the room and opened the oven door. Without thinking, she grabbed the pie pan, burning her fingers. The steaming pie clattered to the floor. She pursed her lips tight to hold back a screech from the searing pain.

"My God, woman," Chance exploded. Rushing to her side, he grabbed her arm and hurried her over to the pump. With several jerky motions, he pumped cool water onto her stinging fingers. Holding her wrist in a tender grip, he kept her hand under the faucet and splashed water onto her fingers.

With her lower lip caught beneath her teeth, she watched as he capably soothed the burn with a gentle touch.

Black hair curled along the back of his wrists and up his arm. Mesmerized by his strong hands, she forced her gaze away and looked up to find him staring at her mouth. Her heart turned over in response.

Chance took a deep breath. He released it through clenched teeth.

With his thumb, he rubbed small circles into her palm, and then turned her hand over. A string of expletives slipped from his mouth when he saw the line of small blisters across the tips of her fingers.

He pulled her hand to his face and pressed a kiss into her palm. The touch of his mouth branded Trixianna with a tingling spiral that danced up and down her spine. Before she could catch her breath, he bestowed a feather-light kiss to the tip of each finger with a velvety, tender warmth. His clear blue eyes smoldered with fire and never once left her face.

She trembled, wrapped in his invisible warmth.

"Better?" he questioned in a hoarse whisper.

She nodded without thinking.

He dipped his head, his eyes closed. He brushed his lips against hers. And then once again, with a sweet tenderness that buckled her knees. His lips were soft and slightly moist. One of his hands came up to cup the back of her head and pull her closer. His breath caressed her heated cheek.

Chance moved his mouth over hers, willing her to open for his seeking tongue. When she did, he thrust again and again, setting her body aflame with rampant desire. Eager for more, she touched her tongue against his, eliciting a groan from deep within his throat. She mimicked his actions with her own tongue. His hand tightened around her neck and he held her snugly.

Her thoughts whirled and spun and skidded out of control. She had never been kissed like this before. Who was she fooling? She had never been kissed at all before, and certainly had never returned a kiss.

She quivered all over like a willow in the wind. She knew it was wanton and terribly wrong to feel this way—out of control and deeply aroused—yet she didn't stop him from kissing her because she wanted the feeling to go on forever. And she wanted more.

When he lifted his mouth from hers, he was panting. His eyes, narrowed and glassy, seemed ablaze with an inner fire. He dropped his hand from her neck. With a bemused stare, he rubbed his own neck.

"Why did you stop?" she asked, her own breath coming in short gasps.

His eyes widened. "Why did you let me kiss you?"

"I . . . well, I know it's wrong, but I've never been kissed before."

"So you wanted to see what all the fuss was about?" he asked with a hint of humor in his voice.

"No. Well, maybe, I guess, but once you started, I found I liked it."

"My God, woman, but you're plainspoken."

"Well, I did like it."

"So did I," he muttered. He bowed his head, still rubbing at the back of his neck. "Way too much."

"It's wrong, isn't it? A woman's not supposed to feel such things."

A look of disbelief crossed his features. "Wrong?" His voice rose an octave. "There's nothing wrong with desire between a man and a woman. Every man hopes that when he marries he'll wed a passionate woman."

Trixianna's cheeks bloomed with heat. Now he was telling her she was acting the wanton.

"But *you're* supposed to be my prisoner," he added. "And *I'm* supposed to be engaged."

"This doesn't change that."

"Well, hell," he muttered. "I guess it doesn't."

He turned on his heel and left the house, leaving Trixianna alone and torn by conflicting emotions.

The sound of shattering glass woke Trixianna. By turns disoriented and frightened, she bolted upright in bed. Pushing tangled hair from her eyes, she squinted against the early morning sun that slanted through the open window. Jagged shards of glass poked out of the frame. Slivers of glass lay glittering on the floor beneath the sill.

The bedroom door burst open. Holding a revolver in one hand and buttoning his trousers with the other, Chance glanced at her. He stood for a moment, barefoot and bare-chested, taking in the broken window.

"Damn," he muttered. He turned on his heel and sprinted out the door.

Trixianna grabbed her wrapper from the end of the bed. She struggled with the sleeves as she stumbled down the hall, following after him.

He tore out the front door and left it wide open. As she watched, he hurdled the picket fence and bolted around the corner of the house.

She scrambled down the walkway and through the gate. She dashed over the dew-damp, cold grass, holding her night rail and robe high to keep them dry. She stumbled around the corner of the house, and came to a halt just beyond the side porch.

Chance stood there panting. He'd stuck his Colt in the waistband of his trousers. In each hand he held two squirming young boys by the scruffs of their necks.

The youngsters were protesting for all they were worth, their voices loud and boisterous in the early morning air.

Chance gave each a none-too-gentle shake, which effectively stopped their grousing.

When he spotted Trixianna, he drawled, "Look what I found. New occupants for the jail."

"Damn, are we under arrest?" the taller of the two asked.

Chance gripped his collar and pulled him up tight. "Watch your mouth, son."

Trixianna stared at the two squirming boys. "Why, they're just children. They're not cut, are they?"

Chance snorted in derision. "No. These so-called children are young men, old enough to know better than to peek into a lady's bedroom window." He stared hard at their faces. "Aren't you Harvey Perry's boys?"

"Yes, sir," the smaller of the two whispered. "I'm Michael."

"And you're—?" prompted Chance.

The older boy ducked his head. "Thomas."

"And just what did you two think you were doing? It's against the law to break into someone's home even if you're just looking."

Trixianna gave Chance a knowing look. He frowned at her. Sheriff or not, he'd broken into her home without a thought about the law, and she was tempted to remind him of just that.

The line of his mouth tightened before he turned back to the boys.

"Gosh, we wasn't breaking in. We didn't mean to bust the window neither. We was just trying to get a better look inside," explained Thomas. He elbowed Michael in the ribs. "This ninny was trying to step up onto a rock, and lost his balance. His elbow hit the glass."

"But why were you looking in?" asked Trixianna.

Thomas's face colored. He rubbed his nose with the back of one hand. He turned to Chance, a scowl on his face. "Do I hafta answer?"

"Yes, you do, son."

Thomas hemmed and hawed, shuffling his feet in the grass.

Chance gave his arm a gentle shake.

The boy stared at the ground. "We just . . . that is, we just wanted to see Miss Lawless's new, you know, her new drawers. The ones she bought at Johannsen's. Johnny Washington tole us they was see-through, real purty and pink and, well, we never seen the like on anybody's clothesline. We was wantin' to see them up close on a real lady."

Trixianna's face flamed, and the tips of her ears burned. She clutched the sides of her wrapper tighter around her waist. Holding her hair away from her face, she glanced up to find Chance grinning at her.

He threatened the boys with jail if he ever found them prowling around his windows again, then released them. They scampered away, hooting with high spirits at their unexpected freedom.

Amusement flickered in his gaze as he took her arm and moved her toward the front door. "Why, Mad Maggie, I believe you're blushing."

"Trixianna," she reminded him. "And you would, too, Sheriff, if young boys were falling all over themselves to get a peek at you in your underpinnings."

He chuckled low in his throat. "I *would* be shocked if young boys were trying to catch a peek at *me* in my drawers without my clothes on."

"It's not the same thing and well you know it."

He opened the front door, and gestured for her to proceed him. "No, ma'am, it's not."

Trixianna tossed her hair over her shoulder and stomped inside. She stopped in the foyer and turned to him, her hands fisted at her sides. "Why, Sheriff, I believe you're laughing at me. Perhaps you're changing your mind about me and thinking maybe I'm not all that bad."

He shook his head. "Perhaps, but then again, maybe you bank robbers have many sides."

"Like the side you kissed yesterday?" Did she really want a reaction from him? She knew that she was probing at emotions better left alone. But what she really wanted was another of his heated kisses.

"Perhaps," came his reply. He stuck his hands in his trouser pockets and rocked back on his heels. He looked her up and down, his eyes bright with merriment. "Those Perry boys are right about one thing."

"What's that?"

"No one around here has drawers like you."

An injury is much sooner forgotten than an insult.
—*Fourth Earl of Chesterfield, Philip Dormer Stanhope*

Chapter Six

Late morning sunshine and a clear, blue sky greeted Trixianna as she jostled her way down the boardwalk. Chance had agreed to let her go about her business if she promised not to run off. Humming to herself, she pulled her baked goods along behind her.

The walkway wasn't designed for wheeled vehicles. Though late and in a hurry, she had to slowly maneuver the small child's wagon through the few people she passed. She dreaded her meeting with Bertram Sinclair. He wouldn't be at all pleased to know that she had dawdled over her morning coffee with Chance instead of firing up the oven and getting to her baking.

She just couldn't help herself. By turns, Chance fascinated and annoyed her. Whenever he gazed at her with those intense pale blue eyes of his, her heart turned over. Aside from the traits she admired—his stubbornness, his unwavering confidence and a total honesty—she had no reasonable explanation for her reaction to him except that he was a good-looking man.

She pulled the cart to a stop in front of Sinclair's Restaurant, then took a deep breath. Brushing aside a wayward strand of curling hair, she tucked it beneath her bonnet. She reached for the door handle. The door banged open, startling her, and Bert Sinclair stepped outside. He presented her with his usual scowl.

"You're late."

"I'm sorry, Mr. Sinclair, but I think your customers will find the wait worthwhile."

The man's florid face flushed with obvious doubt. His glower deepened. "Oh? How so?"

He reminded Trixianna of a toad . . . a red, inhospitable toad with his cheeks and chest puffed out. She wondered how he kept his restaurant solvent with his crotchety disposition. She waved her hand over her baked goods. "I've got five pies—two apple, two cherry and one gooseberry—and one chocolate cake I made especially for you. The cake is my granny's special recipe and it's delicious."

"I don't care if it was Mary Todd Lincoln's favorite recipe. You're supposed to have them delivered by eleven and . . ." He pulled out a pocket watch, snapped it open and squinted at the face. "It's eleven-fifteen."

Trixianna squelched the urge to roll her eyes. She pulled the covering off her pies, releasing an aroma that set her own mouth watering. Sinclair's scowl lessened and his lips turned up in what could almost be termed a civil smile. "My, but those do smell good. My dinner customers haven't arrived yet . . . so, young lady, I'll let it go today."

She refrained from calling him a fatheaded old nincompoop. Instead she smiled, and using all the restraint she could muster, said, "Why, thank you, Mr. Sinclair."

Out of the corner of her eye, she saw him watching her shove the wagon over the threshold and through the doorway. She prayed that she wouldn't dump its contents all over the restaurant floor, although the man certainly deserved it. As she stewed over his lack of manners, she unloaded the desserts onto a sideboard at the back of the room. She noted, with satisfaction, that the place was devoid of customers.

With a look of indigestion on his face, he paid her. She left with a mumbled thank-you and a desire to give him a set-down that even Granny Lawless would have envied. Now *there* was a woman who could put a man in his place. Chance's aunt, Tildy O'Hara, seemed like the same kind of woman. Trixianna admired that in a person.

She stepped outside onto the boardwalk and shaded her eyes from the sun. She gave some thought to doing a little shopping, but knew Chance would track her down if she wasn't home in the time it took to deliver her baked goods. Instead she decided to send a short telegram to Granny Lawless in Abilene explaining her predicament. She'd written once to Jonathan, but not wanting to involve him, hadn't mentioned her troubles. The more she thought about it, though, the more she needed the moral support that Granny could provide. If the sheriff from Dena Valley came for her, it might be a while before she'd be free to contact anyone. Besides, she didn't want to wait until they decided to hang her and it was too late to prove her innocence. Goodness, now there was a horrible thought.

She found the telegraph office closed and the door locked. Disappointed, she hurried home. She needed to be home by noon, and not just for the sheriff. Annie V. would come around then to pick up her apple pandowdy.

When Annie V. left, Trixianna took a cup of tea to the side porch, where she could enjoy the afternoon sun and watch the Grand Fork townsfolk go about their business.

She had just sat down when she spotted Chance standing on the boardwalk across the street. He stood in a small group of men. Even with his head inclined as if listening intently, he towered over the others. He wore his Stetson pulled low, shading his eyes. The star pinned to his blue chambray shirt glimmered briefly as he turned toward a thin man dressed in a dusty shirt and trousers tucked into muddy boots.

She heard Chance's laughter, a deep, throaty sound that sent shivers up her spine. One man said something else, causing Chance to throw back his head and hoot with obvious enjoyment. She watched, mesmerized, as he caught his hat just before it toppled off the back of his head. He held the Stetson in one hand, absentmindedly finger-combing his hair with the other. He shook his head at some quip from another fellow, and again she heard his deep chuckle.

One man, quite ungentlemanly, pointed rudely in Trixianna's direction. All those male eyes turned toward her. The tiny hairs along her arm rose. She swallowed hard.

Chance lifted his head and glanced at her, then said good-bye to the group. They dispersed and went on their way. Meanwhile, Chance started across the

105

street. He settled his hat at a jaunty angle as he walked.

He approached slowly, his steps unhurried. He stopped at the gate, pushed it open and sauntered down the walkway. When he came around the side of the house to where she sat on the porch, he stopped. He leaned against the rail with his arms crossed over his chest. He tipped his hat. "Miss West."

"That's Lawless, Sheriff."

"So you say." He leaned his arms on the porch railing, stared at her and waited for a reply.

Trixianna sipped her tea and kept her eyes away from his discerning gaze. Although he infuriated her and she wanted to make a nasty remark, she refused to demean herself in that manner. She turned her attention to the activity on the street as if her stomach weren't churning or her anger simmering.

"You know, Maggie," he drawled, "you're quite the mystery."

Curiosity got the better of her. She looked up at him. "Oh, how's that?"

"You just drop down here in our little town all by your lonesome. You expect me and all the good folks of Grand Fork to believe that you're just taking a little holiday. Now, that isn't normal. You may be making a little money baking those pies, but it sounds to me as if you're hiding. Maybe it's from the Dena Valley sheriff, maybe not."

Trixianna ducked her head. "I haven't done anything wrong."

"You don't act like it, Miss West. I expect Grand Fork is as good a place as any to hide, but I don't much care for your choice. Besides . . ."

The corners of his mouth quirked up and a devilish

look came into his eyes. "You've got the men *and* the boys all in a muddle. Where you're concerned, they don't know whether they're coming or going."

Truly confused herself, she asked, "Why is that? I haven't had a conversation with any of them, except Burnsey and you."

He chuckled. "That's part of the mystery. They see you walkin' down the street taking your pies and such to Sinclair. You've got that red hair all put up and hidden beneath a hat, and you wear those ugly gray dresses all buttoned up tight. Why, you look prudish, all prim and proper, just like their wives and sisters. You sure as hell don't seem like a hardened criminal."

"Perhaps because I'm not. And my dresses are not ugly."

"And then there's those underthings you wear."

Her cheeks burning, she jumped up and exclaimed in irritation, "That's nobody's business but—"

"In Grand Fork it's everyone's business," he interrupted. His eyes flashed with humor. "You'd best get used to it if you plan on staying around." He quirked an eyebrow. "I guess you don't have much choice 'bout that, now do you?"

Trixianna sank onto her chair. Chance patted her shoulder. "Listen, one of the things those men across the way were discussing is your chocolate cake. It didn't last through dinner. Why, Sinclair himself said it was the best he'd ever tasted, and he never says much of anything agreeable. That should make you happy."

It did. Her mood brightened; she smiled. She picked up her tea and took a sip of the cooled drink. "What did that one man say that had you and the others laughing so hard? Is was about me, wasn't it?"

He cleared his throat, then smiled without malice. If she didn't know better, she'd say it was an apologetic smile. "Maggie, I don't believe you'd care to hear."

"Trixianna," she reminded him.

"Whatever you want to be called doesn't matter. That conversation wasn't for womanly ears."

"Since I'm under arrest, I think I have a right to know what the people are saying about me. After all, they might decide to lynch me or something."

He released a short huff of disgust. "I doubt it. What's the matter? Don't you think I can protect you? This here's Grand Fork, not a big city. Besides, you didn't hurt these folks none. It was those poor citizens in Dena Valley you robbed."

"I didn't rob anyone." She sought his gaze. "But I'd like to know what's being said all the same."

"Fine by me, lady, but don't holler later that I didn't warn you."

"All right. That's fair."

"That Ed James is a clodhopper who can cuss like a mule skinner. His language is so ripe I don't even know all the words he uses." He scratched his chin. "Are you sure 'bout this?"

No, not at all sure. She plucked the hem of her bodice. "Yes."

Chance shook his head, then pulled his hat low over his eyes. He turned away and said in a low voice, "I know it doesn't much matter much to you, but I don't generally talk in front of women this way."

If nothing else, the anticipation would kill her. "Go on, Sheriff."

Chance cleared his throat. "He said he didn't care if you robbed a bank, or stole his dog, you were a damned fine-lookin' gal and he'd take to you warmin' his bed any night of the week."

"You laughed at that?" she said, hurt and disappointed.

"Hell, no." He shifted his stance, then bent forward and clasped her chin with his thumb and forefinger. "I laughed when he said he'd marry you just for your chocolate cake."

His eyes held hers, his hand lingered a moment, then he released her chin.

"I-I don't know what to say."

He chuckled, deep in his throat. "Just say you'll make me one."

"Of course. Anytime," she replied. "But I don't understand."

He straightened away from her. "What?"

"Why would a man marry me just for my cake-baking?"

He snorted in derision. "He wouldn't."

"Then why?"

He shook his head. "You are either the most simple-minded person in the state of Kansas or the most innocent. I can't decide which." His jaw clenched, and she watched, fascinated, as a muscle twitched in his cheek. "Maggie, he wants you in his bed, regardless of your way around the kitchen. It's your ability in the bedroom he's concerned with."

Her cheeks burned. "Oh, my stars."

"Yeah, oh, my stars." He cleared his throat self-consciously. "Now, is there anything else you'd like to know? Maybe a little lesson about the birds and the bees, or maybe you'd like to know how they geld a stallion? I know a story that would curl your—"

"Go back to work, Sheriff."

"With pleasure, Miss West." He started to cross to the other side of the street. Halfway there, he turned and called over his shoulder. "Now don't go running off. You promised me a cake. Chocolate is my favorite."

Trixianna watched Chance walk away, her fingers clutching the teacup, her eyes taking in his purely masculine form. She thought his Levi's fit rather indecently. The muscles beneath the fabric flexed and molded his legs and buttocks as he walked. Why had she never noticed a man's posterior before? Because it wasn't ladylike to look. But more likely, because she'd never been attracted to a man as she was to the sheriff. He moved with long, purposeful strides that accentuated every powerful inch of him. His footsteps echoed off the boardwalk until she no longer heard them as he rounded a corner and disappeared from her not-so-discreet view.

She released her breath. She hadn't even realized she'd been holding it.

Had she been insulted by all that he'd said? She supposed she should be more embarrassed by the men talking about her, but somehow when Chance explained it, it didn't seem so terribly bad. He'd certainly given her some interesting things to think about.

She could understand why they'd be discussing her underpinnings. They were fairly . . . unusual. She'd never felt such luxury against her skin before. When she pulled the chemise over her head and down her body, the fabric caressed her flesh, causing gooseflesh. The pantalets with soft, pink and blue ribbons adorning them were prettier than any she'd ever worn. She wasn't sorry she'd packed so quickly to leave Abilene that she'd forgotten her old things. At the time, she'd been somewhat preoccupied worrying whether Georgette was going to do something dreadful like murder her in her bed.

She sorely missed her sister, but she refused to dwell on it. What was done was done. Only time would heal Georgette's hurt feelings and make her realize that her sister loved her and would never do anything to ruin their relationship.

Trixianna hopped to her feet. She'd better get to the kitchen and start on that cake. Maybe it would soften the sheriff up. Ha! As if anything so mundane as a chocolate dessert would make him forget who he thought she was—a lying, cheating criminal who deserved to be in a real jail, not lying about his home making pies for the restaurant and pandowdy for the saloon gals.

Chance grinned as he sauntered down the boardwalk toward his office. He tucked his thumbs in his gun belt. Why, that saucy Maggie West hadn't even batted an eye. Sure, her face grew as red as a rooster's comb and she squirmed with nervous excitement, but she didn't back down. He gave her credit. She had balls. His grin grew wider. No, she had grit. She certainly did not have balls. She had a bosom that made him think of heaven whenever she heaved it in righteous indignation. Her narrow waist begged for a man's hands. His hands. Her eyes sparkled and shone like light through an open door. He thought he could read her every thought in that tantalizing green gaze. She was keeping a secret, all right, but no one was going to tear it out of her. Not even a stubborn sheriff telling her things no woman should hear. By God, he respected her for that.

*   *   *

After supper, Chance ate half the chocolate cake. And that, after devouring three bowls of bean soup and several slices of fresh-baked oat bread. Trixianna thought by morning he would be sorry.

He pushed back from the table rubbing his belly. "If I ate like that every day, I'd look like Frank Fairfax in no time."

Fanny Fairfax, don't you mean? Trixianna berated herself for having such a mean-spirited thought. But that sweet girl Chance would soon be marrying was a mite plump.

"I think I'll take a stroll round town just to make sure everything's locked down tight." He glanced at Trixianna, up to her elbows in hot soapy water. "If you want to wait, I'll help you with those. I'll only be about ten minutes."

She waved him away with a hand dripping suds all over the floor. "You go on. When you get back, I have something I'd like to discuss with you. Something personal."

He quirked a brow, his Stetson gripped in his fingers. "Would that be a confession by any chance?"

She glanced over her shoulder and gave him what she hoped was a look of disgust.

Apparently it wasn't, because he chuckled. "I'm looking forward to that 'something.' I admire a good bedtime yarn."

He left her then, still chortling. His deep laughter echoed in the room long after he'd departed.

Trixianna arranged her skirts and sat on the sofa. She folded her hands in her lap. Her heart was in her throat, her mouth dry as yesterday's oatmeal. She detested talking about herself, especially when the problem with Georgette really amounted to nothing more than making a mountain out of a molehill.

From the opposing corner of the floral serpentine-backed couch, Chance was waiting for her to speak. His silence seemed to speak volumes about his composure. His arm rested along the back. His booted feet stretched out in front of him were crossed at the ankles. He was the picture of a calm, assessing lawman.

Trixianna thought she knew better. With his hat hung on a peg by the door, his eyes were hers to observe. Caught in the glimmer of the firelight, they flashed with impatient expectation.

"Go ahead, Miss West, I'm waiting to hear your tale."

She released a long breath. "There once were two sisters who lived together. Their mother passed away when they were quite young, and their father only recently. They had a granny living still." Her voice broke with fond remembrance. She cleared her throat and began again. "But their granny preferred to live alone. She was a tad eccentric, and although she loved the girls, she kept pretty much to herself. These two sisters were as alike as any two could be, until one day one of them fell in love."

"You?" asked Chance. His pale eyes glowed with wry contemplation.

"May I continue?"

He bowed his head. "Go ahead. It sounds like a good story already."

"Well, she married, and the new brother-in-law moved in with the two sisters."

His eyebrows rose in amazement. "Whoa! Did they share him?"

Trixianna's cheeks burned. She gave him a hostile glance. "I should say not."

"Hey, don't get riled. I just asked. I want to have my facts straight when I relate this here story to the sheriff from Dena Valley."

She blew out an exasperated breath. He shrugged his shoulders, his wry expression urging her to continue. "The unmarried sister loved her new brother." At his amused look, she shot him a look of distaste. "Not like that. Anyway, they were getting along fine. Her brother-in-law had a good position as an undertaker, and all was fine until three months into the marriage."

"Ah-ha. She wanted him for herself. Am I right?"

"Will you be quiet so I can tell my story?"

"Yes, ma'am."

"Anyway, the man bought his new wife a figurine for their three-month anniversary and—"

"What?" He slapped his thigh with the palm of his hand and gave Trixianna an unbelieving stare. "A three-month anniversary present! Good God. I hope Fanny doesn't expect that. I have trouble coming up with a birthday present once a year. Now I'll have anniversaries, too, but once every month? That's not even good common sense."

"I believe, Sheriff, that this young gentleman loves his wife so much that he *enjoys* buying her gifts."

He shook his head. "No, I can't credit that. Not a bit. Why, no man likes to buy silly frew-fraws unless he's plumb loco."

"Jonathan isn't crazy!"

He stared, complete surprise on his face. "All right, *Jonathan* isn't loco, but I for sure am not buying any

114

presents for my wife. No, sir." He shook his head again.

Trixianna rolled her eyes. This man was so obtuse. She watched him closely. He kept shaking his head, his mouth thinned to a narrow line, his brows drawn together.

He turned his gaze on her. His expression stilled. A thin smile spread across his lips. "All right. That had me going, but you can continue. I'm really riveted to your story now."

"Well, one day when he came home with his lovely gift, he wanted to show it to his sister-in-law. He took her to the bedroom and—"

Chance's brows rose nearly to his hairline. He did a poor job of muffling his laughter, and waved his hand for her to continue.

"And beneath the bed, he pulled out the present. When the two of them heard the wife come in, they hurried to hide it. When they tried to stash it beneath the bed, the sister's dress caught on a loose floorboard and she lost her balance. He tried to help, but they became entangled, he with his back bent over hers, she with her skirt and petticoat revealing more than it covered. It was all very embarrassing, and, of course, shocking to the other sister when she walked into the room. You can imagine what she thought."

Chance took one look at Trixianna and snickered, then chuckled. Before long he was bent over his knees howling with laughter. Tears streamed down his face. His broad shoulders shook with mirth. He stopped a moment, glanced at her again and burst into peals of laughter.

"This isn't funny," she said.

He pulled himself together enough to reply in a shaky voice. "Yes, it is."

"No, it most certainly is not. Why, my own sister flew into a rage. She threatened me with bodily harm."

With the back of his hand, he wiped tears from his cheeks. "She blamed you then?"

"Yes. She said I wanted to steal her husband. Can you imagine?"

"That you would steal someone's husband? Not really. Then what happened?"

"I didn't know what to do. Jonathan and I agreed that the best thing to do would be to just leave for a while and let her cool off. She has a bit of a temper."

"So, you're telling me that the reason you're here in Grand Fork is because of a silly misunderstanding with your sister?"

"Yes. That's it exactly."

He snorted. "That is about the stupidest thing I've ever heard."

"It's the truth." She rose to her feet.

He leaned back against the sofa. A gleam came into his eyes. "Have you thought of taking your little fairy-tale show on the road? I bet you could make a small fortune."

"Are you calling me a liar?"

"I am, and what's more, I believe you're a coward."

"What?"

He jumped to his feet and clasped her forearms. Staring down into her face, he bent his head so their noses almost touched. "I thought we were becoming friends despite the strange circumstances that have you imprisoned in my home."

"I thought so, too," she said in a quiet whisper.

"I hear a grain of truth in your tale, but still, you're not telling me everything."

"But I am." Surprise and uncertainty wrapped around her. She sought his gaze. What she saw there frightened her; he stared at her as if she were something he'd scrape off the bottom of his heel and toss away. "Wh-what do you mean?"

"What I mean is, what were you doing in Dena Valley then, if not robbing the bank?"

"But I was never in Dena Valley."

"How do you explain the wanted poster?"

"I can't," she admitted.

"You're no better than a damn common crook if you won't tell me what you were doing there, and what's worse, you've got no honor."

Without thinking, she wrenched her hand free, reached out and slapped his face . . . hard. The sound reverberated in the small room. Silence stood between them. As she watched, shocked by her action, his cheek turned bright crimson from the blow.

She opened her mouth to apologize, but he raised his hand. She backed away, scared that he might return the favor. He shook his head and said in a quiet voice, "Why don't you go to bed. I think enough has been said here tonight. We'll talk tomorrow."

"I—I'm sorry. I shouldn't have done that, but you shouldn't have said that about my honor and I—"

"Just go," he interrupted. His voice sounded tired and had a slight edge to it.

She turned, tears swimming in her eyes, and trudged down the hall.

At the sound of the bedroom door closing, Chance slumped onto the sofa. He lay down, his feet hanging over the end. He rested one arm over his eyes. His face stung, as though he'd been lashed with a buggy whip. For a small woman, she certainly packed a wallop in that tiny hand of hers.

He'd shamed her, insulted her, even laughed in her face. As part of his plan to get to the truth, he'd goaded her all right. Guilt bit at his conscience. Still she had found the gumption to haul off and give him what for.

He didn't want to believe her . . . but he found himself doing just that. He was more confused than ever. But one thing was fairly certain.

He swallowed the lump in his throat.

She must be telling the truth or a close version of it. It made him feel like three kinds of a fool.

Sweets to the sweet.
—William Shakespeare

Chapter Seven

"Please, Trixianna." Annie V. pressed her fist to her breast and sketched a fanciful bow. The hem of her satin gown brushed along the floor, making a swishing sound. "When you leave town—and don't think I mean at the end of a rope either, 'cause you're no bank robber. You have an honest face and believe me, gal, I've seen all kinds. We'll just have to find some way to convince that mule-headed male of your innocence."

Trixianna shot Annie V. a hopeful smile. "Oh, I do hope so."

"I know so, but soon you'll be gone." She wiped a tear off one cheek. Her eyes twinkled like twin theater footlights. "You'll up and get hitched or just hightail it out of this boring ol' town, and then I'll have nothing sweet to feed my girls. They'll mutiny if I don't keep 'em happy, and the way to those gals' hearts is through their bellies. They are three greedy little pigs when it comes to sweets. I figure it's high time they learned a few of the womanly arts. And pardon me for saying so, not the ones they already know about, like pleasuring a man."

Trixianna's cheeks bloomed with heat at Annie V.'s forthright speech. She shook her head. "I don't know if it's such a good idea to have them here in the sheriff's home."

"Don't you worry none about what the townsfolk will say. Somehow or other, I'll just hustle them in the house the back way. No one will be the wiser. Trust me, I know what to do. I've had plenty of practice getting married men down the back stairs before jealous wives came up the front."

Still, Trixianna wavered. What would the sheriff think of her using his house that way? Before she had the chance to ponder it further, Annie V., right there in Chance's kitchen, fell to her knees. She clutched Trixianna's skirt. "Please, please, please."

Despite herself, Trixianna laughed. "All right, all right, but do get up. You'll muss that lovely gown."

Indeed it was lovely. Trixianna envied Annie V.'s highly improper but oh, so pretty dress. It had a velvetlike shade the color of a dove's breast, silver and satin, with rows and rows of ruching around the hem and cuffs. Lace and fine embroidery edged a square-cut neckline that revealed alabaster skin and an inordinate amount of high, rounded breast. Trixianna envied that also. While she guessed there was nothing wrong with her bosom, it quite simply wasn't as large. Or for want of a better word, as protuberant as Annie V.'s.

"Oh, goody, goody," Annie chortled. She got up from the floor, dusted off her knees and took Trixianna in her arms. She danced her around the kitchen table humming a jaunty tune, until they were both giggling like schoolgirls.

When Annie V. finally stopped, she took Trixianna by the elbows and held her out in front of her. Her kohl-rimmed eyes glowed with honest happiness. "Think of it, Trixianna. What better way to begin than teaching my girls to make their own apple pandowdy?"

"I'm certain they'll be apt pupils."

"Pshaw. They'll be rotten. They haven't got a working brain between them."

Trixianna covered her mouth with her hand to stifle a giggle that promised to burst forth.

"Go ahead and laugh. It's the God's honest truth. Lolly, Gretel and Sasha. I swear, you've never met a bigger bunch of ninnies in all your born days."

"Why do you employ them then?"

Annie V.'s eyebrows shot up. "Why? Honey, if you have to ask, you don't want to know the answer."

"But I do."

She shook her head. "Trixianna, you're a darling innocent. You do know what goes on down there at the Annie V., don't you?"

Trepidation nipping at her, Trixianna nodded. "Besides the drinking?" she asked.

"Mm-hm."

"Sort of."

"Sort of?" Annie V. gave an unladylike snort. "Which parts do you 'sort of' know about?"

"Well, I know that men go there for female company." Trixianna knew she was in way over her head with this frank conversation, but what the heck. In for a penny, in for a pound. How else was a girl supposed to find things out? As usual, curiosity won out over embarrassment and better judgment. "That is, well, I guess it's a bit more than companionship. I don't know precisely what takes place, but I do know about the birds and the bees . . . sort of."

"Whoa right there, honey. That's enough. Don't embarrass yourself anymore. Let's just say that although my girls aren't too bright, they know what to do with their mouths besides talk and they know what to do with their bodies besides dress themselves."

"Oh, my." If her face was as hot as it felt, her head must look like an overripe tomato.

"I've gone way beyond what's polite here, haven't I? I never know what to say to a real lady. Beggin' your pardon, Trixianna, honey, I truly am sorry."

"Don't apologize. Gracious. I find your company very, um, enlightening."

Annie V. hooted with laughter. "Enlightening, eh? That's a new one." She pulled on a hideous hat covered with purple feathers, lavender posies and silver stars. She tied the ribbon beneath her chin at a rakish angle, then sailed out the door with a wave and a promise to be back after the noon meal with her girls.

Trixianna looked forward to the meeting. Other than Annie V., who didn't look or act like what she was, she'd never spoken to a "bad woman." She thought of all the expressions she'd heard used. Sporting woman. Chippie. Tart. Jezebel. Her own personal favorite—painted woman. That always conjured up a humorous picture of Indian women whooping it up on the warpath with papooses tied to their backs. Men thought women didn't know about such shadowy things, and many women didn't really, she supposed, but they certainly discussed it at length. At least she and Georgette had. Back when she and Georgette were speaking.

* * *

"Why, ah declare, this is a delightful way to while away a lazy afternoon," Lolly drawled. With an apron tied around her bed-slat-thin body, she was proving to be the only one of Annie V.'s gals who could talk and stir a spoon at the same time.

Sasha batted her thick, black lashes, and tossed her ebony curls over one shoulder. "I've had worse." She'd only stopped yawning an hour ago.

"Me, too," agreed Gretel, as plump as Lolly was thin, with mousy brown hair, missing teeth and a wide grin that unfortunately displayed that lack of teeth to perfection.

Annie V. was right about one thing, though. They didn't have a working brain between them.

Molasses clung to every available surface. Flour clung to the molasses, making a sticky, gooey mess. Apple slices were scattered from here to Hell and back. Sugar liberally sprinkled the floor and dotted the table.

Trixianna's kitchen—or should she say Chance's kitchen—would never be the same, and she doubted she could get it clean even if she scrubbed every day for a week. She knew the sheriff wouldn't be happy about this filthy mess, and she had no idea whatsoever how she'd explain it.

But four pans of apple pandowdy were finally cooking in the oven.

Trixianna glanced at the tired faces. She wondered what she could say to these working women for the next hour now that the desserts were baking. They had nothing in common.

But she tried. "Lovely weather we've been having."

"Oh, yeah, just peachy," Lolly said.

"How would I know? I sleep all day and fu—"

"Sasha!" said Annie V.

"Well, I don't get out much during the day."

Trixianna cleared her throat and tried again. "Have you seen the lovely new yard goods down at the general store?"

"Lovely?" Sasha said. "They don't have one fabric that's red and they don't have any satin or silk. Can you imagine? We have to order ours clear from San Francisco. Now there's a city that knows how to treat a gal."

"Sasha," admonished Annie V. "You've never set foot in that city."

"Well, that's what I hear."

Annie V. sniffed and gave Trixianna a long-suffering glance. "When you've got the money saved for that trip, honey, I'll gladly put you on the stage."

"We'll see about that." Sasha's sapphire blue dress swished about her as she jumped to her feet. Amid a jumble of ruffled starched petticoats, she stormed out the front door. It slammed resoundingly behind her.

Annie V. rolled her eyes, then turned her flour-smudged face toward Trixianna. "How long till they're done?"

"Oh, about an hour."

"Well, let's teach *you* something then."

"What?" Just the thought of anything that Annie V. and her girls could teach her sent her senses, and her imagination, reeling.

Lolly and Gretel wore identical blank expressions. Annie V. smiled and spread her hands flat on the table. "I've got just the thing. Poker."

She reached into her reticule and pulled out a pack

of playing cards. She brushed off the tabletop and fanned the cards out in front of her.

Trixianna, never having seen any before, leaned forward, fascinated with the tiny figures embossed on them. "Oh, my stars. I couldn't," she whispered. "Could I?"

The pungent odor of smoke drifted in the open doorway of the jailhouse. Chance lifted his head and glanced outside. While the smell was nothing unusual, for some peculiar reason the hair on the back of his neck bristled. His sixth sense warned him that trouble drifted in on that scent.

He strode to the door, grabbing his shotgun on the way. He stood still long to enough to refasten the leather strap holding his holster to his thigh.

Chance settled his Stetson on his head and glanced both ways down the dusty main street. Nothing out of the ordinary.

Yet the burnt smell tickled his nose. Although he wasn't certain, the odor seemed to be coming from the same end of town as his house. Gooseflesh rose on his arms. *That danged West woman.*

He tore off down the street. Raised eyebrows and surprised gasps followed his loud footsteps, but he didn't slow down, even when several people questioned him.

Frank Fairfax stood beneath the awning in front of the Kansas Hotel passing the time of day with the hotel proprietor. "Where's the fire, Sheriff?" he hollered. He gave Chance a good-natured grin as Chance flew by.

Chance just waved his arm and continued on without slowing, his boots pounding the boardwalk.

The scent got stronger the closer he came to the end of the street. As he neared his house, he saw gray smoke billowing out the front window. The sound of a woman's frantic screams came from inside. A tight knot settled in his stomach.

He burst in, throwing the door wide. The scene that greeted him stunned him into momentary speechlessness. Trixianna, Annie V. and two saloon gals scurried around the kitchen like ants at a picnic. Covered in soot and some sort of goo from head to toe, they tossed buckets of water at the smoking stove, missing more often than not. A misty haze hung just below the ceiling and billowed out the open windows. The floor, covered in at least a half inch of water, mixed with whatever was all over the women, looked like a muddy pigsty. He was even more startled to see playing cards spread out over his kitchen table.

Chance took one step inside, attempted to take another and found both feet nearly glued to the floor. He lifted one boot high. Sticky brown matter clung to the sole like a wad of taffy.

He glanced at Trixianna, the obvious ringleader. Who else could cause such a mess? She stood at the sink, pumping water with all her might. Frightened emerald eyes stared out from a soot-covered face. Her hair, the approximate shade of dried mud, lay in ringlets about her head and down her back. Water dripped off the ends and fell to the floor. Her dress and splattered apron clung to her like a second skin.

Oddly enough, Annie V. had removed her dress and stood in her blackened corset, bloomers and high-topped buttoned boots, dousing the poor stove with buckets of water handed to her by Lolly and Gretel. Lolly kept up a continual screech while handing over

126

the water, and Gretel's mouth hung open, revealing large gaps where teeth should have been.

Chance finally found his voice. "What the hell is going on in here?"

The screeching stopped and four identical sooty faces turned as one to stare at him.

The silence was deafening.

Then they all began explaining at once. He couldn't understand a single word among the multitude of female voices. He slapped his Stetson against his leg. "Shut up, all of you!"

The caterwauling stopped.

"You." He pointed to Trixianna.

Oh, damn. Damn, damn, damn. Chance was going to expect a perfectly reasonable explanation and Trixianna didn't have one. He probably thought she'd meant to burn his house down on purpose, particularly in light of their argument last night, when all she wanted to do was a neighborly thing like teach a few women how to cook.

He continued to stare at her. "Stop throwing water on that damnable contraption. If it hasn't drowned yet, it's not going to. I reckon that whatever fire was in it, or on it, is out by now."

Trixianna glanced at the dripping stove and nodded. She drew in a deep breath.

"Just what the hell happened?" he demanded.

The fright caused by the fire in the oven hadn't quite dissipated. Her heart thudded in her chest and her hands shook. She opened her mouth to reply, but she had no idea what to say. She hesitated a moment trying to find the right words.

"I can explain, Chance," Annie V. said, coming to

Trixianna's rescue. Her hands on her hips, she inclined her head.

"No." He swiveled back to Trixianna and pointed a finger at her. "I want to hear this from you."

Trixianna swallowed the rather large lump in her throat. "I was simply showing Annie V.'s girls how to make apple pandowdy."

He gave her a look that could curdle milk. "Why would you want to show a bunch of damn—"

"Chance," Annie V. interruped in a warning voice.

His cheeks bloomed with color; then he gave her an apologetic look, before swinging back to Trixianna. "A bunch of good-time gals how to cook. They have no need for such as that."

"What makes you think so, Sheriff?" Lolly asked.

Chance must have been surprised to hear her gentle, yet accusing, Southern tone, because the tips of his ears became pink along with his cheeks.

"We might up and marry someday," Lolly continued. "It's not so uncommon. Some of us even have children, and God knows, we all got to eat."

"I never meant . . . what I mean was, well, I never intended—"

"We know what you meant, Sheriff, *and* what you intended," Annie V. interrupted again. Her hands were fisted at her side. "You think we have no life other than the one you and all those high-and-mighty Grand Fork men see . . . flat on our backs right where you like us."

"Now, Annie. That's not what I meant. Hang it all, you're not the one I'm mad at, it's Mad Maggie." He frowned, then bestowed Annie V. with a disgruntled look. "Where the hell's your dress?"

Annie V. looked down at herself as if she'd forgotten

her unclothed state. She shrugged her shoulders and gave him a nonchalant smile. "It was one of my favorites, too. I'm afraid it caught fire."

Chance's right brow rose, and his mouth dropped open. He looked her up and down, then once again more slowly. "Are you all right?"

A wry expression crossed Annie V.'s face as she answered, "I'm fine, but that dress will never be the same again. I tore it off faster than a cowboy on Saturday night."

Chance shook his head, raw amusement crossing his face. He ducked his head as he ran a hand through his hair. It stood up in ebony waves. He glanced at Trixianna, then pointed a finger at her. "It looks like she tried to burn my house down."

"I did not!" Of their own volition the words shot from Trixianna's mouth. She had the insane urge to reach out and bite that accusing finger. It took all her resolve not to do just that. "It was an accident, pure and simple."

"*You* are an accident pure and simple."

Trixianna glared at Chance, unable to come up with an appropriate reply.

"Now, Chance," Annie V. said with a sympathetic glance at Trixianna. Trixianna realized Annie was trying to come to her rescue before Trixianna did or said something stupid.

Annie V. wrapped an arm around his and looked into his stern face with a slow, secret smile. "I was just learnin' Trixianna here how to play poker. We were having us a rip-roarin' time and just plain forgot about the oven. That is, until it started belching smoke."

Chance, his lips set in a straight line, his body taut with suppressed anger, unclasped Annie V.'s arm and stepped away. As he moved, his booted feet made a sucking sound that caused Trixianna to wince. He swallowed hard before settling an angry glare first at her, then at Annie V. "My God, Annie. Didn't you smell anything?"

She shrugged her shoulders, then shook her head. "Well, as a matter of fact, no, we didn't. Pretty odd, wouldn't you say?"

"Odd?" He snorted derisively. "Were you teachin' her to drink liquor as well? Or maybe our *Mad Maggie* already has that vice."

"Why, Sheriff," Lolly drawled. "We—"

"Were just leavin'," Chance finished.

"Yes, we were," Annie V. agreed with a nod of her head. "And Chance."

He looked at her.

"We weren't drinking either."

Annie surprised Trixianna by struggling into her ruined dress right in front of Chance. He seemed totally oblivious.

Without a word, Lolly and Gretel gathered up their bonnets and wraps and waited for Annie V.

The front of her once-beautiful dress was all but missing, singed beyond repair. She stood before Trixianna with her hands holding the bodice to her chest, a bemused expression on her face. Trixianna took one look at the ruined garment, then rushed to her room. Grabbing a knit shawl, she hurried back to the kitchen. She gently draped it around Annie's shoulders to cover the fire-damaged bodice.

Annie V. gathered Trixianna in a hug. "Don't you worry about the sheriff none," she whispered. "His bark is worse than his bite . . . and I've heard tell that his bite isn't all that bad either."

Annie turned, and she and her brood carefully

stepped through the muck, holding their hems off the floor. Although by this time it didn't matter, for the gowns were beyond hope: scorched, filthy and irreparable. With a wave of her hand and a light chuckle, Annie ushered her girls over the threshold and out the door.

Trixianna stole a quick look at Chance. *His bite isn't all that bad?*

He'd dropped into a kitchen chair, and as Annie departed, he absentmindedly shuffled the deck of cards.

Her face grew hot as she contemplated Annie's ribald comment about him. She wasn't sure about the context of that statement, but her imagination painted vivid pictures. She couldn't help wondering how Georgette would have explained the phrase. Since her marriage, Georgette had been much more knowledgeable of the ways between men and women.

Trixianna eyed Chance, gauging his mood. He wore an expression of complete unconcern, his anger apparently dissipated. She was beginning to realize that Chance's temper flared suddenly, then disappeared just as fast.

He swung around in his chair. With eyes that flashed a firm warning, he gestured to Trixianna to sit across from him. Reluctant to inflame him again— now there was a great choice of words—she did as he silently ordered.

"Well, we've had a busy day, haven't we?" he said, stating the obvious. His voice held a trace of humor and his eyes twinkled.

"You could say that," she agreed.

"You didn't try to burn my house down?"

She straightened her shoulders. "Of course not."

Chance sucked in a quick breath as his gaze, soft as

a caress, dropped to her breasts. Then, just as quickly, he jerked his gaze back up to her face. A dark flush worked its way up his neck. He cleared his throat. "Of course not," he repeated.

The tenderness on his face surprised her. Had he forgotten who she was? It took a moment to compose herself enough to speak. "I really am sorry about the mess. Those ladies are a mite rambunctious, and they clearly don't know their way around a kitchen."

His gaze grew cynical as he took in the untidy condition of the room. "Now that's the damned truth. Those *ladies* nearly burned my house down around my ears."

"I know and I'm sorry. I'll clean it all up, I swear. The stove, the floor, everything."

"Um-hum."

"Really, I'm sorry."

His head shot up. "For Christ's sake, quit apologizing."

"I'm sorry."

He shook his head and rolled his eyes. A glint of humor crossed his face.

"You're not angry then?" she asked.

"Not by a jugful."

"Thank goodness." She jumped to her feet. "I'll start right away."

He reached out and clasped her wrist. His eyes held her, more surely than his hand. "Now just hold your horses." He let go of her hand and motioned for her to sit.

Trixianna dropped into the chair. She held her breath as a wave of apprehension rippled through her. One thought danced through her head. *He's going to put me back in that horrid jail cell.*

He arched an eyebrow, then with one thumb pushed his hat to the crown of his head. He scratched his forehead where a lock of ebony hair had fallen across his temple. He hesitated, blinking his eyes, before his gaze settled on her. "You know something? You've been nothing but a pain in the backside since I first set eyes on you. You've near done me in. I almost wish you'd run off just so I'd have a good excuse to shoot you."

Her stomach churned with anticipation. Blood pounded in her head. Now what would he do?

He stood up and pushed away from the table. He stepped across the room with exaggerated steps, and tossed his black Stetson on the peg by the door. He turned and looked at her, then shook his head. From somewhere deep in his chest, she heard a rumble of laughter. "Have you seen yourself?"

"No."

He undid the buttons on his cuffs and rolled up his sleeves. Propping his hands on his hips, he glanced at her. His lips quirked in a smile, and he laughed as if sincerely amused. "I've seen cleaner hogs wallowing in the mud. You look like you had a tussle in a pigsty . . . and lost."

She jumped to her feet.

He held out his hands in a placating manner. "Now, don't go gettin' riled on me. I meant no harm."

Trixianna headed for the bedroom, where she could see for herself. He headed her off by taking her arm. "I believe I know women well enough to know you don't want to see. Did you see Annie V. and her girls before they left?"

Trixianna's cheeks burned as she thought of their

appearance. They'd been covered in soot and flour and muck, and soaked from head to toe.

He led her to the sink, then pumped water into the basin.

"Is there any hot water left on the stove?"

She shrugged.

He crossed to the stove, brought back the kettle and added part of it to the cold water in the basin. He tested the water first, then dunked a dish towel in the water.

He wrung it out, turned to her and began washing her face. He held her hair away from her face with one hand, and with the other gently scrubbed away the grime. His calloused hands were warm on her skin.

She closed her eyes, remembering. She well recalled the two of them standing in this very spot when she'd burned her fingers and how he'd kissed her with such tenderness. How he had gazed at her. She opened her eyes, looked into his face and wondered if he remembered, too.

Chance remembered, all right. Her nearness, her female scent, almost brought him to his knees. Despite the fact that she looked like a drowned, bedraggled pup, he wanted her. His thoughts were very un-sheriff-like where she was concerned. He'd wanted more, much more from her. He'd known then, just as he knew now, that it was wrong. All wrong. Guilt rocked his gut. Why did this woman, instead of Fanny, the one woman who should bring out his desires, have the ability to make him tremble with passion?

He couldn't help liking her. Bank robber or no, she

had spunk, a fire and glow that caught his senses and sent him staggering.

Unlike other females he'd known, she didn't break into tears at the smallest setback. No matter what, she couldn't be cowed.

His feelings had nothing to do with reason. And everything to do with desire.

He backed away, his hands clenched.

"Let's get this mess cleaned up. I've got work to do." His voice came out gruffer than he intended, but he got her attention. She backed away, her eyes wide, her lips parted and moist.

It took all his control to keep from wrapping her in his arms and kissing her senseless. God, she was something.

He handed her a scrub brush and a bucket. "Go to it, Maggie."

Soft words are hard arguments.
—Thomas Fuller, M.D.

Chapter Eight

Before he arrested Mad Maggie West and settled her in his own home, Chance used to walk the streets of Grand Fork twice a day. Nothing of consequence ever happened, but it put him where the townsfolk could see him and talk to him if they wanted. Everyone felt better knowing he was doing his civic duty. He felt better just getting out of his stuffy office.

After he arrested *that woman*, he made his rounds six times a day, making sure he walked by his own place each and every damned time. Most times all he needed to do was take a deep breath to know she was inside. The smells of her cooking made his mouth water and his stomach grumble. Generally speaking, and with no qualms whatsoever, he sneaked a look in the windows. He felt reassured by her presence, which only confounded his feelings about her more—after all, he still considered her a criminal. Didn't he?

Today he froze at the window when he saw Mad

136

Maggie holding a long-handled blade in one hand. *And it was no kitchen utensil.*

To Chance it looked more like an Arkansas toothpick. He had seen a few in his younger days, and knew firsthand that the weapon bore a deadly double-edged blade. The knife shut into the handle and could be easily sheathed. This particular dagger was not used to slice carrots.

She stood with her back to him, the knife raised at shoulder level. The knife looked lethal even in her small hands. Over her shoulder, Chance could just make out the shape of a man seated at the table. With a force he wouldn't have believed if he hadn't seen it with his own eyes, she slashed the blade down, and then brought it up again. The man didn't move so much as a muscle when she brought the weapon down. Her voice was pitched low, and Chance couldn't make out her words. The man seated at the table seemed to be listening and not replying, nor did he display any visible reaction. What in the name of Hades was going on? Was she in danger . . . or was the man with her in danger?

Chance strode around the side of the house, and drew his gun. He reached the side porch, leaped over the steps and landed with a muffled thud upon it. He pushed the door open quietly and stepped inside. Cautiously, he strode down the hallway, his pistol leading the way. Anticipation thrummed throughout his body. His heart pounded with each breath he took.

"I'm sorry, Trixianna, but James is no solicitor."

"What?"

"No, I must confess, he's my valet."

Her knuckles whitened as she clenched the weapon even tighter in her small grasp. "Then how am I going to get out of this mess if I don't have a lawyer? I simply can't do this anymore," she said.

Chance entered the room on silent feet.

"Balderdash." Even with Burnsey's back to him, Chance recognized that distinctive British accent. "Your sister will come around."

Surprised that Burnsey sounded so calm considering he was conversing with a woman who held a blade above his head, Chance stepped further into the room.

The floorboards creaked beneath his feet.

Mad Maggie swiveled and in one clean motion, released the knife. It sailed through the air with a quickness that left Chance startled.

The blade lanced through the thick leather of his holster. The pointed tip just nicked his leg. The solid leather held the quivering blade straight out from his thigh.

Keeping his gun aimed at Mad Maggie, he glanced down at the shuddering blade . . . stuck not six inches away from his private parts. He swallowed the lump that clogged his throat.

"My God, you have a wicked aim," exclaimed Burnsey. He half-rose from his chair, glanced at Chance and sat back down.

Her eyes wide, she started toward Chance. He lifted the gun and pointed it straight between her eyes. She stopped dead in her tracks, her hands held out to her sides.

"You startled me," she whispered. Her voice trembled.

"I startled you?" With his free hand, he jerked the dagger from the leather. Beneath his denim trousers, warm blood trickled down the outside of his thigh.

138

"Are you out of your mind? You could have sliced my manhood clean off!"

Chance heard Burnsey snicker. He shot him a look guaranteed to cow lesser men. The laughter stopped, then silence met his stony stare.

"I'm sorry," Trixianna said.

"You're sorry? Hell, if you weren't already under arrest, I'd do it again. Where'd you learn to throw a blade like that?"

She waved a hand at his pistol. "Why are you still pointing that thing at me?"

"I'm asking the questions here."

She brushed her palms against her dress, then clasped her hands together at her waist. In a fragile, shaking voice, she said, "My papa taught me."

"What the hell for? Is he a wanted criminal, too?"

"Now, Sheriff," began Burnsey.

Chance pointed the dagger at him. "You stay out of this. I'll get to you later."

He turned back to Mad Maggie. "Well?"

"My papa's dead." Tears glistened on her eyelashes. He watched her visibly swallow.

Chance felt like a mongrel dog. Her low, tormented voice ate at his innards. He knew he should apologize, but the words escaped him. This strange woman had lacerated more than his leg. She'd punctured his pride and while she hadn't done him any serious harm, his ego couldn't take much more. Not once, but twice, she'd nearly killed him, and it galled him no end.

And what was more annoying, it didn't seem as if she'd done it on purpose either time.

He holstered his gun and folded the blade. She flinched when he took her by the arm. He kept his grip light and led her to the table. He pulled out a chair and gently pushed her into it. Her body shivered beneath his hand.

He pulled another chair around and, crossing his arms over the back, faced her. Tears glistened on her lashes, but he could tell she was fighting their release by the way she bit her lower lip. With her body stiff as a railroad pike, she sat with her hands folded in her lap.

"Take a deep breath and start at the beginning."

"Why?" She stared at him from eyes brimming with unshed tears. "You don't believe a word I say."

He wanted to take her in his arms and kiss her furrowed brow. He wanted to rub her back and console her with warm words. He did neither. He held himself still and waited. The cool steel of the knife in his hand reminded him that she was no ordinary woman.

"You can cry if you like," Burnsey said.

Trixianna jumped to her feet. Her chair teetered, then clattered to the floor. She refused to be mollycoddled. She knew Chance was just trying to get her to confess and Burnsey was acting like her father. She straightened her shoulders and glared at both men. "We Lawless women do not cry. No matter what."

One of Chance's brows rose in amusement. "Oh?"

"That's right, Mr. Magrane. My departed papa taught my sister and me how to shoot a gun and throw a knife so we could take care of ourselves. He taught us to never back down from a problem, but to face it head on. He knew there would be men out there like you—"

"Like me?" He sounded offended.

"Yes. Men exactly like you who'd take advantage of our gentle natures."

He grimaced, then partially rose to his feet. His clear gaze came level with hers. "Gentle nature? What gentle nature would that be?"

"Mine. I've told you and told you, in the most polite way I know how, that I'm not this West woman. I don't even look like her, but you insist on keeping me here thinking I'm some . . . some, I don't know, some common outlaw like Jesse James."

"Sit down." He righted her chair, then pointed at it until she sat. "Until you prove me wrong, that's exactly where you'll stay, too. You're not helping yourself none by shooting me, burning down my house or this latest"—his face turned fiery red—"disaster."

"Disaster, Sheriff? Not quite, but it's very quaint phrasing," murmured Burnsey.

"Shut up, Burnsey. Don't you have a bottle waiting someplace?"

Grinning, Burnsey bowed his head as if in studious contemplation of the contents of his teacup.

"I thought I explained, Sheriff," said Trixianna. "You just startled me. I've never actually thrown a knife at a real person before."

He released a disgusted huff. "What'd you use?"

"That same knife you're holding," she explained.

"No." He rolled his eyes as if beseeching heaven for patience. "What did you throw *at?*"

"Oh. A scarecrow."

"Um-hmm," he began. He rubbed his chin thoughtfully. "You've never knifed anyone before. Then just what the hell were you doing with it this time?"

"I was just—"

"Good Christ," he interrupted. "Where have you been hiding it all this time? If I'd been doing my job you shouldn't even have had a weapon on you."

141

"It was in my reticule."

"You keep a knife in there?"

Trixianna nodded. Maybe it was unusual for a lady to have a knife on her person, although she'd never given it a thought until today. Both she and Georgette had always kept a hidden blade. Georgette's knife was even bigger, and she handled it with deadly precision. Trixianna decided to keep that little bit of information to herself, however. "I was showing Burnsey how to fillet a fish."

Chance stared at her a moment, his mouth gaping. He blinked several times, then snapped his mouth shut. He turned his head to stare at Burnsey. "Did you ask her to show you?"

Burnsey nodded. "Yes. Since coming to the West I've found fishing to be a delightful way to relax, but I didn't have the foggiest notion how to make the fish edible. Trixianna actually knew how, and was in the process of showing me when you interrupted. She is a fount of information."

The beginning of a smile tipped the corners of Chance's mouth. Amusement flickered in his pale blue eyes. "It's a mite hard to picture you fishing, Burnsey. Will you hold the pole in one hand and your umbrella in the other? Or maybe you'll just let your lawyer do the holding . . . and the filleting?"

Chance burst out laughing. Then Burnsey joined in.

Chance's laughter, full-hearted and warmly infectious, set off a tingling in Trixianna's stomach. She couldn't help but smile.

Before long they were all laughing like fools.

Trixianna watched with fascination as tears of mirth rolled down Chance's face. Shaking his head, he wiped them away with a thumb. Genuine astonishment etched his features as he said in a voice choked with humor, "You are the most unbelievable woman I have ever met."

"I am?" *What is unbelievable about me?* She was as common as dandelions in July. Or did he mean that as an insult, not a compliment? Was he insinuating that she couldn't be believed or that she was just unusual? She couldn't tell, even by the relaxed expression on his face.

"I totally agree," said Burnsey. He reached across the table and took her hand, brushing a kiss across the knuckles. "Although I consider it a fortunate turn, not a misfortunate one."

"You haven't had her living under your roof," murmured Chance.

Burnsey winked at her. "I should be so fortuitous."

Trixianna felt herself blushing.

"You wouldn't feel that way if she'd shot you, poisoned you and then tried to emasculate you."

Trixianna gave Chance her meanest look. He just grinned. Disgruntled, she tried again to the same effect. She'd been practicing her most hateful face in front of the mirror and had thought she had it down pat. Apparently not.

But the sheriff had no manners at all. It was most ungallant of him to speak such foul language in front of a lady.

She stood up. Both men followed suit, Chance at a more leisurely pace. Taking her time, she smoothed the front of her dress, straightened her cuffs and removed her apron. She hung it on a wall peg, taking down her bonnet at the same time. Deliberately turning her back on Chance, she turned to Burnsey.

"Would you escort me down the street? I feel the need for some fresh air."

"I would be honored, my dear." He offered her his arm.

She placed her hand on his elbow, and waited while he adjusted his hat and put on his gloves.

Out of the corner of her eye, she saw Chance turn his chair around and drop into it. He propped his feet on the table and grinned at her. "Don't go far now, Mad Maggie. I wouldn't want to have to chase you and haul your little backside back here in front of God and everybody. You know how people gossip." His voice fairly dripped syrup.

She forced her lips to part in a stiff smile. "It's Miss Lawless to you, Sheriff, and I won't be gone long . . . just long enough to get this bad taste out of my mouth."

A lazy chuckle chased her out the door.

Mayor Fairfax stumbled out of the doorway of Jane's Fine Dresses for Ladies as Trixianna walked in front of it on her way home. His arms flew skyward as he sought a foothold on the uneven boardwalk. He caught hold of her sleeve and held on until he righted himself.

"I am so sorry," he managed, gasping for breath. His face became pink as he apologized for nearly running her over. "Do forgive me." He straightened his hat and adjusted his spectacles. Both had become askew when he'd lost his balance.

Trixianna pushed her bonnet out of her eyes. In the mayor's mad rush out the door, he'd knocked the bonnet down over her face. She adjusted the brim, then replied, "No harm done, Mayor." She patted his arm. "Is there a problem?"

He tilted his head and said in a whisper, "I shouldn't admit this, but I'm in hot water with the missus. She's as mad as a March hare right now."

"Mrs. Fairfax?" Trixianna had never had the privilege of meeting the woman. She wondered what she was like. Trixianna gestured at the door of the ladies' dress shop the mayor had spilled out of. "Is she inside?"

"Oh, yes, indeed she is." He retrieved a kerchief from his inside vest pocket and mopped his brow. Awkwardly, he cleared his throat. "She's about to have a conniption because I don't agree with her taste in dresses."

"Oh?"

He nodded, his misery apparent. "Mrs. Fairfax asked me to help her choose a gown for Fanny and Chance's wedding."

"I see." A wave of apprehension swept through Trixianna. Just thinking about Chance marrying put a knot in her stomach. She didn't quite understand the reaction. She would have to decipher it when she was alone.

"Eloise can't wear green," the mayor confided. "It makes her look downright sickly. I tried to tell her, but she went and tried on that dress anyway. Then she asked my opinion." He rolled his eyes. "You'd think, after twenty years of marriage, I'd know better, but no, I told her just what I thought."

"And what was that?" Trixianna grimaced, waiting for his answer.

"That she looked like a wrathy bullfrog wearing feathers."

"Oh, my stars."

He shook his head. "As soon as the words left my mouth I knew it was a mistake."

"Is she angry?"

"Angry?" His face paled. "She is mad enough to spit nails. Pardon me for saying so."

"That's quite all right, Mr. Fairfax. What are you going to do now?"

His face brightened. He took her arm and pulled her toward the door. "You're coming with me, young lady."

"Oh, no. I couldn't."

"Yup. Mrs. Fairfax needs another opinion and yours is as good as any. Besides, you're a woman. She'll trust your advice."

"She doesn't even know me," Trixianna protested.

"She will now."

"But everyone thinks I robbed the bank in Dena Valley. Surely Mrs. Fairfax won't value my opinion."

"No one believes you robbed that bank except Chance Magrane. He's a stubborn man and is unmovable once he sets his mind to something."

She couldn't disagree with that statement. Chance was as stubborn as she was.

"But that's neither here nor there," continued the mayor. "Right now you're gonna settle this dispute between Mrs. Fairfax and myself. An impartial party is what's needed and you're that party."

Trixianna didn't want to be a party to anything, especially the Fairfaxes' marital disagreement. She opened her mouth to refuse. Instead she found herself being hauled over the threshold and into the ladies' establishment. The bell over the door tinkled, announcing their presence.

Two ladies at the back of the store turned at the sound.

One was tall and dressed in the latest style, an exquisite sapphire satin and velvet gown. The bodice was square-cut velvet trimmed with needlepoint lace at the neck and cuffs. Six velvet-covered buttons closed it. The skirt was pulled up high in the back with panniers and a fashionably large bustle. She smiled as Trixianna entered, and then she glided toward her, her skirts swishing. She extended her hand. Her eyes sparkled with a mischievous glint.

"Welcome to my shop, I'm Jane Knapp." She took Trixianna's hands in hers, then turned and winked at the mayor. "I see you've brought back the wayward husband."

The other woman, of medium height with hair as black as night and a frown nearly as dark and forbidding, stepped forward. She wore what Trixianna guessed was the "frog dress." The mayor was right. It was a dreadful chartreuse color that made the woman look like she'd eaten too many green apples. "I thought I asked you to leave, Frank," the woman said.

"Now, Eloise," he said. He extended his hands, palms up.

She stepped forward and slapped one of them away.

Jane snickered, then concealed her smile behind a lace mittened hand. She excused herself and disappeared behind a curtain at the back of the shop.

Trixianna wished she could follow.

She would have been disconcerted by the reaction from his wife, but the mayor recovered without batting an eye. "Eloise, dear, have you met Trixianna Lawless?"

The woman's frown evaporated. Her brows rose in

surprise. She stepped forward and peered closely at Trixianna. "Oh, so you're the one everyone in town is talking about. Why, you're a lovely young woman. Such beautiful red hair you have."

"Thank you, Mrs. Fairfax."

"I simply can't imagine why Chance thinks you're that bank robber."

"Neither can I," agreed Trixianna. "We look nothing alike."

"Men." She glared at her husband. "They can be so vexing sometimes."

Trixianna nodded.

"Tell me, my dear. What do you think of this gown?" She twirled around so Trixianna could get the full effect. It looked frightful from any angle. The high neck grazed her chin, the color reflecting onto her face. Her features were the color of pea soup.

Without a doubt, it was the ugliest ensemble Trixianna had ever laid eyes on. "It is an unusual color," Trixianna finally said.

The mayor cleared his throat. He gave Trixianna a look of pained tolerance. When she stood in silence and waited for Eloise's reply, he nudged her arm none too gently.

"Well, of course, I'm no expert on fashion, Mrs. Fairfax," Trixianna went on. "But it seems to me that on your daughter's wedding day you'd want to let her be the one to shine. I'm afraid that in that dress everyone's eyes will be on you."

"You think so?"

"Yes, I certainly do."

"Jane," called Eloise.

On catlike feet the woman glided out of the back room. "What is it, Mrs. Fairfax?"

"Do you have anything else?"

"I've the perfect thing." She curled her arm around Eloise's and escorted her to the back. Over her shoulder she grinned, then gave Trixianna and the mayor a wink. "This is all the rage out East, Mrs. Fairfax. Sedate yet elegant and cut with exquisite lines. It's a lovely shade of nutmeg. I believe it's the only frock that will do for Fanny's wedding."

They disappeared behind the curtain. Trixianna could hear the two of them chatting like old friends.

Beside her, the mayor heaved a heartfelt sigh. "My dear, you have saved my hide today. If there's anything I can do, just let me know."

"Mayor, the only thing I want is my freedom. I'm not Mad Maggie West, you know."

He took her arm and escorted her to the door. "I'll see what I can do. If I hear anything, I'll let you know." He brushed a kiss on her cheek as she reached for the door handle.

"Thank you, Mayor."

"Thank *you*, Miss Lawless."

She stepped outside and stopped a moment to allow her eyes to adjust to the bright sunshine.

Behind her the mayor threw open the door and called out, "Of course, you're invited to the wedding. It's just three days away." The door banged shut with a thud, leaving Trixianna reeling.

She walked a block or two before the shock sank in, and she dropped onto a bench in front of the livery. Her heart thundered inside her chest.

Chance and Fanny?

In less than a week they would be husband and wife. The thought left a sour feeling in her stomach. Her

149

head pounded. And what was worse, she wanted to cry.

Chance figured he'd given the woman long enough to cool off. What she didn't need was enough time to make her escape from Grand Fork. Damn her. She should be back by now. He shoved his Stetson on his head and stomped out of the house, slamming the door behind him.

He came across the mayor and his wife exiting Jane's, the ladies' shop. The mayor held a brown-wrapped package and his wife wore a big smile.

Chance tipped his hat and tried to skirt the pair, stepping aside to allow Mrs. Fairfax room to pass on the boardwalk.

The mayor grabbed his arm before he had the chance to get by. "Sheriff, I just want you to know you've got quite the diplomat living under your roof. She'll make a splendid politician one day."

"What?"

"Trixianna Lawless."

"What'd she do now?"

"Why, Sheriff, she's a treasure, an absolute treasure," gushed Eloise Fairfax. She took Chance's arm and pulled him close. The scent of lemon verbena assailed his nose.

He inclined his head to listen. He liked the woman, but she could be a bit long-winded. He took a deep breath, waiting for what was sure to be a detailed story.

"I believe that woman saved my marriage."

"Oh?"

"Yes, indeed. The mayor and I were trying to pick

out a dress for your wedding, and we were having a somewhat quarrelsome disagreement."

"Somewhat?" the mayor said, astonishment obvious in his voice. "You were ready to murder me."

"Don't be silly, dear. It was just that I had my heart set on this lovely green gown, but Mr. Fairfax made it plain that he didn't like it."

"Like it? It was just plain ugly, Eloise."

She frowned at him before continuing. "I had to ask him to leave Jane's before I lost my temper."

"You didn't ask, you ordered."

"Well, anyway, he left, but he came right back in with Trixianna Lawless."

"Is that right? What did she do?" Chance asked.

"Why, she convinced me that the green wouldn't do at all. And she was right! Wasn't she, Frank?"

"She sure was and she saved my goose, too."

"Not only that, but the wedding will be all the better because the gown I chose won't be the one noticed. Instead, it will be Fanny's beautiful wedding dress, as it should be."

"You mean to tell me that you think she actually helped?"

"You sound surprised, Sheriff," observed the mayor. He slapped him on the shoulder, chuckling. "I've heard you've had some problems with her, but she seems all right to me."

"You mean, for a hardened criminal?"

"Why, Chance," declared Eloise. "I'm sure you've got the wrong person. There is nothing hard about that woman at all. She is most kind and very generous. Why, we certainly wouldn't allow her to stay with you if we didn't trust her, would we, dear?"

"No, siree."

"Well, hell," muttered Chance. He made his good-byes to the Fairfaxes, and continued his search for the kind and generous hardened criminal Mad Maggie West, who called herself Trixianna Lawless.

Still trying to sort through her disorienting feelings, Trixianna shook her head. The sight that met her eyes across the dusty street made her forget what she'd been thinking. Her heart jumped up into her throat and her pulse pounded.

Fanny Fairfax and Burnsey were strolling down the boardwalk, Fanny's hand on Burnsey's arm. Her head was tilted as she stared into his face. The sound of her lilting laughter and his deep chuckle resounded in Trixianna's ears. To most observers, they looked like casual friends, but Trixianna instantly recognized the look on Fanny's face. She'd seen Georgette gaze with big cow eyes at her beloved Jonathan in just such a fashion.

Fanny Fairfax was in love with Alistair Burns.

Never was cat or dog drowned,
that could but see the shore.
—Italian proverb

Chapter Nine

Trixianna wiped her beaded brow with a crumpled cotton towel. Staring at the squares on the oilcloth-covered table, she traced the pattern with her index finger; first one red block, then one white block. On what should have been a crisp autumn afternoon, the sun battered the roof with heat, turning the house, especially the kitchen, into an enormous, stifling oven.

Her baking finished and delivered for the day, Trixianna sat in the kitchen, longing for a cool spot to relax. And wishing she could go home to see Georgette and Jonathan and Granny Lawless. Wishing that things were different between her and Chance. Wishing. Wishing. Wishing.

She recalled seeing a meandering creek not far from town. She could think of no better way to spend the rest of the afternoon—with a light lunch, Angel for company and the lovely shade of a willow tree. Maybe even a book to read so she could stop feeling sorry for herself. With a smile, she remembered a saying of Granny Lawless's. Feeling sorry for oneself was "about as useless as feathers on a hog."

She wrote Chance a note explaining her whereabouts so he wouldn't call out a posse when he found her gone. She left it in the middle of the kitchen table beside a plate of molasses cookies where even he couldn't miss it.

With Angel in one basket and lunch and a book in the other, she wandered past the few houses near the edge of town. She kicked at the gold and bronze leaves scattered on the ground, and her spirits lifted with each step.

Soon the ruts in the road were little more than a memory as she left all signs of Grand Fork behind. She climbed over a slight hill, then down through a stand of hackberry and ash trees, their foliage just starting to turn and drop from the branches. She found a spot beneath the shade of a cottonwood where the embankment of the creek gently eased down to the slow-moving water.

Trixianna set both baskets down and released Angel. He sauntered off, his tail high, his whiskers twitching. She smiled as she watched him stalk some poor unsuspecting creature near the creek's edge.

She unfolded a blanket, shook it out and sat down. As she tried to remove her bonnet, it pulled several hairpins free and her bun fell to her shoulders. Too impatient to fix it, she yanked the remaining pins out and tossed them in one of the baskets.

She removed her boots and stockings and drew her dress up to her knees. Free of propriety, she savored the warm, humid air as it caressed her bare legs. She undid the top three buttons on her dress, exposing her neck and chest. Lying back on the blanket, she closed her eyes.

Slowly, like the creek drifting in front of her, she relaxed and let the sunshine and the gurgling water calm her. A wren warbled in the branches above her head, and grasshoppers chirruped nearby. A slight wind whispered through the prairie grass. The current bubbled and swept along. The air didn't seem as still and hot as it was in town. Trixianna thought this must be heaven on earth.

Her predicament with the law didn't seem quite so serious out here under God's loving eye. She knew in her heart that Chance would soon discover that she wasn't Mad Maggie West. The sheriff from Dena Valley would arrive soon, or her family, and either could verify her innocence. She would be free to go back home to Abilene. If that was what she wanted. She wasn't sure. Although she missed her family, the thought of leaving Chance left a lump in her throat and a twisting in her stomach. Could she be falling in love with the sheriff? She doubted it. In actuality it felt more like a case of dyspepsia.

She knew little about love, but doubted it made one ill.

Mad Maggie West was going to drive Chance to some serious drinking. No, much worse, she was going to prod him into murder. Hers. She had no business wandering off. She was probably having a tryst with her band of cutthroats. Well, maybe not. In all honesty, he didn't know that she had a gang, and furthermore, he couldn't imagine her riding with one. In fact, he couldn't even see that woman atop a horse.

But somehow, in his wild imaginings, she was off plotting a dirty deed. Something to do with harming his body. He rubbed his thigh where she'd etched a half-inch scratch into his skin with her knife. Six inches to the left and she'd have gelded him. He shuddered at the appalling thought.

He crushed her note in one hand and picked up a cookie. While munching, he took a look around the kitchen. She kept it neat and tidy, unlike her own room. He walked past it on his way to the kitchen every morning. And each and every time he peeked in, stared in surprise, then slammed the door shut, his heart pounding. Her room reminded him of a bordello bedroom after a hard night of lusty bed play. Mussed sheets, quilt wrapped around the footboard, clothes tossed in all directions. A warm flowery scent that startled his senses. Worst of all, her silky-soft pink nightgown puddled on the floor. He shook his head to scatter the wayward thoughts arousing his body.

He picked up another cookie and chewed it thoughtfully as he left the house to search for her. Damn, she made a fine cookie. And she had the prettiest green eyes this side of the Mississippi. And the cutest freckled nose.

And, by God, he had to steer clear of her. He had a fiancée who was a fine upstanding woman and deserved better. He had responsibilities as the sheriff in Grand Fork. He needed to haul Maggie's wayward carcass back home where he could keep a careful eye on her.

And that seemed to be his biggest problem at the moment. He couldn't keep his lecherous eyes *off* her.

He trudged down the hot, dusty road, his Stetson pulled low over his brow, his irritation with himself and with her growing. He'd thought he was easygoing, but since that woman had come into his life and turned it upside down and ass-backward, he hadn't been an easygoing man. He'd been edgy and either growling or snarling at the slightest provocation.

Chance frowned and brought his head up, his ear cocked to the unfamiliar sound. What was that infernal racket coming from over the hill? It sounded like hell had turned loose one of its inhabitants.

He scrambled down an incline and crossed through a thicket of trees. He stopped at the edge of the creek and looked downstream.

Unless he was mistaken, that was Mad Maggie in the middle of the creek attempting to walk downstream through the moving current. Water lapped at her knees. She held her arms up to keep her uncertain balance, though she didn't appear to be in much danger. In one hand she clutched her skirt, giving him a startling view of slender legs clad in transparent silk. He stood gawking like a schoolboy.

The god-awful screeching came from farther down the creek. He ran down the length of the stream and called her name. "Maggie!"

She stopped suddenly and turned at the sound of his voice. As she turned, she lost her balance. She fell to her knees, drenching her dress and splashing her face and head. Her dark red hair hung down her back in curling wet ribbons.

She pulled herself up and staggered to her feet. Her wide eyes sparkled with fright. "Oh, Chance! Angel's floating away."

"An angel?" He glanced at the sky. "Where?"

"No," she shouted. She pointed downstream and

trudged awkwardly through the churning water. "Down there."

He looked, seeing nothing but leaves and broken twigs floating on the water. The creek angled right and veered from sight. He kept pace with her from the shore. "I don't see anything."

"It's Angel. Can't you do something? I'm afraid he's going to drown."

Angel? What angel? He was dumbfounded. However, fear radiated from her, and pushed him to run past the curve in the stream.

Then he saw her cat. Of course—Angel! The danged feline had managed to perch on a floating log, and now found himself moving downstream with the current as it picked up speed at every turn.

His high-pitched yowling hurt Chance's ears. He thought about letting the stupid beast drown, but then remembered the look of terror on Maggie's face. He ran alongside, yanking his boots and socks off as he scrambled down the steep embankment.

He stepped in and gasped. The cool water took him by surprise. It brought an instant numbness to his skin. The mud sucked at his feet and made maneuvering difficult. It seemed the harder he worked, the further away the cat floated. Finally, Chance just gave up and plunged beneath the water.

Trixianna rounded the bend, her legs tired and aching. Her skin tingled with the cold. Fatigue threatened to overcome her. She winced, then shivered when she saw Chance dive beneath the water. He came up mere inches from Angel. She hurried forward as fast as she could.

He submerged again, and this time when he popped to the surface he held the hissing, scratching cat by the scruff of the neck in his outstretched hand. Angel, bedraggled and dripping, didn't look too grateful. Chance shook water droplets from his face and hair, then grinned.

Trixianna slogged forward to take the cat. As she did, she slipped on a mossy stone and stumbled. Simultaneously with the start of her fall, her hand collided with Chance's extended arm. He dropped the mewling cat. They bent over at the same time to retrieve him, and their heads bumped with a resounding thwack. Chance lost his balance and fell over backward, striking his head on the incline of the creek bank. His eyes rolled back and he collapsed, unconscious, his legs folding beneath him, his head lolling onto one shoulder.

Oh, no, not again.

Trixianna tossed Angel up onto the bank, where he scampered away. She put her hands under Chance's arms and pulled his head and shoulders out of the water, then dragged his body as far as she could from the creek. She dropped to her knees beside him, cradling his head in her lap. She shivered with fear for his welfare. He lay so still, so quiet.

She patted his chilled cheek and brushed wet hair from his eyes. "Chance? Dear God, answer me. Please be all right."

She slapped his cheek a little harder, terrified of doing more harm than good. His blue-tinged lips parted and he moaned. His eyelids fluttered. *Thank God.* "Chance? Can you hear me?"

He came to, sputtering and coughing up water. His pale blue eyes opened, then widened. He tried to lift his head, but Trixianna refused to let go.

"Damn. You did it again, woman." He turned his

head and looked around as if unsure of his whereabouts. Uttering an impressive obscenity that under different circumstances might have shocked Trixianna, he glanced back at her with a look of complete irritation.

She heaved a heavy sigh of relief. He was going to be fine. "Are you all right?" she asked.

"Hell, no."

"What's wrong? Is it your head?"

"Yes. No. Dammit, it does hurt, but that's not it. I passed out again, didn't I?"

"No, no," she reassured him. "You just banged your head on a rock or something. You knocked yourself out. You didn't faint."

He snorted. "I don't see much difference."

She patted his cheek again and smiled.

He grabbed her hand and sat bolt upright. "Your hands are like ice, woman." His gaze traveled down her body and then up again, taking in her soaked, shivering condition. "Did you happen to notice we're sitting in six inches of damnably cold water and conversing like we're at a church social?"

Trixianna shrugged her shoulders. "I couldn't lift you any farther."

His black brows shot up. "You actually moved me? I weigh twice what you do."

"Maybe, but I couldn't let you die, not after you saved my dear Angel."

"And almost drowned doing it," he muttered. He paused. "I do appreciate it, but I seriously doubt I'd have drowned."

"You never know."

He swiped a droplet of water off the end of his nose. "Besides, aren't cats supposed to have nine lives?"

"Yes, I guess so." She smiled. "Regardless of that, you jumped right into the water without even thinking about your own welfare." Overwhelmed with gratitude and something more indefinable, Trixianna leaned forward and framed his face with both hands. His breathing quickened, and his moist breath caressed her face. She parted her lips and pressed her mouth against his jaw. Her lips brushed against his rough beard and her eyes drifted shut. She heard his quick intake of air, and turned her head ever so slightly. His cool lips, soft and pliant, met hers; then they heated, and his mouth covered her own. His tongue slipped inside, delving, exploring, caressing.

Amazingly, his body gave off a warmth that penetrated Trixianna's chill. Her own body grew flushed and heavy. She kissed him back with an eagerness that surprised her. With a tentative touch, she stroked her tongue against his. He tasted like sweet, warmed honey.

Chance angled his head and took the kiss deeper, melting her insides and making her tremble. He clasped her waist in a gentle grip. His thumbs rubbed tiny circles against her ribs. Gooseflesh broke out on her skin.

Trixianna lifted her palms to his hard chest, feeling his heart's reassuring steady rhythm. She eased her hands to the back of his head and plunged them into the thick black hair there. Kneading the back of his neck, she relished the feel of his scalp beneath her searching fingers.

He made a growling noise deep in his throat, then moved his mouth from hers. His hands tightened at her waist. His eyes shimmered with a pale sky-blue light, the pupils dilated. He swallowed hard. "Why did you kiss me?"

"I-I don't know," she lied. She peered at him, unable to tear her gaze away from his features. She did know, but would die of embarrassment before she ever told him. She'd wanted his kiss, and felt like a terrible wanton for even admitting it to herself.

He stared back at her, appearing completely and utterly surprised. Spots of crimson washed the upper half of his face. A muscle twitched at his jaw. She saw him swallow again.

"Stop looking at me like that," he murmured, his voice raspy. His gentle tone conveyed little conviction behind the harsh words.

"Like what?" she whispered. Her heart thundered; her lips throbbed with the remembrance of his kiss. A fevered wanting like nothing she'd ever experienced coursed through her veins. She licked her dry lips.

Chance shook his head. "And stop that, too."

He propped one hand on the slope of the bank, and wrapped the other one around Trixianna's waist. He rose to his feet. Mud clung to his trousers and shirt. "We've got to get you out of those wet clothes. Can't have you dying on me before I get the chance to hang you."

Although he smiled, his deep voice reminded Trixianna of her circumstances and brought her back down to earth with a start. "Thank you for your concern," she said bitterly. Disconcerted, she pulled away. She'd almost forgotten she was kneeling in a cold, muddy creek. Now, as reality set in, she shivered from head to toe.

With his hands on her bottom, he unceremoniously shoved her up the bank, then scrambled after her. He looked around, and saw Angel grooming himself on the blanket beneath the cottonwood tree. "Damn fool cat."

Chance jerked the blanket from beneath the cat's paws and sent the feline flying. Then he wrapped the warm covering around Trixianna's shoulders. She offered him a corner of it, but he shook his head as he gathered up her things.

Chance started walking toward town, acting as though nothing had happened between them.

In his mind, had anything occurred? Probably not. To him, she was the notorious outlaw Mad Maggie West, and the sheriff had no real interest in dallying with that kind of woman. She was available, and he'd simply returned her kiss.

It meant nothing to him.

She knew she would never forget his generosity in saving Angel. She would never forget his tender yet dangerous kisses. She couldn't forget either that she was his prisoner and that he reminded her of it daily.

Later that afternoon, Jones's Laundry and Bathhouse had never had a more thankful customer than one Sheriff Chance Magrane.

Grand Fork was fortunate to have Jones's Laundry and Bathhouse. It seemed a strange combination to some folks, but both businesses required hot water and plenty of it. To Hiram Jones, they went together like ham and eggs.

When the sheriff dragged his soaked, tired body into the place, Hiram didn't have to ask twice what he wanted.

Hiram kept a steady stream of hot water pouring

into the tin tub before the water had a chance to cool. Chance didn't complain.

He leaned his head against his knees, closed his eyes and willed himself to relax. Steam swirled around his upper body and dripped off his chin. Although his muscles were beginning to relax, his thoughts weren't. They kept darting through his mind like a humming-bird at full speed.

Images of Mad Maggie kept popping into his head. *She*, with her wet dress clinging like a second skin, a vision close enough to see her perfect, round breasts and hard buttonlike nipples begging for his touch.

She, with soft lips and a pliant mouth. *She*, who kissed like she'd never kissed a man before.

She, the notorious outlaw Mad Maggie West, who most definitely wasn't his fiancée.

And never would be.

Chance ducked his head beneath the water until he couldn't hold his breath any longer without drowning. He came up sputtering. "Damn! Damn that con-founded woman."

"And who might that be?"

Chance's eyes flew open. He wiped water from his face, and stared into the grinning countenance of Al-istair Burns. The Englishman was weaving from side to side, eyes blurry, derby missing and hair standing on end. Drunk as a lord.

Would the man never give up drinking? Chance doubted it. "Burnsey."

Hiram sauntered in behind him, burdened with two steaming buckets of water, and dumped them into the tub next to Chance's. A cloud of steam rose to the ceil-ing.

Burnsey wasted little time stripping off his clothes . . .

or trying to, anyway. He tripped, lost his balance and grabbed the side of Chance's tub to keep from toppling inside and joining him. He finally settled on the floor, where he undressed with careful deliberation, scattering his wrinkled clothing to all four corners of the room.

Hiram rolled his eyes heavenward when he caught Chance's amused grin. "Maybe the hot water'll sober him up," Hiram muttered. "Then again, maybe pigs will fly." He left the room, muttering to himself.

Chance chuckled. He leaned back and tried not to watch Burnsey in his clumsy attempt to disrobe.

Finally, naked as the day he was born, Burnsey stepped gingerly into the hot water.

"Ahh, 'upon the seraph-wings of ecstasy.'"

Sheriff-wings? What the hell did that mean? Chance laughed again, then shook his head. Burnsey could put away a gallon of whiskey and keep right on bending a person's ear, his speech unaffected until he passed out, usually with one last word of wisdom, upon the floor.

Chance closed his eyes. "Burnsey, you've got quite a vocabulary for a drunk."

"Now, Sheriff, is that any way to speak to me? It just sho—" he said, then stopped. He cleared his throat, inhaled, then began again, carefully enunciating each word. "It just so happens I had a royal-like education. The great poets were required reading. Would you care to hear more?"

"Thanks, but I believe that's not necessary."

"Undoubtedly, you are unappreciative when it comes to the arts."

Chance snorted. "I just don't want to argue with a drunk."

"We're not arguing."

"That's right, we're not. Now shut up and let me take my bath in peace. I haven't had much of that lately."

"I've heard. Is Trixianna more woman than you can handle, Sheriff?"

"*Mad Maggie* is more woman than any half-dozen men can handle."

The Englishman chuckled, then paused before speaking again. "She's a grand, upstanding woman and you two do make a fine couple."

Startled, Chance turned to peer at his bathhouse companion. Burnsey had his head tilted back and eyes widened. He seemed to be staring with avid fascination at the ceiling overhead. Chance glanced up, too. He saw nothing but rising steam amid the wooden beams and rafters. He glanced away, shaking his head. Next thing he knew, he'd be seeing pink elephants right along with the old rummy. "Maybe you haven't heard, Burnsey, but I'm engaged to be married."

"Yes, yes, I know." His face took on a faraway look. "Fanny Fair."

"That's Fairfax."

"Yes, of course. A beautiful girl."

Fanny? Beautiful? Were they discussing the same woman? She was many things, but Chance didn't think beautiful was one of them. Honest and intelligent, pleasant and generous, good-hearted. She would make a satisfactory wife. However, meaning no offense, Chance put her a mite closer to homely than beautiful.

"She's not for you, though," Burnsey said.

Chance sat up quickly. Water spilled over the sides of the tub and gushed onto the floor. It seeped between the cracks in the floorboards and disappeared below. He plopped back down. "What the hell does that mean? Not for me?"

"You don't love her." He no longer sounded like a drunk. Although Burnsey stared at Chance through bloodshot eyes that had recently seen the bottom of a whiskey bottle, they contained gentle warmth and complete understanding.

"No, I don't," Chance said, unsure why he was admitting it. He couldn't keep the regret from his voice. He gripped the sides of the tub with both hands and clenched his eyes shut tight. "God knows I've tried."

Burnsey released a long, drawn-out sigh. "And your plan is to carry through with this loveless marriage?"

"Of course."

"Of course," Burnsey repeated in a low whisper. His expression stilled. He picked up a cake of lye soap off the table between the two tubs and began sudsing his chest.

"I made a promise," said Chance. "And I would never humiliate Fanny by backing out at the last minute."

Burnsey's hand stopped in the middle of his chest. He leaned toward Chance. "Have you ever told her how you feel?"

"Are you crazy, man? I don't talk to her about such things."

"What *do* you talk about?"

Chance scrubbed his hands down his face. "Hell, I don't know. The usual stuff."

"You should tell her. Doesn't she deserve that much?"

Chance stiffened, irritated and uncomfortable with the intimacy of this particular conversation. He liked Burnsey, but this was really none of his business. "What she deserves," Chance said, "is a husband who comes home every night, isn't unfaithful and provides a solid roof over her head. That's it. And that's all I have to say about it. Now shut up and leave me be."

With a significant lifting of his brows, Burnsey went back to vigorously soaping his body. "Whatever you say, Sheriff."

Chance went back to trying to relax. Unfortunately, he now had two women on his bedeviled mind.

Trixianna lay her head back on the edge of the hip bath. Lavender-scented soap bubbles floated about her and tickled her chin. The comfortable, warm kitchen and the low light cast from the lantern surrounded her in a soothing atmosphere. The hot water swirled about her, making her limbs tingle and coaxing her body to relax.

Although she tried, she couldn't forget Chance. Those two simple words—Chance and relax—could never be put together in the same sentence as far as she was concerned.

He, with his persuasive, knowing kisses.

He, with a voice, husky and silky-smooth at the same time, that sent her heart skittering every time she heard it.

He, with a laughing smile and a gentle, beckoning, all-male touch.

He, who was engaged to marry Fanny Fairfax in less than three days' time.

Trixianna closed her eyes and moaned. How had she ever gotten herself into such a confounded predicament? She'd fallen in love with a man promised to another. He thought she was the deadliest bank robber Grand Fork had ever seen . . . the only bank robber Grand Fork had ever seen, she amended. What was she going to do?

Something would happen soon, she thought. She would just have to put her mind to work—what would Granny Lawless do in this situation? It was something to ponder.

That decided, Trixianna continued her bath with only troubling thoughts of the sheriff to contend with. They weren't really troubling, though. More like confusing, exciting, restless.

Trixianna compared these new feelings of desire for Chance to drinking a hot cup of chocolate. It soothed and warmed her insides, making her feel loose and relaxed, yet happy at the same time. She liked the feeling.

She couldn't help groaning aloud at the mess she'd made of her life. She ticked the occurrences off on the fingers on her hand. One, she'd run away from her problem with Georgette instead of staying and working it out together. Two, she'd been arrested for something she hadn't done. Three, she'd complicated the sheriff's life in every way imaginable. He thought she was a menace to his well-being and most of the time, she was. Four, she'd fallen in love with him. And five . . . what was five? she wondered. It didn't matter. Chance was engaged to Fanny: a woman Trixianna liked, a woman that Trixianna didn't want to hurt. Fanny had been so understanding, even allowing her to stay with Chance in his home.

Trixianna wouldn't betray that trust, that kindness.

First she had to get Chance to drop the charges against her, and then she had to leave Grand Fork, as quickly as possible. Before her heart broke.

She feared it was already too late.

*The abstinent run away from what they desire
But carry their desires with them.*
—Bhagavadgita

Chapter Ten

The sheriff from Dena Valley was due in Grand Fork tomorrow or the next day to take Mad Maggie West alias Trixianna Lawless off his hands. But did he want her taken off his hands?

Chance stared at the print on the telegram until the words blurred before his eyes. Rain blew against the side of the building. Falling off the roof, it splattered noisily into a nearby rain barrel. The sunless, gloomy end to the day only added to Chance's foul mood. He scrubbed his tired eyes with the palms of his hands, then stared out the window at the rain.

Out of the corner of his eye, he caught sight of the framed photograph of Fanny and her silly pet goat, Bluebeard. He frowned at the serious, reserved expression on her face. He gave Fanny a grudging nod. The sheriff from Dena Valley would be here, all right. Just in time for his wedding.

So why, if he was getting rid of *that* woman, did he feel so heart-sore? Why did he feel as if he were losing his best friend? And why, if in just a matter of days he'd be marrying the woman he thought he'd always wanted, did he feel like kicking some mongrel dog into the next county?

He was a coward for refusing to acknowledge the answer that lay right in front of him. He had fallen in love with another woman while engaged to Fanny. Dishonorable and shamed was how he felt . . . and guilty as sin.

Jerking to his feet, he shoved his Stetson on his head and made for the door. He didn't ordinarily drink during the day, but right now he needed a drink. All right, he *wanted* one. There was little difference at this point. And not one Grand Fork busybody better say a single damn word about it. That is, if they didn't want to find their butts kicked up around their necks.

He stormed out the door and stalked down the boardwalk. Rain soon soaked through his shirt, but he didn't care. Eyes widened and feet moved quickly out of his way. He received a "howdy" from the blacksmith, Luther Inman. Apparently he was the only man in town brave enough, or foolish enough, to speak when Chance's face was deliberately set in such a dark, vicious expression.

As he passed two young boys playing marbles under an overhanging roof, one looked up and his eyes widened. Chance heard him whisper to his friend, "Look at Sheriff Magrane." His eyes shimmered with admiration. "He 'pears madder'n a rained-on rooster. Do ya suppose there's gonna be a real doggone shootout right here in the street?"

"Darn right, kid," Chance muttered. He stopped

172

long enough to say, "Better clear the streets." Like spooked cattle, they jumped off the boardwalk and shot off in opposite directions, dodging puddles as they scrambled down the muddy road.

He stomped into the Annie V. Standing with feet planted wide, he shook the rain off his hat, then hung it on a wall peg. One single-minded intention played in his head. To get so drunk he could forget he'd ever met a certain rusty-haired woman with kissable freckles all over her kissable nose. And eyes the color of the first spring blades of grass. He groaned aloud. He sounded like a lovesick cowboy who'd been out on the range too long. Next thing he knew he'd be scribbling poetry and wearing those fancy scarves that Burnsey wore around his neck.

He strode over to the bar, settled his elbows on the counter and ordered a whiskey. He glanced around. It might be too early for Annie's girls to be strutting their goods, but the place was humming all the same. The packed room buzzed with hearty, male laughter and the sound of serious monkey business. Annie V.'s saloon was no different than most; it was dark and dank, smelling of stale whiskey and unwashed bodies. Choking smoke hung above the room like a gray cloud. The mirror behind the wall was cracked, the floor muddy. The piano player knew five songs, only one of which was recognizable.

But Annie V. knew how to keep 'em happy, and she knew how to keep 'em coming back for more.

During the nooning she supplied thick beef or ham sandwiches for a nickel. Set up on a long table against the back wall, and large glass jars of pickles and eggs accompanied the sandwiches. All a man had to do was order a drink and he could keep on eating.

During the evenings, Annie's girls smiled and cooed, whispering compliments in the men's eager ears. They displayed their assets with low-cut dresses and short hems, thereby allowing them to cajole the men into drinks, money and a go-round upstairs. Everyone went away with a smile on his face.

Today, however, Chance wasn't interested in them. He was here not to think about Trixianna.

"It's good to see you, future son-in-law," said a sadly familiar voice.

Chance groaned.

Mayor Frank Fairfax stepped up to the bar and slapped him on the shoulder. He called for a beer, then settled in on the closest stool.

Apparently, thought Chance morosely, there were two men brave enough—or stupid enough—to beard the lion in his den. First the blacksmith, and now the mayor.

"All set for the big day?" Frank asked.

No. Chance nodded.

Frank angled his head at Chance's empty whiskey glass, and cocked an eyebrow. At his nod of agreement, the mayor ordered one for each of them. "Last chance to sow some wild oats?"

"Frank, I reckon you're just being friendly, but would you mind leavin' me be?"

The mayor chuckled. "What's the matter, son? Have a spat with Fanny?" He shook his head. "That girl can be quite a trial sometimes."

"No. Fanny's done nothing wrong." Fanny never did anything wrong. Fanny was above reproach. She was good and right and honorable. That was part of his problem.

"Why, she's so het up about this wedding, she's

about to make me crazy," Frank said. "One minute she's laughing, then she's crying. Hell, that's why I'm drinking in the middle of the day myself. I had to get away from those two blubbering women of mine."

He glanced at Chance beneath lowered brows, then whispered, "Grand Fork's illustrious mayor and no-nonsense sheriff gettin' *educated* together in the Annie V." He threw his head back and roared with laughter. "Don't that beat all?"

It sure as hell did. Chance downed his second whiskey in one gulp and ordered a third.

He glanced up at the sound of voices. The bat-wing doors swung open. In strolled Burnsey, dapperly dressed as usual, and his dour companion, the lawyer, James . . . what the hell was that man's last name?

Unfortunately, they, too, strolled over.

"Well, do tell, James," Burnsey said. "Chance Magrane imbibing in the pub and it isn't even . . ." He pulled a gold watch from his vest pocket, snapped it open and checked the time. His face lit with a grin. "My, my, it isn't even one o'clock. What's the occasion? Have you arrested another beautiful woman?"

Burnsey and Frank burst into howls of laughter, slapping each other on the back. Tears of mirth rolled down Frank's cheeks.

"Well, hell," muttered Chance. "Can't a man have a drink without the whole damn town wondering what for?"

"No, sir," came the simultaneous reply.

"At least not you, Sheriff," Burnsey said. A Cheshire cat grin tugged at the corners of his mouth. "You never drink during the day. We should get a table. This calls for a celebration."

"Why?" groused Chance. He wanted to get drunk, and he preferred to do it alone.

No such luck. Before he had a chance to get away, Burnsey grabbed the mug out of Chance's hand, ordered another round and dragged him over to a table. He pushed him into a chair. "Drinking in the middle of the day. The revered sheriff . . . and the mayor. Think of it. It will probably make the headlines of tomorrow's gazette."

"Shut up, Burnsey."

The afternoon hours rolled on and Chance kept drinking. Burnsey wandered off to join a poker game. It wouldn't be long before he began shedding his dandyish clothes. The man was an incorrigible gambler, and a lousy one to boot. Besides, he didn't have the sense God gave a damned fence post.

Earlier James had joined the piano player, and Chance had been surprised to hear him playing a pretty fine tune. He had put the current musician to shame. His head hanging in dejection, the humbled piano player had left the saloon, apparently having lost his position to a better candidate.

The sun began setting, yet Frank matched Chance drink for drink, his face becoming redder with each swallow. His laugh became louder, his jokes more absurd, and his words less intelligible.

Meanwhile, Chance remained sober. Cold stone sober. Unaccountably so, for he'd drunk enough to down three good-sized men.

He glanced at Burnsey, then shook his head. He'd lost track of him for a while, but the man was now down to one sock, red long underwear, and his expensive derby hat. He hated to see him lose another of those all-fired hats that he sent all the way to London for.

Chance rose to his feet, surprised to find them steady. He grabbed Frank in one arm and Burnsey in the other, leaving Burnsey's lawyer banging away on the piano. He hauled them both out the door and into the downpour. He didn't lock Burnsey in the cell, but he knew he wouldn't get into any more trouble, even without locking it. The Englishman passed out as soon as his head hit the mattress.

Chance turned to the mayor, whom he'd left propped against the wall while he helped Burnsey into his cell. Frank's spectacles had slipped to the end of his reddened nose. His eyes were no more than narrow slits in his face. Chance smiled. "Frank, let's get you home."

Unbalanced, the mayor teetered on his feet. If not for Chance's grip on his arm, he would have toppled face first onto the floor. Glassy bloodshot eyes met Chance's. "I don't reckon the missus will like my drinking the afternoon away."

"I don't reckon," Chance agreed.

"What she doeshn't know won't hurt her," the mayor slurred. He gave Chance a knowing, buck-toothed grin.

"I believe she'll know."

"How?"

Chance rolled his eyes. "Oh, just a wild guess, Mayor."

Frank stumbled as Chance pulled the door open. He grabbed Chance's sleeve. "We'll shee."

Chance tightened his grip around Frank's shoulder. "I can hardly wait."

By the time they made it to the mayor's house, both

men were drenched from head to toe and shaking with cold. Frank, muttering something about weddings and debtor's prison, stumbled through the front door as Mrs. Fairfax yanked it open. He dropped into a wet heap on the foyer floor. His eyes drooping, his hands limp at his side, he sat in a puddle, oblivious to the wrathful look on his wife's face.

"What has happened to my husband, Sheriff?"

Chance swallowed a knot of apprehension. If icicles could form on people with cold stares, Eloise Fairfax would have been an ice statue. "I'm afraid the mayor may have had a mite too much to drink."

With hands on her hips, and eyes as chill as last winter's snow, she asked, "A mite?"

"Well, maybe more than a mite," Chance amended. He felt his chance for a civil relationship with his future mother-in-law dwindling by the minute.

He heard a gasp, and saw Fanny step into the foyer, her smile fading as she surveyed her bedraggled father. She clasped a hand against her chest, her startled gaze seeking her mother's. "What's wrong with Father?"

"The danger of drink, my dear." She turned a hostile glare toward Chance. "Mind you don't do this to my daughter once you're married, Mr. Magrane."

"Yes, ma'am." Belatedly remembering his manners, Chance yanked off his Stetson. Rain poured off the brim, further ruining the foyer floor.

"Don't look so melancholy, Chance. I sincerely doubt that you held my husband at gunpoint and poured liquor down his throat."

"Well, no, ma'am." Despite his being chilled, Chance's cheeks flamed. So why did he feel guilty about Frank getting drunk?

"It's too late to cry over spilled milk." Eloise shook her head, a look on her face that could have curdled that very liquid. "Would you mind taking him upstairs and putting him to bed? I'll get towels and dry clothing. Then you'll stay and have supper with us."

It wasn't a suggestion. Chance nodded. He leaned over, grabbed a still-muttering Frank beneath the arms and hauled the near-deadweight over his shoulder.

"First door on the right," said Eloise through lips pinched tight. She tossed her skirts aside and marched down the hall to the kitchen. Fanny followed her mother. Over his shoulder Chance caught a glance of her—eyes wide, mouth hanging open.

Mumbling as Chance tossed him over his shoulder, Frank continued his incoherent harangue all the way up the steps and into the bedroom. Chance tossed him on the bed. He lay where he landed. Chance arched his aching back, then leaned over to remove Frank's shoes. Wouldn't want to soil the missus's ivory bed coverings. The mayor's shoes clung tight to damp socks that pulled off at the same time. Chance wadded up the soggy pair and tossed them into the corner.

The sound of a window-rattling snore followed Chance out the door. Fanny met him in the hall holding a towel and a clean, dry shirt of her father's.

Her cheeks colored as she held them out to him. "Mother said you could clean up across the hall." She indicated the door. "If there's anything else you need, let me know."

Chance had no idea what possessed him to say, "There is one thing."

"Oh, what's that?"

"A kiss. I'd like a kiss from you."

179

A momentary telling look of discomfort crossed her round face before she replied. "Of course." She held her arms stiff at her side. Her eyes fluttered shut.

He'd kissed her before, but had purposely kept the kisses chaste. He hadn't wanted to frighten her with a passion she was unaccustomed to. But now he needed to know something. He bent forward and placed his hands on her shoulders. She flinched, but recovered quickly. Her eyes opened and she gave him a wan smile.

Her eyes squeezed shut just as Chance's mouth grazed hers with the barest of touches, giving her time to adjust to him. He traced the fullness of her taut, dry lips with the tip of his tongue. She shuddered, and he knew instinctively that it came from his touch. He waited for the instant reaction he received when he kissed Mad Maggie—a hot fevered rush that went straight to his groin.

Nothing. He felt nothing. Tame as dishwater, her kiss had no effect on him. An unreasoning irritation drove him on. He deepened the kiss, his tongue stroking hers, his lips molding the shape of her unwielding mouth.

She moaned, then twisted out of his grasp. An anguished grimace crossed her features. She wiped the back of her hand across her mouth. The look on her face told him everything he needed to know, and sent his stomach plummeting to his feet. Was this going to be his life then? Spent with a woman who found his kisses disgusting, his touch repulsive?

Cheeks flaming, she said, "My goodness, Chance. I'm somewhat shocked."

"By what?"

Obviously flustered, she stammered, "B-by your, well, by your—your ardor."

"You didn't enjoy it then?"

She shook her head. "It wasn't that I didn't enjoy it. I was just surprised is all."

It was a blatant lie, an attempt to soothe him. "I'm sorry, Fanny." His voice sounded hoarse, hollow, even to his own ears. The way he felt inside. "I had to know."

"What?" she asked. She sounded perplexed. She honestly didn't understand.

"Do you still want to get married?"

Her eyes widened. "Of course. Don't be silly. You weren't out of line, just impulsive. It's understandable."

"Even knowing you hate my touch, my kiss, you still want to marry me."

"I said yes, didn't I?" She shoved the towel and shirt into his midsection. Her gaze darted away from his searching one. Grabbing the hem of her skirt, she sailed down the stairs without a backward glance, her back ramrod straight.

He sighed and hung his head. He stared at the spreading puddle beneath his feet, his hands tucked beneath his armpits. He'd never heard that caustic tone of voice from Fanny before. He didn't understand what she was thinking. Why did she still want to marry him? She didn't love him any more than he loved her.

He wondered now why he'd believed their partnership would work. He'd thought it out so well. But then he'd never really given the idea of passion within the confines of marriage much consideration.

When you married, you went to bed. When you

went to bed, you made love. When you made love, passion arose. Didn't it? Did loving the person you made love with have something to do with passion? He could see it wouldn't be that way between Fanny and himself. Not only would it be loveless, their union would be a cold, emotionless affair. Two overly polite people stepping around each other . . . both figuratively and literally.

It would take the high heat of August and a minor miracle to thaw her out. Although she was a fine woman, Fanny Fairfax had no passion for him at all.

His heart heavy, he stepped across the hall into the room that Fanny had indicated. He sank onto a trunk and stripped off his damp shirt. He towel-dried his chest and head, his mind reeling.

He heard Eloise call his name, but ignored it. He knew he should go downstairs, but didn't have the stomach to face Fanny and her mother again. *Coward.*

He wondered if the house had a back stairs.

No. By God, he'd made a commitment to Fanny and he would stick to it. She would be the one to break the engagement. He'd face her and make the most of it . . . and hate himself tomorrow for being a spineless snake.

He pulled on Frank's crisp white shirt, which was two sizes too small. He rolled up the sleeves, but had little choice with the top buttons. They'd have to remain undone, revealing his chest and damp, gray undershirt. Tucking the tail into his trousers as he descended the stairs, he wondered if Mad Maggie would miss him for supper. He would miss her bright, smiling face, that was for sure.

*   *   *

Where was Chance?

Trixianna's supper of ham and beans was cooked, and now staying hot in a big cast-iron pot on the back of the stove. The cornbread lay cooling on the sideboard. The apple pie was ready for dessert.

If Chance didn't come home soon, all her hard work would be wasted. She checked her watch, pinned to her breast, as she had every ten minutes for the past hour. Eight o'clock.

She sighed. In all the time she'd stayed at his home, he'd never promised to be there for supper. He'd always had some excuse or other—he needed to check on a prisoner, or talk to the mayor, or stop a fight. But regardless of his excuses, he'd also been there every single night, smiling, laughing, and complimenting her on her cooking. She could happily spend the rest of her days just watching that man eat.

Trixianna looked at her watch again. Eight-ten. He'd never been this late before. She paced the floor, wringing her apron strings.

What if something had happened to him?

What if he had gotten shot by someone with a better aim than hers?

What if . . . she never saw him again?

She sank into a kitchen chair. Staring out the window into the dark night, she willed her mind away from all the things that could go wrong. As the sheriff, Chance probably faced danger all the time, she reasoned. And nothing had happened to him before she came along.

A knock startled her. She jumped to her feet and rushed to open the door. Swinging it wide, she stared across the threshold at a tall, thin man. Several days' growth of dark beard shaded his lean face. He stood still, his hat in his hand, his clear eyes direct, yet gentle. He seemed familiar to Trixianna, but she didn't think she recognized his chalk-white face and drawn features.

"Is the sheriff home?" he drawled. He studied her with intense, pale blue eyes that hinted at amusement. He sported a graying, bushy mustache, but his hair was as inky black as Chance's. His muddy clothes and tired demeanor spoke of quite a few miles spent on horseback.

"No, he's in town," she replied. Usually wary of strangers, for some unknown reason Trixianna found herself warming to this man.

"I see," he said, his lips quirking into a smile. He leaned forward, his hands on his spare hips. "And you are?"

"Trixianna Lawless."

"Should I know you, ma'am?" he asked, his voice courteous yet obviously curious.

"I can't think why."

He chuckled. "Me neither. I'm Rider Magrane, Chance's little brother."

"Oh." Trixianna heaved an extreme sigh of relief. He wasn't a criminal out to do Chance harm. She glanced behind him. "Have you a horse?"

He waved a hand down the street. "I stabled him at the livery down the road and walked here."

She beckoned him into the light-filled room. "I didn't even know Chance *had* a brother."

He followed her, tossing his hat on the wall peg as he passed. He kicked the door shut with the heel of his boot. "Thought he crawled out from under a rock, did ya?"

184

Her cheeks heated. "Well, no, of course not, but he never mentioned he had a brother."

"I reckon he might not."

What a strange thing to say! "Please sit down, Mr. Magrane. I'm sure he'll be home soon."

"Call me Rider, ma'am."

Trixianna nodded. "All right. Would you like coffee while you wait?"

"Coffee sounds good." He dropped into a chair, then heaved a deep sigh. He scrubbed his face with both hands. "Damn. Pardon my language, ma'am, but it's good to be off that pitiful, spavined excuse for a horse. Now I know why I got him so cheap. I haven't ridden that many hours for quite a spell. There isn't a bone in my body that's not complaining."

Trixianna turned from the stove and looked over her shoulder. "Is Chance expecting you?"

Amusement flickered momentarily in his eyes, then passed. "No, I reckon not. He sent me a wedding invite just because I'm family, I expect, but I doubt he thought I'd be coming."

"A long trip then?"

"You could say that, ma'am," he murmured. He sighed again. "A very long trip."

Trixianna walked across the room with the coffeepot in one hand and two cups in the other. He watched her, a smile on his face. She poured one steaming cup, then handed it to him. He thanked her with eyes bright with pleasure.

Trixianna sat down across from Rider and studied his features. He held his coffee with both hands wrapped around the cup, his eyes narrowed. She saw the family resemblance; the same black hair and thick black brows, the same pale blue intense eyes that didn't miss a thing. Rider was much thinner, though, and his complexion was pale, almost sickly, instead of bronzed and windburned like Chance's.

Suddenly, Rider's eyes lit up. He turned a beaming smile upon Trixianna. "Is that ham and beans I smell?"

"Why, yes, it is."

"Hot damn! I haven't eaten in a spell. Could you spare a plateful?"

Trixianna smiled, and was halfway out of her chair before she replied. "Of course."

"I don't mean to be nosy, ma'am, but what the devil are you doing here in Chance's house at this time of night? You a housekeeper or cook or something like that?"

Trixianna contemplated her answer as she spooned beans onto a plate and placed a wedge of cornbread beside it. She set it in front of Rider before she answered. With both hands clutching the back of a chair, she looked him square in the eye. "I'm under arrest."

His eyes bulged and he choked on a spoonful of food. She rushed around the table and slapped his back a few times. He coughed, then took a noisy swallow of coffee. His eyes watering, his spoon stopped midway to his mouth, he said, "What the hell for? What are you doing here? Why aren't you in jail? Dammit it all, I've got so many questions, I almost forgot how hungry I am."

"It's all right." Trixianna sat down across from him and patted his outstretched hand. "You eat. I'll talk," she said.

He nodded. Breaking off a piece of cornbread, he plopped it into his mouth and chewed. His watchful eyes never left her face.

"You see, the sheriff, that is . . . Chance, he mistook me for that bank robber, Mad Maggie West."

"Yeah? I've heard of her."

"We do look a little alike. I saw the wanted posted, and I suppose I can see a slight resemblance, but really . . ." Trixianna waved her hand in a dismissive gesture. "That woman has a big nose and her eyes are squinty like this." She narrowed her gaze and puckered her mouth to show him what she meant.

Rider laughed. "No offense, ma'am, but she must be an ugly cuss if that's what she looks like."

Trixianna joined in his laughter. "I guess so. Anyway, Chance came to my house early one morning to arrest me, and he so scared me that I shot him."

"You what!"

"Oh, don't worry, I'd never shot a gun at a man before, so I didn't kill him or anything, just wounded him in the shoulder, but I'm sure it hurt a great deal."

Rider shook his head, a smile turning up his lips in a mischievous grin. "I'd say."

"Anyway, the townsfolk of Grand Fork—they're really wonderful people—wouldn't allow Chance to put me in the jail. They said it wasn't fit for a lady. I'm staying here until the Dena Valley sheriff comes to take a look at me. I'm sure he'll straighten out this awful situation."

"Hmmm." Rider's brows lifted in an expression so like Chance that Trixianna smiled. He smiled back. "So in the meantime, you're holed up here with Chance. What does his bride-to-be think of this cozy little arrangement?"

"Fanny?"

He nodded. "Yeah, Fanny. I'd forgotten the name of Chance's bride."

"She's a lovely person, very understanding, as has been everyone. She hasn't said a word against me. Actually, I think you could say we've become friends. She doesn't believe I robbed the Dena Valley bank either."

"She must be agreeable, all right. Is she pretty?"

Taken aback, Trixianna stammered, trying to find the right words to describe Fanny. She stalled by pouring more coffee into Rider's empty cup. She glanced at his face.

His lips turned up in an amused smile. Then he gave her an infectious grin. "No, huh?"

Trixianna bit her lip to keep from returning that charming smile so like Chance's. "Fanny has many fine qualities."

"I'm sure she does or else Chance wouldn't be marrying up with her."

"That's right. Did you know she's the mayor's daughter?"

"That might explain a few things," he murmured. "Have you got more beans?"

"Yes indeed."

Trixianna jumped up to refill his plate. This time she brought back one for herself. She glanced at her watch. Nine-thirty. Where was Chance?

"Late, is he?"

"Oh, I'm sure he's just busy and lost track of the time. His stomach will remind him soon."

"Yeah, that's Chance all right." He chuckled, shaking his head. "When he was a kid, he'd get right cranky when he was hungry. I expect he likes having a woman to cook for him."

"He hasn't complained about my cooking."

Rider cocked his head to one side. "I hear a 'but' there."

"Well, we've had a few problems adjusting to living together."

Rider snorted, then burst into laughter. "I can well imagine."

"Have you a place to stay?"

"Well, if it's all the same to you, I'd thought I'd just bed down on the floor. I'm a little strapped for cash."

"I'm sure Chance wouldn't mind. I'm just sorry I've taken over the extra room."

His expression darkened. "I'm not so sure about Chance minding, but what's he gonna do once I'm bedded down and snoring on his floor? Kick me out?"

"I guess not." Trixianna picked up the plates and cups from the table. She put them in the sink to be washed in the morning. As she turned down the fire on the stove beneath the beans, she hoped Chance would smell them when he arrived home.

She turned to Rider, who stood beside the table watching her. "I'm turning in for the night," she said. "Is there anything I can get you?"

"No, ma'am. I'll sit up awhile and wait for Chance. I don't know how long I can keep my eyes open, though. It's been a hard trip."

Trixianna started down the hall. "Well, there's hot water on the back of the stove if you'd like to clean up, and there's bedding in the chest by the fireplace. If there's anything else you need, please let me know."

"Don't you worry 'bout me." He stretched his arms and yawned, then gave her a boyish grin. "I've been taking care of myself for a few years now."

She smiled. "I'm sure you have. Goodnight then."

"Goodnight, ma'am, and thanks again for supper. Chance will be sorry he missed out."

"Oh, he'll show up sooner or later. If I know his appetite, he won't even mind eating them cold."

Rider chuckled. "I reckon not."

Rider turned down the lamp on the kitchen table. He wandered around the kitchen, then the parlor, looking at Chance's possessions and wondering about his brother's life here in Grand Fork. He yanked off his new calfskin boots, then stretched out on the sofa. His stocking feet dangled over the end. He clasped his hands behind his head. Staring at the ceiling, he thought about his only sibling. What would Chance think when he found out his baby brother was finally out of prison?

A man surprised is half beaten.
—Thomas Fuller, M.D.

Chapter Eleven

Several hours after midnight by the meager light of a waning moon, bounty hunter Sam Smith skirted the main road and trotted into Grand Fork, Kansas. He rode down a silent alley, deftly avoiding anyone's notice. He slowed down in front of a surprisingly quiet saloon. Thin light shone out the bat-wing doors and spilled across the boardwalk. The sign above the swinging doors proclaimed it The Tanglefoot in bright red lettering.

Smith eased himself out of the saddle. He looped Jezebel's reins around the hitching post and stepped stiffly up onto the walkway.

His body ached from every pore, and he felt about as lively as a day-old corpse. Three days on a horse could make a man wish he'd taken up an altogether different profession—one which didn't require a man to bust his butt on a hard saddle day in and day out.

But a plentiful reward called. Rumor had it that

Mad Maggie West was holed up in Grand Fork, and by God, Sam planned on taking her in and collecting on that mighty fine reward.

He took one look around and wondered what would make anybody think they could go unnoticed in this one-horse town. Hell, he could spit from one end to the other without going dry. He knew from experience that most desperadoes weren't known for their brains, but to hide out here? Well, what could you expect from a woman?

Women just didn't think like men. Sure as shootin', they could be devious and contrary on occasion, but they weren't good criminals. The upright women he knew were quiet, well-behaved and mild-mannered, and the bad women . . . well, they weren't *that* bad. He couldn't comprehend a female holding up a bank, much less shooting someone, but that was what they said she had done, and that was why he was here. Come hell or high water, he was taking this woman to Dena Valley and collecting the five hundred dollars.

He had thought long and hard about Mad Maggie as he'd ridden toward Grand Fork. He figured the law had it all wrong and it wasn't a woman at all, just a small man with a high-pitched voice. That made more sense to him.

They said Mad Maggie West had not only robbed that one bank, but others as well. Why, over at the Dena Valley bank, the poor man that she had shot, a bachelor fellow, would now probably stay unmarried, would more than likely never father children. Just the thought of that particular gunshot wound made Smith wince.

He looked at poor Jezebel, whose head drooped like a sunflower in a drought. Smith felt guilty pushing the mare hard, but damn, that reward was a whole piss-load of money.

As soon as he washed the trail dust from his throat, he'd settle Jezebel in the livery, but right now he needed a drink.

Then, after a short night's sleep, he'd find that bank robber and become a rich, lazy gentleman rancher. Maybe he'd even marry that sweet filly in Sweet Springs with the big brown eyes who thought he was "the handsomest man she'd ever laid eyes on." Of course, she was a working gal, and probably called all the men handsome even if they were plug ugly. She sure knew how to please a man in the hay, though. Even if she couldn't make hotcakes, Smith could live with her pleasing him for the rest of his life.

He strode into The Tanglefoot and stepped up to the bar. The place was all but empty. Years of ground-in dirt covered the wooden floor, making it the color of tar. Tobacco stains near the spittoons spoke of more than a few near-misses. There was no piano, no faro tables and no dance-hall gals. The mirror over the bar was cracked and several jagged pieces were missing. The room held a few scarred tables and a couple more broken-down chairs. There seemed to be nothing to do in The Tanglefoot but drink.

The barkeep was leaning on his elbows and talking with one lone customer who looked about ready to collapse. The bar counter was the only thing keeping him upright.

"I's telling ya, Jim, she's prim and proper on the out-side, but underneath, she's wearing nothing but a sportin' gal's duds."

Jim, the bartender, nodded in agreement. He turned

toward Smith and lifted his head. "What'll you have, stranger?"

"Give me a beer and a shot of your cheapest whiskey."

Jim, a bushy-yellow-haired older man, chuckled as he poured the drinks. "It's all one price, pardner. What you in town for?"

"Business," Smith said as he settled against the counter. Business with Mad Maggie West.

The drunk made his way down the bar, shuffling his feet and fighting to keep a grip on the rail. He sidled up next to Smith. Alcoholic fumes wafted up Smith's nose. "Hey, wanna hear the news?"

What he wanted was the man to move away so he could breathe without choking. The man smelled like the back end of a bull.

"Leave him be, Peterson," advised the bartender as he set the two drinks in front of Smith. He waved a meaty fist at the drunk, who didn't so much as blink.

Peterson moved closer. Smith stepped back a pace. "What's the news?" he asked.

Jim snorted. "Peterson's all het up about the prisoner the sheriff arrested." His bushy brows rose a fraction and he gave Smith a knowing grin. "A woman."

Smith returned the smile. He drained the shot of whiskey in one burning gulp. Heat burst inside him as it hit his empty belly. He took a slow swallow of the beer, and eyed the bartender. "Oh? What'd she do? Sneeze in church? Cuss at the ladies' sewing circle meeting?"

Jim laughed outright. He wiped his hands on the front of a dirty gray apron tied carelessly over a round belly. "A bit more serious than that, I'd say."

"Ain't right, I'm tellin' ya," Peterson said.

Jim nodded at the drunk. "It don't matter what she done. He don't allow as how a woman should be thrown in jail no matter what the charge."

"And what would that be?" Smith asked in a friendly tone, practically salivating over his good fortune. This might turn out to be the easiest money he'd ever make. The only woman who could be arrested in Grand Fork had to be Mad Maggie West.

"Bank robbery." Jim's wide face broke into a bewildered frown. "They say she robbed the bank over to Dena Valley and shot up a man while doing it."

"That so?"

"Yep. Hard to believe, ain't it? But the townsfolk here in Grand Fork didn't rightly agree with putting a woman in jail alongside men, even if she is a bank robber. So until the sheriff in Dena Valley can come fetch her, the townsfolk made our sheriff keep her in his own home. Don't that beat all? Poor Sheriff Magrane."

"Magrane, did ya say?"

"Yep, Sheriff Chance Magrane."

Damn. The one and the same. Smith drained his glass, pulled a few coins from his pocket and dropped them on the counter. "Where can I get a room and a bath?"

Jim gave a short bark of laughter. "This time of night the bathhouse is closed, but you're in luck, stranger. Annie V.'s is just down the alley a ways, and she can give you both plus a woman that'll put a smile on your face."

"Thanks." As he turned away from the bar and headed for the doors, a tall man with a black Stetson pushed them aside and stepped in. He turned to look at Smith, but Smith ducked his head, murmured hello and passed him without meeting his eye.

Smith paused outside the door and listened to the conversation.

"Hey, Sheriff," called Jim. "How does Grand Fork look tonight?"

"Quiet," came the familiar voice of Chance Magrane.

"Want a drink?"

"Nope. Just making my nightly rounds before I head on home."

"To that purty red-haired gal?" joked Jim. Smith heard him chuckle.

"That purty red-haired gal is a criminal and well you know it, Jim."

The barkeep laughed outright, obviously not the least bit disturbed by the sheriff's intimidating tone. "Chance, I walk by that house of yours at the end of the street every day on my way here. And every day since you arrested that woman, I slow down when I get to the picket fence. I just mosey by real slowlike and take a long whiff. Whoo-ee, the smells comin' from inside like to bring a man to his knees. If that woman robs banks as well as she bakes a pie, she's a real danger. But I'd be willing to forgive and forget for that cooking."

"Maybe you would, but the law wouldn't."

"That may be so, but I tell ya, even when I close up here early in the morning and go home, I can still smell apple pie when I walk by. I don't rightly know how you get any sleep at all, Sheriff."

Smith climbed onto Jezebel and walked her down the deserted street. So much for a bath and a room. Right now would be a good time to snatch Mad Maggie West. The sheriff was busy and probably wouldn't be home for a while. The timing couldn't be better.

Smith guessed he wouldn't have any trouble finding the sheriff's place either. He'd simply follow his nose.

Trixianna rolled over and blinked in confusion. Something had wakened her from a sound slumber. Disoriented and half-asleep, she glanced uneasily around the room. Inky black surrounded her in a cocoon of shadowy darkness. She remembered the Perry brothers, and wondered if they were up to their old mischief.

She reached for the oil lamp by her bed. A dark figure stepped from the shadows, knocking her hand away. Trixianna scooted back, but a gloved hand gripped her wrist. She opened her mouth to scream for Chance, when another hand, smelling of horse and leather, clamped over her mouth.

She thrashed her legs to get free, but encumbered by the bedcoverings, it had little effect on the man, now leaning across her body holding her down. His body odor turned her stomach, and he smelled of whiskey. Terrified, she clenched her free hand into a fist and punched his chin with all her might. Pain flew up her arm. She drew back her hand, then unfolded her stinging knuckles against her chest. Her hand throbbed with sharp pin-needles of pain. Surely, she'd broken every one of her fingers.

She heard him grunt, then draw a quick breath. With a deftness of motion, he covered her mouth with a piece of cloth and tied it around the back of her head. He trussed her wrists and legs in separate lengths of rope. Strong arms tossed her over his shoulder. He moved to the window, and easily held her against his body while crawling over the casement. As he moved like a wraith in the darkness, his silence and determined, unknown purpose chilled her to the bone.

Trixianna, her heart hammering, could scarcely draw breath through the bound cloth over her mouth. Icy fear thudded in her chest like a fist. Several feet in front of her nose, the ground loomed. Afraid he'd drop her on her head if she fought him, she didn't move, and instead waited for a better opportunity to escape.

The kidnapper stopped not six feet from the window. A horse, ground-reined, chomped at the meager grass. She and the horse met eye-to-eye. Trixianna noticed the dew sparkling on the grass in the moonlight, and heard an owl hooting in a tree overhead. She thought she might be losing her mind; she kept thinking she would wake from this dream, but it seemed frighteningly real.

Trying to keep her head while fighting for composure, she concentrated on remembering details so she could relate them later . . . after she'd escaped. She had no doubt that she would. Then she would hit him over the head with something other than her fist.

The man stepped into the stirrup and hoisted her across his thighs, her bound hands on one side of the horse and tied legs on the other. With a jarring gait, he took off, one large hand splayed intimately across her bottom.

Dressed in her thin night rail, she shivered as drafts of cold air skittered up her exposed legs. Her head bounced up and down against his denim-clad knee. Certain she would be sick to her stomach in minutes, Trixianna held on as the horse galloped out of town in total darkness.

* * *

The stranger in The Tanglefoot had looked familiar to Chance. His stance. His gait. The way he wore his hat cocked at an angle. Chance was sure he knew him from somewhere. His mind kept playing with the image of the man leaving The Tanglefoot. He would recall it sooner or later. He'd always prided himself on never forgetting a face.

He'd put off going home, too. Fanny's reaction to his kiss still swirled around his mind. Thoughts of his impending marriage, looming like a disaster on the horizon, kept him away. Thoughts of Mad Maggie in her warm, cozy bed, an empty reminder of the love he could never have, also kept him away.

Grand Fork was quiet for the night. He had no more excuses. He started home, his thoughts bouncing between Fanny and the stranger in The Tanglefoot. It hit him like a blow to the jaw. He stopped stock-still, stunned with the realization.

Sam Smith.

He was well known as a plodding, not overly bright bounty hunter. And they'd crossed paths before. The man would do just about anything for a buck. What might he do for five hundred dollars?

Chance sprinted the rest of the way home. He arrived at the front gate, uneasy, surrounded by a chilling black silence. He'd no more than stepped over the threshold when a shiver of apprehension skittered up his spine and settled in the pit of his belly. He drew his revolver and stood motionless, listening, waiting. As his sight adjusted to the dim light, he crept through the house, his eyes searching. He stopped outside Mad Maggie's door, and held his breath. He heard nothing but the pounding of his heart, and turned the handle. The door swung open. Inside the room, the bedcovers

lay snarled on the floor. The window was flung wide.
Smith.

Cussing to himself, Chance lit a lantern and dashed
outside. He examined the dirt beneath the windowsill.
Two sets of footprints were clearly visible, one coming
toward and the other going from the house. Large
men's boots.

She'd made an escape, all right, but unless his in-
stincts were shot to hell, she'd not gone willingly. His
gut tightened at the thought of that single-minded
bounty hunter putting his hands on Trixianna.

So furious he could hardly see straight, Chance sad-
dled his horse and was on their trail within minutes.
He knew exactly where Sam Smith was going. Toward
Dena Valley and that five-hundred-dollar reward.

Simmering with mounting rage, he headed south
toward Dena Valley, pushing his horse dangerously
hard through the night darkness. Angry thoughts
raced through his head as well. Once before, the man
had stomped on Chance's dignity. He wasn't going to
let Smith do it twice. And he wasn't going to let Smith
lay a hand on Trixianna. Chance would kill him first.

Rider sat up on the sofa. He rubbed his eyes and
looked around the dark room. He'd slept like the dead
for the first time in five years, but something woke
him. As he strained to listen, he heard nothing but
ordinary night sounds—an owl hooting, a dog's bark.
Maybe what he'd heard was Chance coming in, although he was surprised Chance hadn't seen him,
woken him and thrown him out into the night.

It wasn't like Chance to be so unobservant. Of
course, Rider thought with a grin, maybe Chance was
anxious to look in on his female houseguest.

Rider sank back and closed his eyes. Tomorrow morning was soon enough to face Chance's wrath.

Bile burned in Trixianna's throat. She knew she was going to be sick, and with the cloth covering her mouth, she'd surely suffocate. She thrashed her arms and legs, and released a muffled scream.

The silent kidnapper jerked back on the reins, and they skidded to an abrupt stop. She turned her head to stare at the man and tried to wriggle off the horse. He clamped a hand around her waist.

He must have seen the panic in her eyes. He dismounted, helped her to the ground, removed the covering over her mouth and deftly untied the rope around her ankles.

She rushed to the side of the road, sank to her knees and emptied the contents of her stomach into a patch of weedy ground. Her head ached, her stomach rebelled and fury coiled hot and heavy in her belly. "Who are you and why have you done this?"

When she looked up, she found him standing close, no discernible expression on his face. He untied her hands and gave her a dampened neckerchief; then he squatted on the ground beside her. She wiped her face and handed it back. He stuffed it in his coat pocket. Reaching for a blade of grass, he began chewing. His eyes followed her every movement.

"Sam Smith," he finally answered.

Trixianna shivered. From the cold or his odd behavior, she wasn't certain. He didn't frighten her as she might have expected. He just didn't seem that menacing or calculating. Just annoying. Or maybe annoyance had simply overridden her fear. Still, he had kidnapped her. Determined not to show her anxiety, she took a deep breath.

"Mr. Smith, what are you going to do with me?"

He chuckled. With a fluid motion he stood up, pulled her to her feet and escorted her to the horse on the other side of the road. Reaching inside a saddlebag slung across the horse's withers, he yanked out a thin army blanket. With careful deliberation, he wrapped it around her shoulders.

"Well?"

He said nothing, just chewed and stared off down the road.

"Aren't you going to answer my question?"

"No, ma'am." He retied her hands in front of her, lifted her onto the horse's back and climbed on behind her. "I'm leavin' your legs free so you can sit astride, but don't try nothing . . . and don't talk neither. I can't abide a gabby woman."

They cantered along the dark, dusty road. One mile. Trixianna stewed. Two miles. Trixianna simmered. Three miles. Irked beyond belief, she turned around and confronted him. "I am not gabby, and besides, I have a right to know where you're taking me."

He looked down his nose at her from disbelieving smoky gray eyes.

"I want to know what you're going to do with me and I want to know right now."

"Hmff." He stared down the road and made no reply.

"You are insufferable."

"And that's a bad thing, ma'am?"

Trixianna glared at him, then became the victim of his steely glare. "I demand to know what your intentions are."

"Hmff."

"You're not going to answer, are you?"

He slowed the horse to a walk, then turned her by the shoulders so she could see him. He stared at her as if he'd never seen a woman before. She swallowed a nervous lump in her throat. Maybe it wasn't a good idea to bait one's kidnapper. "I recall telling you I can't abide gabby women. Now ma'am, if'n you don't shut up, I'll do it for you."

"What does that mean, Mr. Smith?"

He shook his head. "Ma'am, you're awful damn polite."

"Thank you . . . I think."

He shook his head again. "I'll cover your mouth again, that's what it means. Now shut up."

"Well, I never . . ."

"That's what I'm hoping, ma'am," he muttered.

Trixianna gave him a tight-lipped smile, then turned forward. She pulled the blanket close around her shoulders. An uneasy silence fell between them. She didn't know if this had something to do with her being mistaken for Mad Maggie West, or if the polite Mr. Smith had some other nefarious notions in his pea-sized brain.

The sun would be up soon, and the thought of riding down this public road with her bare legs showing and clad in only her thin nightclothes made Trixianna more than a little uncomfortable. To say nothing of being in close proximity to the taciturn Mr. Smith and his closemouthed demeanor. She tried not to think about his intentions.

Her head bobbed to the steady rhythm of the horse's hooves, and she soon found herself falling asleep. Trixianna couldn't believe she could actually fall asleep under the conditions. She mentally gave her posterior a hard kick. She simply wouldn't allow it. She needed a plan. A damn good one. She though about Chance. What would he do if he were in her place? Huh! He would never be in this predicament. Where was the man when she needed him?

She soon came up with a means of escape so simple, she even allowed herself to smile. She could escape this man's evil clutches without much trouble at all.

Dawn soon broke over the horizon in a dazzling array of pink and gold. It cast the surrounding fields and pastures in an amber glow. Trixianna waited until they were alongside a wide stretch of prairie grass as tall as her shoulder. She pretended to yawn, then glanced over her shoulder, giving her captor an agonized expression. "Mr. Smith, I, um, I need to, that is . . ."

He actually blushed. His neck and cheeks turned a fiery shade of crimson. Hauling back on the reins, he vaulted off the horse before the beast came to a complete stop. He reached up, grabbed her by the waist and settled her on the ground in front of him. He untied her wrists. "Go," he instructed.

She turned around, picked up a stone the size of her fist and glanced over her shoulder. He stood with his back to her beside the horse, leaning over to adjust the cinch. Before he could react, she stepped forward and brought the rock down hard on his head.

He turned, his eyes narrowed. He fingered his bleeding forehead, a questioning look on his face.

With an unpleasant realization of what she was about to do, she brought her knee up forcefully into his groin. He gave a keening moan and dropped to his knees, one hand on his head, the other clasped around his bruised personal parts.

"I am truly sorry," she whispered. She spun on her heel and fled into the high prairie grass, putting as much distance between them as she possibly could. She ran, her legs pumping madly as she dashed through the tall grass. She didn't stop, and she didn't look back.

Chance caught up to Sam Smith around dawn. The man stood by the road, bent over at an awkward angle, relieving his bladder. He glanced over his shoulder, a pained expression on his face. As Chance drew closer, a startled look came across Smith's features. He finished his business in a rush, buttoned up his britches and hobbled toward his horse as if he had just stopped for this reason alone and was in a hurry to get on his way. A purple bruise marred his chin, and a bloody gash cut across his temple.

He tipped his hat as if they were standing on the boardwalk in Grand Fork passing the time of day. "Looks like it's going to be a nice day, sir."

"Don't humor me, Smith. I'm not in the mood. Where's Trixianna?"

"Trixianna?" he asked, in an exasperated tone of voice. "I thought that was Mad Maggie West you were holding."

"I knew you had her, you low-down skunk."

"I don't know what you're talking about." He lifted his leg, winced and stepped into the stirrup. Chance drew his revolver and leveled it at Smith's chest.

Smith lowered his leg and moved away from his mount. He folded his arms across his chest, a belligerent glare on his wounded face.

Still astride his own horse, Chance leaned on the saddle horn. From his vantage point, he gazed down at Smith. "Throw down your gun."

"Now wait a dang minute."

"Do it," Chance ordered.

The man obliged. "Dammit, Magrane, I—"

Chance drew the hammer back on his Colt.

The loud click startled Smith. He visibly swallowed, but otherwise didn't move.

"Where's Mad Maggie?"

Smith released a heavy sigh. "She said she had to go . . . you know." He ducked his head, blushing like a schoolboy.

Chance nodded, then smiled. It sounded like one of her ploys. It took someone as feebleminded as Sam Smith to fall for it, though.

What was he saying? She'd brought him down a few times with less trouble than it took to cross the street . . . or eat a slice of cranberry pie.

"I turned around to give her some privacy and before I knew it, she cracked me over the head with a rock, then kneed me in the groin. Before I could breathe again, she took off like a jackrabbit with his tail on fire. I never seen the like. I figured as soon as I could stand up without puking, I'd just lope on into the weeds and track her down. She wouldn't be hard to find, wearin' her night things and all."

Chance couldn't believe his ears. "She's not dressed?"

"Nope."

"Is her hair down?"

"Sure. She was sleepin' when I took her."

"Well, hell," muttered Chance. He heaved a sigh of relief. Thank God she was all right. But his blood heated and thundered through his veins at the thought of that thin nightgown she wore to bed and her russet hair flying loose as she ran. "You know, Smith, I'm not even sure that she is Mad Maggie. The sheriff from Dena Valley is due in town tomorrow."

"I guess I won't get that five hundred then?"

"What you get is to ride away without me putting a bullet in your backside. What made you think you could get away with it anyway?"

"I never figured on you catching me. I didn't mean no harm."

"You were headed for Dena Valley, weren't you?"

He nodded.

"Not too smart, Smith."

Smith jumped on his horse, shaking his head.

"I'll be seeing you, Magrane."

"Stay out of Grand Fork, Smith."

The sound of Smith's laughter and the clip-clop of horse's hooves drifted away on the wind, leaving Chance wondering where he'd find Mad Maggie in a never-ending sea of Kansas prairie grass.

Trixianna ran until she thought her legs would collapse beneath her. Then she ran some more. Finally, panting and out of breath, she crumpled to the ground in a dry, narrow gully. She lay there listening, her ears perked for any unusual sound. She heard the wind whispering through the grass and the grasshoppers chirping around her. Above her head, a hawk circled and then dove out of sight. The sun shone bright just over the eastern horizon in a cloudless sky. She heard no horse's whinny. No angry, masculine voice called for her. She released a deep, shuddering sigh of relief and closed her eyes.

How close had she come to . . . what? She still didn't know what he'd wanted. Reward money? She started to shake. Tears pricked the back of her lids. She gulped hard trying not to release them, but the big, wet tears slid down her cheeks, scalding her face. Hard, gut-wrenching sobs tore from her throat. She couldn't hold the emotion back any longer. She lay down in the tall grass, her head on her arm, and wept with anguished relief.

Chance heard her before he saw her. Deep, tortured sobs brought a shiver to his spine. His ears twitched as cold fear clenched his stomach in tight knots. He dismounted and ran toward the sound of her voice, afraid of finding Trixianna harmed: beaten, bloodied or worse.

He ran through the tall grass, and almost tripped as he descended into a dry, rocky basin where a creek used to flow. She lay on her side there, surrounded by rocks and large boulders. With her head in her hands and her gown up around her knees, he couldn't see her face. But he could still hear those heart-wrenching sobs.

He stumbled across the dry stream bed and dropped to his knees beside her. "Trixianna?"

A stumble may prevent a fall.
—Thomas Fuller, M.D.

Chapter Twelve

Chance jerked Trixianna to a sitting position, his fingers squeezing her arms. He met her startled gaze, which revealed scared, misty-green eyes glistening with tears. He stared at her pale face, each freckle standing out in sharp, vivid contrast. She'd never looked more beautiful.

He pulled her roughly into his embrace. His Stetson dropped off the back of his head. He ignored it as he listened to her try to muffle a sob, then another. He lifted her onto his lap, cradling her head against his chest.

"Go ahead," he said in a broken whisper. Her anguish consumed him, ripping his heart to shreds. "Cry. Let it all out. You're safe now."

Chance rocked her in his arms as she wept like a small child, hiccuping and gasping for breath between sobs. A ragged lump lodged in his throat. God, he'd done this by leaving her unprotected. Doubt about her identity plagued him anew. Who was this woman? Right now, regardless of who she was and how it affected his future, he'd gladly take her pain as his own.

She lifted her head to the hollow between his shoulder and neck, where it fit to perfection. Her trembling arms clung to him, her tears soaking his chambray shirt. He brushed his hands through her hair, allowing his fingers to tangle in its silky length, He dropped his hands to the small of her back, where he held her close.

Eventually her sobs slowed until all he heard was her soft, even breathing. He closed his eyes and relished the feel of her soft unbound breasts against his chest, her thigh pressed against his knee. The warmth of her sighs tickled his neck. She lifted her head. Tears still glimmered on her lashes, and her reddened cheeks were puffy, her nose pink. But those freckles on her face still lured him. . . .

Chance clenched his hands into fists to keep from reaching down and lifting the thin barrier of cotton that kept his hands from her soft, smooth skin.

"I'm sorry," she whispered. "I never cry."

"I guess you're entitled once in a while," Chance said. A bleak smile crossed her face, frightening him. He had to swallow the apprehension in his throat before he spoke. "Did he hurt you?"

"No," she replied. Her voice sounded tired, almost resigned.

He fought the urge to kiss away her unhappiness and make her forget everything but what lay unspoken between them.

She met his gaze. "Did you think I ran away?"

"No. I knew Smith took you."

"Who is he?"

"A bounty hunter after your reward money. He's long gone."

Her eyes brightened. "I'm glad you didn't think the worst of me."

He chuckled. After what she'd just been through, he admired her spunk. "Not this time."

A glint of amusement danced in her eyes. She looked at him with a gaze of such intense pleasure that his stomach lurched. He released a long, ragged sigh.

Then she dropped her head to his shoulder again. She moved one of her hands, splayed against his stomach, across his ribs with a caressing, circular motion that sent a shiver rippling through his body. He swallowed hard, then squeezed his eyes shut and hoped to God she wouldn't notice the way his body reacted to her innocent touch. He refused to betray her unqualified trust in him. A trust he was beginning to have in her, too.

A powerful instinctive response to finding her alive and unharmed enveloped him. He fought it hard . . . and lost. Brushing his lips against her cheek, he whispered, "I'm going to kiss you now unless you object."

Why would she? Right now, she wanted it more than life itself. Trixianna's breath caught in her throat. She stared into Chance's irresistible eyes, and saw only longing and tenderness in his gaze. "I'd like you to. Can you do one thing for me first, though?"

He gathered her tight in his arms, his brow furrowed. "What's that?"

"Call me Trixianna."

He gave her a startled look just a second before plunging his hands into her hair. He seemed to be studying the strands intertwined in his fingers. Then he pressed a light kiss on her brow. Brushing a line of kisses over her cheeks and on the tip of her nose, he said, "I've been wanting to kiss that stubborn nose of yours since the first day I saw you in my jail . . . Trixianna."

Her name on his tongue sent shivers up her spine, and down to the very tips of her toes. Anticipation tingled in the pit of her stomach "Why?"

"Well, hell, woman. Those freckles of yours are darned sexy, that's why."

"Oh, my."

"Trixianna, I'm going to kiss you now," he breathed just before he claimed her lips. And he did kiss her, with a thoughtful exploration, a tender journey. Then he became more thorough, and before long, his kisses consumed her. He used his whole mouth—velvet tongue, sharp teeth, warm breath—to wander, to travel, to capture her with a slow, sensual seduction.

She wrapped her arms around his neck and buried her hands in his thick, black hair. "Chance," she choked out, feeling weak and trembly. Confused by her tumbling emotions, she sought his gaze.

"Kiss me back, Trixianna," he demanded, his voice thick, his eyes appealing. His thumb rubbed a tiny circle against her collarbone. She stared into his face, shivery with expectation.

Her knees weakened, her heart thundered. She returned the kiss, following his unspoken direction, nibbling his lips with her teeth, drinking in the sweetness of his mouth. She lifted her lips from his, panting, and wanting more.

He cupped the back of her head, then slid his hands through her hair. Catching a strand, he brought it to his mouth to kiss it. He stroked it across his cheek, his brow. He slowly closed his eyes.

Conscious of his warm touch, rough and seeking, through the thin covering of her gown, Trixianna placed her hands against his chest. His heart pulsed beneath her palms. With shaking fingers, she undid the top buttons of his shirt and slid her hands inside. The muscles of his powerful chest, hot and sleek, twitched beneath her exploring. When her thumb grazed his nipple, it puckered and hardened. She felt, then heard, his indrawn breath. She looked up.

"Trixianna," he whispered in an agonized voice. "This feels so right, but God knows, it probably isn't."

She had no answers for him. She couldn't think of right or wrong for she was confused herself. She only knew that she wanted him to touch her and kiss her.

He shook his head as though clearing it, then closed his eyes. Reclaiming her lips again, he pulled her to him, and gave her a hungry kiss. His demanding lips and thrusting tongue forced her mouth open. She savored the unfamiliar sensations spiraling through her.

Chance lifted her gown and slid his calloused hand up her shin, passing over her knee to the tender flesh on the inside of her thigh. She felt his fingers tremble as they stroked her skin, his hand easing higher up her leg. Her knees fell open and she pushed her hips forward . . . wanting, needing his touch.

Trixianna gasped as his hand cupped her between her legs, his fingers stroking the moist curls, his thumb caressing in a circular motion.

"Ah, honey," murmured Chance. His breath against her lips. "Relax . . . there, that's it . . . now let it happen. Just relax and let it happen."

She didn't understand the insistent way her body

was responding to Chance's questing fingers, but she willingly followed his instructions. She bit her lip and let go.

Suddenly a sparkling pattern of colored lights lit up behind her eyelids. Her muscles contracted and spasmed around his fingers, holding them tight inside her body. A quiver shot through her like a bolt of lightning. She went taut, then slack, her whole being upended and spiraling.

Trixianna opened her eyes to find Chance staring at her. His gaze was so piercing, so intensely absorbed on her face, that it sent another tremor coursing through her limbs.

He lowered his gaze. She heard him swallow. He inhaled a deep breath between parted lips. Slowly he took his hand away and gently pulled her night rail back down over her hips and legs. He pushed away, leaving her mouth and flesh burning with fire. He shoved against his denim trousers with the heel of one hand, as a crimson flush covered his cheekbones. His bronzed features now held an expression of such hopelessness that she wanted to weep for whatever he felt. Guilt? Shame? Regret? She couldn't tell. Despair plucked at her heart.

His head drooped and sank to her shoulder. Taking her hand in his, he said in a thick raspy voice, unlike his usual confident tone, "This has got to stop now."

She nodded. "I know."

He brought one of her hands to his lips and gently kissed the knuckles. "You know this is wrong."

She nodded again, too miserable to reply.

"But damn," he whispered. "How can it feel so right when I know in my gut it's not?" He turned his gaze to her hand, flipping it over and then back. He stared at her swollen, bruised knuckles. His brows shot upward. "What's this? What'd you do to your hand?"

She stared at it, surprised by the injury. She remembered hitting her kidnapper, but it seemed such a long time ago. So much had happened since then. "I-I struck that awful man."

Her answer seemed to amuse him. His countenance brightened. "By any chance on the chin?"

"How did you know?"

He chuckled, then kissed her palm. "That's not all you did either, is it?"

Heat stole into Trixianna's cheeks. "Well, no, not exactly."

"He was as green as frog sh . . . well, hell, what I mean is, he was green as a frog's overcoat when I came across him."

"Was he very angry? I was afraid he'd come after me."

"No. He seemed more dazed than anything."

"So he's really gone?"

"Yep. He's really a harmless sort. He just thought he could make some easy money. You cured him of that." Chance stood up and pulled her to her feet. He searched the ground until he found his hat. He slapped the dust off against his thigh, then settled the Stetson on his head. Reaching down again, he picked up the discarded blanket. With tenderness in his every touch, he wrapped it around her. His hands rested lightly on her shoulders. "What do you want me to do now?"

Kiss me? Touch me? Make love to me? How about marry me instead of Fanny Fairfax?

Believe in me?

Trixianna wanted to shout at him to do all those

215

things, but she knew it was wrong to even want them, much less ask them of him. He'd made a promise to Fanny, and being an honorable man, he would keep it. She stared into his gentle, caring eyes, wanting him to believe in her more than anything she could imagine. "Do you think I'm Trixianna Lawless now?"

He shook his head, a perplexed frown drawing his brows together. "I'm not sure what I think. I'm as confused as Sam Smith right about now, but even knowing it's against the law, I'd be willing to let you go if that's what you want."

"You would? But why?"

He grimaced, his eyes narrowed with obvious frustration. "Because I care too much about you to turn you over to the sheriff from Dena Valley and let him throw you in jail." He shook his head again. "You don't belong there."

"But you still don't believe me?"

He took her hand. "I have to know the truth about Mad Maggie. And I know you're keeping secrets. Whether they're against the law or not, I can't say."

"I'm not a criminal," she insisted. She felt as if she could die inside. What they had just shared was special, wasn't it? How could he dismiss it so easily? "I have told you as much."

He nodded. "And I want to believe you. But my judgment is clouded. Besides everything else that's gone wrong, I want you . . . badly, and that's not right." His misery etched in each word, he continued. "Not when I'm engaged to marry another woman."

He wanted her! Chance wanted her, but he was too much of a gentleman to act on his feelings or renege on his agreement with Fanny. She couldn't help but respect him for that even when it broke her heart into tiny pieces. "Then I suppose I have to go. I have to leave Grand Fork."

He surprised her by giving her a lopsided grin, his gaze roaming over her figure. "Well, not like that you can't."

Trixianna looked down at herself. Her night rail was ripped and dusty, and the hem had been dragged in the dirt. Her hair lay tangled about her shoulders. Yet she didn't mind Chance seeing her this way. She loved him regardless. It seemed right somehow, even knowing that it wasn't proper in most people's minds. She managed a choking laugh.

Chance cleared his throat. "I can get you back to Grand Fork before long without anyone the wiser."

"Then what?"

"We can do this any way you like. It's your decision."

"What do you mean?"

"I can say I arrested the wrong woman or you got away or—"

"But wouldn't that make you look inept?"

"Inept?" His mouth quirked in a lopsided grin. "Thanks for thinking of my reputation, but I'll survive. After all, Mad Maggie West is supposed to be a dangerous woman."

Trixianna's temper flared at the mention of the criminal. "If you want me, Chance, then why are you marrying Fanny? Of course, what could I expect? You don't even believe me when I tell you my own name." Feeling hurt and rejected, she lashed out. "I'm setting out of this town. You're nothing but a hypocrite, Sheriff Magrane. And right now, I don't think I can watch you marry Fanny."

"Dammit all to hell." Chance jerked his hat off his

head and slapped it against the side of his leg. "You're right. I am a hypocrite, a damned foolish one."

Trixianna hadn't expected him to agree. She stared at him. Her anger dissipated, replaced by deep sorrow and a heartsick feeling.

"We'll work it out," he stated.

"I don't know how." Trixianna followed Chance to his horse. He mounted, then pulled her up in front of him. They stayed off the main road on the way back to Grand Fork, making their way in abject silence.

Rider woke late, his bones aching, his mouth dry and his stomach grumbling. The house lay still as a graveyard. He didn't have to be told that he was the only one about. He didn't think Chance had come home last night. And where was that beautiful red-headed outlaw?

While he waited for the water to heat for a much-needed bath, Rider shaved, then explored the kitchen. He found the previous night's cornbread and finished it off. He was just dressing after his bath when he heard a knock at the door. He debated answering it at all. He didn't know where either Chance or his captive were.

Oh, well. It was about time the gentle townsfolk of Grand Fork found out that Chance had a not-so-shining little brother. He doubted that Chance had bothered to tell anyone about him . . . or where he'd spent the last five years.

He pulled open the door to find a young woman and a goat—yes, by damn, and it was on a leash—standing on Chance's porch.

"Hello," she said. Her large nut-brown eyes sparkled. She gifted him with a friendly smile. Rosy, plump cheeks reddened further as she gazed expectantly at him.

He couldn't help noticing that she had large buck teeth in a rather tiny face. They took a little something away from her earnest smile. Still, he grinned in return. "Hello yourself."

"I'm—"

"No, ma'am," Rider interrupted. "Let me guess."

She giggled. "All right."

"You're . . . leaving milk."

"No, sir." Her face flushed. "Bluebeard is a boy goat."

"Excuse me, ma'am. My mistake," Rider said. He leaned a shoulder against a column on the porch. "Then you're selling raffle tickets for the church social."

She shook her head.

"You're taking names to petition the governor to get women the right to vote here in Kansas?"

Her face lit up. "No, I'm sorry, that's not why I'm here, though it's a splendid idea. One I'll have to take up with my father."

"You're . . ." Holy hell! This was Chance's intended. Friendly and nice but, good God in Heaven, homely as a mud fence! "You're Fanny!"

"Yes, yes, yes." She giggled. "I'm Fanny Fairfax. How do you do?"

Rider swallowed down his surprise and shook her outstretched, gloved hand. "I'm real pleased to meet you, ma'am. Would you sit here on the porch with me?" He wanted to get to know the woman Chance had chosen for his bride.

He took her hand and helped her sit beside him. She tied the goat to the lowest porch railing, where he proceeded to munch on what little grass grew at his feet.

"I'm Chance's younger brother, Rider."

"Chance's brother?" One gloved hand flew to her breast. Those unbelievably large, liquid brown eyes of hers widened in astonishment. Her mouth dropped open. She recovered her composure quickly and replied in a small, offended voice, "He didn't even tell me he *had* a brother."

"Well, we don't stay in touch much."

"Still, I can't think why he wouldn't have told me." She hesitated a moment. "Then you're Tildy's nephew, too."

It was Rider's turn to be surprised. "Tildy O'Hara?" At Fanny's nod, he continued. "That old battle-ax? I thought she'd kicked the bucket long ago."

"Oh, no, Tildy's just fine. She couldn't be better. We love her dearly here in Grand Fork."

"Well, that's good news, I guess," muttered Rider.

"She's out of town right now, but she'll be back in time for the wedding."

Wonderful news. Rider remembered her as being an interfering, overbearing, talkative old woman . . . who'd disapproved of every little thing he'd ever done, none of it aboveboard in her mind. Sure, she'd been right most of the time, but he was reformed now and he wasn't anxious to renew their acquaintance.

"I stopped by to see Chance," Fanny said. "Is he about?"

"Call me Rider," he stated, stalling for time. All right, Chance hadn't come home at all last night. He didn't recall his brother as being the kind of man to spend much time with fancy women, and as he remembered, Chance seldom drank, at least not to excess. Grand Fork shouldn't have the kind of trouble that would keep the sheriff away all night. So where the hell was he then? And where was that so-called bank robber, Trixianna?

Chance cantered up to the back of his house. Upon hearing voices on the front porch, he put his fingers to his lips. Trixianna nodded as he helped her off the horse. He slowly pulled the back door open and scooted her inside without being seen. She ran on tiptoe down the hall to her bedroom, where she could change clothes. His last sight of her brought a smile to his face: her hips swaying as she scrambled down the hallway.

He walked around and tiptoed onto the front porch. Caught off guard by the man before him, he stared tongue-tied as he heard him speak.

"Ma'am, I don't know but—"

Chance leaned against the door. It creaked open from his weight. Fanny shrieked in fright. Rider jumped to his feet and whirled around. Chance saw him reach for a gun that wasn't there. Obviously, old habits died hard. Rider lowered his arm and locked expectant eyes on Chance.

Chance gazed into a pair of familiar blue eyes . . . the same color that he stared at every morning while he shaved. He held the door open with one hand, his body frozen in place.

A smile tugged at his lips, then broadened with exuberance. He bounded down the steps and grabbed Rider in a bear hug guaranteed to break every one of the younger man's ribs. Chance surprised himself with his emotional outburst, the outpouring of love he felt for this, his only brother. He had tried for years to forget that he even had a brother—this man who had caused Chance to leave his hometown under a cloud of suspicion and doubt. He'd made a new place for himself in Grand Fork, and now all the anger and humiliation that he'd felt then died with just one look at Rider.

Chance wrapped his arms around Rider and closed his eyes, fighting tears. He felt as if his breath was being cut off.

He glanced at Fanny. She'd risen to her feet. Tears ran down her crimson cheeks. She dabbed at the corner of one eye with a lace handkerchief. She sniffed, then gave Chance a look of annoyance. "You never told me you had a brother."

Chance whispered in Rider's ear. "I'm sorry, little brother, but I never told anyone here in Grand Fork about you. I never expected you to live very long in that stinking hellhole I put you in, much less want to see me when you got out."

"I understand, Chance. Honest. I had five long years to think about what you had to do and about what *I* did, and I'm not holding a grudge." His voice sounded husky, tear-filled, much like Chance's own.

Rider backed away, then slapped Chance on the shoulder. "I'm here to see a wedding. Isn't that right, Miss Fairfax?"

"So, you've met my Fanny?"

Chance watched Fanny cringe at his softly spoken words. Rider didn't seem to notice her reaction.

He grinned. "She and I were just getting to know each other."

Fanny blushed at Rider's teasing, her ill humor seeming to fade.

"You'd better watch out, Chance," Rider added. "I might just steal her away."

Brash as ever, Rider pulled her into his arms and bussed her cheek soundly. With his arm still around her, he asked, "So when is the big day?"

She pushed out of Rider's exuberant embrace. Reaching out a gloved hand, she scratched the goat's neck with open affection. "The day after tomorrow."

Rider turned to Chance. "You ready, big brother?"

"Ready as I'll ever be."

Fanny fixed Rider with a thin-lipped smile. "Not much for the groom to do, Mr. Magrane."

"Call me Rider," he said again. He winked at Chance. "All the groom has to do is show up with a big smile on his face, I guess."

"Rider!" Chance croaked. "You go too far."

Rider flushed, then rubbed the back of his neck. "Beggin' your pardon, ma'am. I've been away from polite society a while."

Fanny remained mute, her cheeks pink, too embarrassed to speak. Chance doubted she understood the implied meaning behind Rider's words, but she knew enough to recognize an implied vulgarity when she heard one.

"Is that goat gonna be in the wedding?" asked Rider in an obvious attempt to change the direction of the conversation.

Fanny's head bobbed up. "Of course. I couldn't have a party without him."

"He is?" Chance knew she was partial to the animal, but to bring him inside the church? Bluebeard ate everything that wasn't tied down, and even some objects that were. In point of fact, he was munching on Rider's trousers at that very moment.

Rider saw him and cuffed him on the nose. It didn't deter the beast. He kept right on chewing. "Well, hell," he muttered. His eyes met Chance's with an appeal to help.

Chance grinned, then shrugged his shoulders. "You're on your own, little brother."

"Some things never change," Rider grumbled. He stepped away from the goat, and the material ripped and stayed in the goat's jaw. Rider now sported an obvious hole in the seat of his denim trousers. He clapped a hand over the exposed skin, then rolled his eyes.

Chance bent over his knees and burst into laughter.

Fanny giggled, then covered her mouth.

Bluebeard nibbled the fabric, oblivious to their humor.

Rider chuckled. "Remind me to steer clear of that trouser-eating beast. It could get a mite breezy."

Chance turned to Fanny, his laughter easing. "Was there something you came by to see me for, Fanny?"

She waved her hand in a gesture of dismissal. "It can wait. I really must be going." She then walked over to Bluebeard. As she leaned over to untie him, she cooed childish gibberish in his ear.

Rider watched her, his mouth gaping. He caught Chance's gaze. Chance shrugged his shoulders. What could he say? She loved the goat more than she loved him? Rider wouldn't believe him anyway. Who in his right mind would?

Fanny waggled her fingers and ambled off, her skirts swishing, her ample backside swaying. "It was nice to meet you, Rider," she called over one shoulder.

"Same to you, ma'am."

Bluebeard chose that moment to take a swipe at the enticing fabric of Fanny's skirt, but she snatched it out of his eager grasp.

"Well, big brother," Rider drawled. He sat down on the bottom step and propped his elbows on his knees. "That isn't exactly the woman I pictured when you wrote me that you were taking a wife . . . in your one and only letter in five years."

Chance dropped down on the porch beside him, and decided to ignore that last jab. He leaned his elbows on the stair behind. "What did you have in mind?"

Rider grinned. "That fetching redhead I saw last night. The one you've arrested and kept all to yourself."

Chance felt his face heat. "You were here last night and saw her?"

"Yup. You sure as hell weren't. I slept on your sofa." His grin widened. "You know, you aren't very observant for a lawman. What were you up to?"

"None of your damned business."

"Oh? One of Grand Fork's good-time gals?"

Chance punched Rider on the shoulder. "Hell, no."

"Ouch." Rider rubbed his arm. "Where is that lovely bank robber anyway?"

"She's inside, and she's not what you think."

Rider's eyebrows rose a fraction. "The hell you say. She wasn't here earlier. I searched your little house this morning, top to bottom, before I took a leisurely bath. Unless my eyesight's failing, I was all alone."

Chance cleared his throat. The tips of his ears burned. "She wasn't there before, but she's there now. I expect she'll be out soon."

Rider leaned against the porch railing, his hands pushed deep in his pockets. He narrowed his eyes. "Just what the hell is going on here, Chance?"

Chance inspected the peeling paint on the underside of his porch roof. "Nothing that concerns you."

Rider bent over, his face inches away from Chance's nose. He poked a finger at Chance's chest. "I can always tell when you're lying, big brother. You refuse to meet my eyes. And right now you're lying like a pet dog."

Trixianna stopped with her hand on the door, dressed in her best Sunday gown and ready to face Chance and his brother. Determined to keep her feelings inside where no one could suspect how she felt about Chance, she screwed up her courage and stepped out the door. In a bright voice, she asked, "Who's got a dog?"

Chance jumped to his feet. He stared at her. "I didn't know you even owned a dress that wasn't as gray and ugly as a cemetery marker."

"Why, brother, you are quite the charmer," Rider said. "Is that any way to speak to your lovely houseguest?" He removed his hat and held it over his heart. "Ma'am, you're as lovely as a buttercup."

"Thank you, Rider."

"Yellow," muttered Chance. "That dress is yellow."

Rider swatted Chance on the posterior with his hat. "What's wrong with you? Of course it's yellow."

Chance shook his head, then met Trixianna's eyes. His pale blue irises shone with tenderness. "Why, honey, you look darned pretty."

Remembering the way he'd intimately touched her and aroused her earlier, Trixianna felt the heat of a blush steal into her cheeks.

"Honey?" asked Rider, his voice obviously puzzled. His gaze skipped from Chance to Trixianna, and back again.

Chance visibly swallowed. He turned a flushed face

toward his brother. "What I meant to say is that her dress is the color of honey."

Rider stared at Trixianna's gown, and folded his arms across his chest. "It isn't either. It's as yellow as an ear of corn."

"That's been out in the sun too long," explained Trixianna. "Honey is a very good description. So, who's got a dog?"

Both men stared at her as if she'd lost her mind. Rider found his voice first. "I said the town was quiet as a sleeping dog."

Chance nodded in agreement. "It usually is this time of day. Too early for the drunks and too late for much of anything else. Why don't we all go inside and have coffee?" he suggested. He stepped up onto the porch. Then he turned around, snagged Rider's shirtfront, and dragged him bodily up the steps.

"Good notion," Rider replied. He slapped Chance's hand away and straightened his shirt. Following Chance inside, he said, "Then you can explain what the devil is going on around here. A fellow goes away for a few years and he feels like a stranger among decent folks."

Trixianna had put the coffee on before she'd come outside. Now she stopped in front of the stove, one hand on the pot, and turned to stare at Rider. "What do you mean—decent folks?"

Trixianna watched as Chance frowned, than shook his head. Rider frowned in return. "She's got a right to know," he said.

"Why?"

"If she's staying here and I'm staying here, maybe she'd like to know what kind of man she's sharing living quarters with."

Chance gave a huff of exasperation.

Trixanna stomped her booted foot on the kitchen floor, rattling the glass panes in the window. She glared at the two silent men as she crossed the room with the pot and three cups. She set them noisily down on the kitchen table. "Would you quit talking about me like I'm not even in the room? 'She's this, she's that.' My name is Trixianna. I would appreciate it if you would use it. Now, if you've got family matters to discuss that don't concern me, I understand that, but please don't treat me like I'm the invisible bank robber come to stay." She glared meaningfully at Chance.

He looked at her with a calculating expression in his blue eyes. She met his clear-eyed gaze, her cheeks flaming, her heart pounding. She'd surprised herself with her forward behavior, but she wasn't the least bit sorry.

"Hey," hollered Rider. He made a slight gesture with his right hand. "I don't mean to cause any big ruckus here. It's not a big secret, Trixianna." He smiled at her.

She smiled in return. She began pouring the coffee, her gaze drifting between her task and the brothers' intense expressions. She heard Chance groan.

"I've been in prison up at Lansing the past five years," Rider explained.

Trixianna gasped, stunned by Rider's admission. She missed the cup. Coffee poured all over the table. It ran over the side and dripped unnoticed onto the floor.

"And Chance put me there."

*Wise men have their mouths in their hearts,
fools their hearts in their mouths.*
—*15th-century proverb*

Chapter Thirteen

Chance wanted to throttle Rider for involving Trixianna Lawless in their personal business, but even more than that, he wanted to throttle her. He glanced at the wanted posted that, upon closer inspection, looked nothing like her. She'd messed with the neatly ordered plan he'd made for his life. A plan it had taken him years to arrange and execute . . . he winced at the use of that word, but right now it seemed damned appropriate.

Less than two days from realization, his life's plan was in total chaos. Complete and utter ruin because of the way he yearned for one woman—one particular woman.

He propped his legs on his desk, steepled his hands over his stomach and stared at the tips of his dusty boots. He shook his head and smiled.

He loved her.

Hell, what's more, he enjoyed being with her. He appreciated her rambunctious, unpredictable nature. And that truly confounded him.

Chance Magrane, the quiet, no-nonsense, all-business sheriff, had fallen for a woman who was the out-and-out opposite of the wife he'd imagined he wanted: a steady, placid, reserved woman. A church-going, lawabiding, quilt-sewing woman. A quiet woman who would stand by his side agreeing with every word he uttered, nodding and smiling and speaking only when spoken to. Ha!

So much for his ordered life. What had Trixianna said to him? *What point is there planning your life if you're not living it?*

He'd never thought about it, but she was right. He was planning, always planning, and always looking ahead. He didn't enjoy each day as it passed by. He just let it go. In fact, until she had come along, he'd seldom laughed. Since she'd arrived he'd done little else . . . even at his own expense.

But now he had a problem. A big problem. He'd made a binding promise to Fanny. Could he back out without humiliating her? Not likely. Was he willing to do that to her? No. He had a moral obligation.

Because of what he felt for Trixianna, how she'd made him feel alive, the joy she carried with her and spread around like so much Christmas cheer, it brought an unbearable ache to his heart to even think of losing her. Regardless, he still couldn't embarrass Fanny in front of her family and friends and the whole town of Grand Fork.

Besides, what kind of man would that make him?

It all came back to the same thing. Whatever he decided to do, he was a coward.

But a coward who dreaded spending the rest of his life with a woman he didn't love.

He lowered his head and stared at his steepled fingers. His stomach knotted with a deep, unaccustomed pain. He'd never felt so low.

The sound of the office door opening brought his head up.

Rider stood in the doorway, shaking the light drizzle from his coat. As he peered at Chance, the grin Rider wore upon entering the room slowly faded from his face. "Who died?"

Chance shook his head, then lowered his legs to the floor. "What do you want?"

Rider shrugged his shoulders. "I thought we were meeting at Sinclair's for dinner."

Chance pulled out his pocket watch. Twelve-thirty. He'd forgotten he'd promised to meet Rider at noon. What with his newfound feelings for Trixianna, he'd be hard put to remember his own name. "Sorry," he mumbled. "Got involved in work."

Rider snorted. "Looks to me like you like've got woman problems—two of 'em, in fact."

Chance stiffened, remembering how easily Rider could read his face. "What the hell would you know about women? You haven't so much as smelled one in the past five years."

"And don't I know it." Rider gave a mighty sigh. He swept his hat off his head and brushed back his damp hair. "Let me take you to dinner and I'll tell you everything I know. It won't take more than five minutes. Then you can tell me everything you know. That won't take more than ten. By then, we'll both be experts and we can eat."

"Well, hell," muttered Chance. He rose to his feet

and reached for his rain slicker. "I haven't got anything better to do."

Fanny Fairfax pulled up to the front gate driving a stylish black buggy with a fringed top. She held a lavender parasol in one hand, the reins in the other. The morning drizzle had stopped, but the road was muddy and rutted, difficult to traverse.

Although surprised to see Fanny, Trixianna waved her over. With much difficulty, Fanny started to climb down still clutching the parasol. As she stepped from the buggy onto the muddy road, her foot slipped out from beneath her and she lost her balance. The horse skittered sideways, and Fanny fell in a tumble of white petticoats and purple silk—kerplop—right onto her plentiful backside. Her flat-brimmed straw bonnet, decorated with lavender and violet flowers and a large hideous blackbird, plopped into the muck beside her. Fanny took one look at the hat; her face crumpled and she broke into anguished sobs.

The flighty horse galloped off down the road taking her buggy with it. Trixianna scampered across the yard to Fanny's side.

Fanny hid her face in her pudgy hands, her head bent. The parasol lay forgotten in the road beside her. Trixianna dropped to her knees. She patted Fanny's quaking shoulder. "Are you all right?"

Fanny shook her head and sobbed louder.

"Have you hurt yourself?"

Fanny shook her head again. The sobs subsided a bit as she glanced at Trixianna through tear-filled eyes. "I . . . I, I—." She dropped her head and smothered a sob. "What a g-goose I am."

"No, you're not. Are you worried about the hat?"

Trixianna picked it up, rubbed ineffectually at the muddy brim and handed it to Fanny. "It's almost like new," she lied.

"Oh, bother. I should just give it to Bluebeard to eat." She stared at the bonnet a moment, then plopped it on her head and shoved it down with both hands. She glanced at Trixianna, her brow furrowed.

Fanny's big wet eyes put Trixianna in mind of a spaniel she once had as a child. Stifling the urge to grin, she asked, "Who's Bluebeard?"

"My pet goat." She gave Trixianna a tremulous smile.

Of course. The goat in the photograph on Chance's desk. What an odd choice for a pet.

"He's going to be in the wedding."

In the wedding? Trixianna couldn't imagine such a thing. He would eat all the flowers and chew on the guests' finery. She stared at Fanny, stunned into silence.

"Can you help me up?" she asked in a choked voice.

Trixianna grasped Fanny's elbow and tried to lift her. It proved impossible by herself, but between the two of them, and with quite a bit of inelegant grunting and groaning on Fanny's part, Trixianna got her to her feet.

Tears continued to run down Fanny's scarlet cheeks as she allowed Trixianna to escort her to the porch. She helped Fanny to a chair, then went inside and made tea. She already had the water on for herself.

When she returned, Fanny had somewhat composed herself. Tears still glinted in her eyes, but she'd wiped her face dry with a lace handkerchief she now clutched in her fingers. She gave Trixianna a meager smile and accepted the cup of hot tea. Trixianna sat down opposite her and waited to hear the reason for the tears. She had a feeling it wasn't because Fanny had fallen in the dirt and the horse had run off. She didn't have long to wait.

"I know I don't know you that well, but you have a kind face and I needed to talk to someone. I have no close girlfriends, and I'd die of embarrassment before I could bring this up with Father or Mother. Since you don't really know anyone in Grand Fork, you can't gossip. You don't look like the sort of person who would stoop to such a thing anyway."

"I would never do that." What a fib that was! One of her and Georgette's favorite pastimes was gossiping.

Fanny leaned forward. A disapproving smile played about her lips as she confided in a troubled voice, "I've found out that Chance often visits the Annie V. Saloon and stays quite late."

Trixianna waved her hand in a dismissive gesture. "All men like to have a drink once in a while. I suppose they enjoy the camaraderie a saloon provides."

"I don't believe Chance goes there to drink," Fanny stated. She cast her eyes downward, plucking at a loose thread on her bodice.

"Whatever do you mean?"

Fanny's head shot up, her eyes widened. "Trixianna, where are you from?"

"Abilene," she answered, surprised by the question. "But what does that have to do with the sheriff?"

Fanny shook her head. "My goodness, Abilene. I thought that was a wicked town."

"It was once not so long ago, but the law has taken care of most of those cowboys and such who were causing the problems. Granny Lawless used to tell my sister and me such stories. Oh, my stars! But now, today, it's a lovely, quiet town."

"Is that so?"

Trixianna clasped her hands together in her lap. "Fanny, I don't understand what Abilene has to do with any of this."

Fanny leaned forward and whispered in a conspiratorial voice, "Men seek out comfort at the Annie V."

"Comfort?" Realization hit Trixianna like a kick in the shin. She gasped aloud, her cheeks burning. "However did you find out such a thing?" she whispered.

With a weepy expression on her face, Fanny slumped in her chair, her ample bosom heaving and tears sparkling on her lashes. "My witless brother, Frank, Jr., and I were having a disagreement over whose turn it was to set the table last night. I believe he told me about those women just to peeve me."

"Well, then, perhaps it isn't true."

Fanny gave a sigh of resignation. Tears poured from her big, brown eyes and coursed down her plump cheeks. "Oh, it's true. Men are very lusty, you know. Chance is no exception."

How well she knew! Struggling with the guilt she felt at knowing Chance so intimately, Trixianna tried to steer Fanny in a different direction. "But is that a reason to weep?" At Fanny's look of disbelief, Trixianna continued. "What I mean is, you shouldn't cry about it. You should tell him how you feel and that you want him to stop going to the Annie V. That's the solution. Just make him stop."

"Oh, I couldn't *make* him do anything."

Trixianna flattened her palms against the arms of her chair. Irritation flared at the young woman's immaturity. "Of course you can. He's your betrothed, isn't he? He should listen to what you have to say. After all, you'll be married and then he'll have no choice." *Neither will I. I have to get away from Grand Fork.*

"Oh, I couldn't." Tears continued unabated down Fanny's cheeks. She patted her breast, trying to catch her breath. "I'm a little afraid of Chance."

Trixianna raised an eyebrow in disbelief. Afraid of Chance?

"It's true." A tremor touched her lips. "He's so big and tall, and sometimes he raises his voice and he gets so gruff and mean-sounding. When he looks at me he scares me so bad I can hardly think straight."

"However did two such mismatched people become engaged?"

Did I actually say that out loud? Trixianna gasped and shot to her feet. She clasped Fanny's gloved hand. "I am so sorry. That's entirely none of my business."

"I asked him."

"Don't tell me any more."

"No, it's all right. Really. I don't mind telling the story. Sometimes I ask myself the same thing. It's just that I so wanted to get married and have a family of my own. Father was always saying, 'That Chance Magrane is sure a fine man. He would make a good husband.' And I thought he was right, so I'd find ways of getting Chance to walk me home or dance with me at a barn dance or a wedding. Pretty soon everyone in town assumed we were engaged, so one day I just said to him, 'Are you ever going to ask me to marry you?' He looked at me kind of funnylike and said, 'Is that what you want?' I said, 'Of course.' He didn't say anything for a while. Then he scratched his head in that way he does when he doesn't know what to say. Finally, he said, 'Well, it fits my plan.' "

"Oh, my."

"Not very romantic, is it?"

"Do you love him?" Trixianna asked, not caring that it was none of her business.

Fanny blinked, and two glistening tears coursed down her round cheeks. "N-no," she blubbered, her tears once again turning to sobs. "B-but I d-don't know how to break off the en-gagement without humiliating myself." She cradled her head in her lap, covering her face with her hands.

Trixianna stared at Fanny, and her heart ached for Chance.

The clip-clop of shod hooves brought Trixianna's head up. *Oh, dear God.*

Chance.

He stopped his horse in front of the porch and stared at Trixianna. His knowing blue eyes caught and held hers just a second before he turned his gaze toward Fanny. He pushed his black Stetson to the back of his head and scratched his temple. "What's going on here?"

Fanny's head bobbed up. She dabbed at her face, but there was no disguising the red nose and puffy eyes.

He dismounted, casting a frown at Trixianna as he jumped onto the porch and knelt at Fanny's side. He took her hand and held it easily in his big, work-calloused fingers. He glared at Trixianna. "Did you say something hurtful?"

"Of course not." How could he think such a thing of her after all this time? The man could be such a beast.

"Are you all right, Fanny?" he asked in a gruff, yet

oddly tender voice. When she didn't reply, he reached his hand up and with one finger tipped her chin so she had to look at him.

Big, wet tears coursed down her cheeks and fell onto his hand. She blubbered something unintelligible, wiping at her eyes. Chance waited patiently with a quiet assurance that surprised Trixianna. "Take your time," he said, his voice calm and steady. His gaze never left Fanny's puckered face. A single tear trickled from the corner of her eye. With the tip of his finger he wiped it away.

Trixianna stared tongue-tied, her heart in her throat. Maybe he wasn't such a beast. He obviously cared for Fanny. He was being so tender, so kind, she fought an involuntary reaction to reach out and pull him away. She stared with longing, and remembered his work-roughened fingers on her cheeks, her eyelids, her chin, caressing, stroking, whispering in her ear. Guilt came down on her like a blast of frigid north wind. Fanny's voice brought her up short.

"Really, Chance, it's nothing. I lost control of Pansy when I was climbing down from Father's new buggy. I fell into the road, hurting nothing more than my pride. Then Pansy ran off without me."

Aren't you going to tell him? Trixianna wanted to scream at Fanny. Was she just going to let him go on believing she loved him and wanted to marry him? Even now as Fanny regained control of her emotions, Trixianna could see her distancing herself from Chance as if his touch, his nearness, annoyed her.

Chance rose to his feet. He glanced at Trixianna, his expression tight with obvious strain. "I'm taking Fanny home. I'll speak with you when I return."

"All right," she said. Maybe Fanny would tell him how she felt when they were alone.

But what would she and Chance talk about when he returned? His wedding the next day? Whether she would attend that wedding and be a witness to her undoing?

Or the fact that she loved him with a desperation that bordered on madness?

Chance escorted a quiet, almost sullen, Fanny to her home. She quite obviously wasn't happy riding double. She resisted his efforts to hold her, to comfort her, instead pushing her plump body as far away from his as she could while on the back of a horse. She spoke when addressed, but otherwise was as quiet as a saloon on Sunday morning.

He walked her to her door, kissed her cool cheek and bade her goodbye. She didn't even acknowledge his departure, simply turned and trudged inside.

Chance heaved a sigh of relief. He mounted his gelding and cantered home.

Rider and Trixianna sat at the kitchen table eating molasses cake when he walked into the kitchen. He tossed his hat on a wall peg by the door and sat down to join them.

Rider grinned hello, his mouth stuffed full. He mumbled something unintelligible.

"Don't talk with your mouth full," admonished Trixianna.

Somewhat surprised by her authoritative tone of voice, Chance stared at her. She and Rider had to be close in age, but she sounded just like a mother. He thought, with a pang of regret that he wouldn't be the father of her children, that she would make a good mother someday.

Rider smiled again, his good nature obvious. He reached for the glass of milk at his elbow. Downing the milk in one swallow, he wiped his lip with his sleeve when he finished. "Ma'am, that cake was somethin'. The best I ever ate."

"Thank you, Rider. That's kind of you to say, but your manners leave something to be desired."

"Amen to that," Chance added.

Rider's eyes rounded. Then he gave Trixianna a boyish grin. "Well, hell. If I'd known I was going to be mothered like this when I came to Grand Fork, I might have stayed in jail."

He stood up and walked to the door. With one hand on the handle, he said, "I'm going into town to get my hair cut and see the many sights Grand Fork has to offer."

Chance rolled his eyes. Ever the clown.

"Then I'm going to a saloon I heard about, the Annie V." He cast a sideways glance at Trixianna, whose face bloomed with color at the remark. Rider ducked his head and beat a hasty retreat.

The door slammed, and an uncomfortable silence settled over the room.

Chance broke the stillness. "Uh, you know he's been without female companionship for a spell. He means no disrespect."

Trixianna nodded, her cheeks still flaming. She knew full well what Rider would be doing at the Annie V. Fanny had explained that diversion in plain enough English. Still, she was chagrined that Chance had witnessed her embarrassment. She wanted him to think of her as a worldly woman who knew of such goings-on.

"Oh, it's quite all right," she said, "I understand."

"You do?" he asked, his eyes wide with surprise. "It isn't all right and you shouldn't understand."

"I understand that men have needs."

"Good Lord, woman!" He slapped his palm on the tabletop. The tips of his ears turned pink. "I forget how honest you are sometimes, but I do not want to have this particular conversation with you."

"Well, as I recall, you were the one who wanted to talk, or so you said when you took Fanny home," she retorted. She spread her arms wide. "Here I am."

He rose to his feet. Placing both hands flat on the table, he leaned toward her, his face mere inches from hers. He stared at her, his eyes fixed upon hers. In a silky voice wrought with unspoken challenge, he said, "I do want to talk to you, but I have work yet in town. Burnsey made me promise I'd take supper with him, so it'll have to wait. But this will be our last night together." He swallowed visibly. "I want your company."

"I'll be here when you return."

"I know you will."

The door shut quietly behind him, leaving Trixianna alone with her thoughts.

Damn. Chance hadn't been able to escape Burnsey's incessant chatter about, surprisingly, everything but Chance's upcoming nuptials. Finally, the Englishman had drunk himself into a stupor and Chance had locked him up. Now it was well past midnight. He trudged home, his head lowered, his feet dragging. Trixianna would be in bed by now. He so wanted to talk to her, and explain his reasons for marrying a woman he didn't love.

He also wanted to tell her that he hadn't been taking advantage of her, either when he'd saved her cat from drowning, or when Sam Smith had tried to steal her away. Both times he'd lost the use of reason. She had the power to make him forget things . . . like his duty as sheriff, his obligation to Fanny, his common sense.

He entered the house quietly. Thoughtful as ever, Trixianna had left a lamp burning low on the kitchen table so he could find his way to his room. He sat down on a kitchen chair, and yanked off his boots and wool socks. He pulled his shirt off over his head. Trudging down the hall, holding his clothes in one hand and the lantern in the other, he stopped just outside Trixianna's room. As always, she'd left the door ajar. He squelched the insistent urge to peek in.

Chance stepped across the hall to his own room, and tossed his clothes on the foot of the bed. As he set the lamp down, he heard a muffled moan.

Dashing across the hall, he drew his gun. He threw the door wide. Trixianna lay with her feet entangled in the bedcoverings, thrashing in the throes of a dream. Twisted around her hips, her night rail glimmered pink in the dim light of the lantern. Her legs, long and sleekly tapered, lay displayed for his intense scrutiny. Her coppery-colored hair—how he loved that hair—spread about her head and beckoned him. Called to him like the sea sirens sailors spoke of. He watched her sleep, his heart in his throat. Holstering his gun, he unbuckled the gun belt and placed it over the footboard. He sat down on the side of the bed and stroked her cheek. His calloused fingers caught on a fine strand of hair next to her face. The rasping of her breath sounded loud in the still of the quiet night, and she stirred.

Trixianna woke. She heard breathing. Then a familiar odor filled her nose. Chance. Leather, spearmint, his own distinctive male scent. She rolled onto her back and gazed into his compelling blue eyes. She opened her arms to welcome him. He hesitated a fraction of a second before stretching across her, his chest covering hers. Heat radiated off his body. To be so close to him was like being cocooned in a scratchy wool blanket, his hair-roughened chest scraping across her tender breasts.

Wrapping his arms about her, he buried his face in her neck. "Oh, God," he moaned. "Tell me to go away. Tell me to leave you alone, now, before it's too late."

"It's already too late," she whispered.

"Don't," he warned, his voice thick and unsteady. "Don't say that."

"I can't help it, Chance," she insisted. "Stay with me tonight, just tonight."

"You don't know what you're asking. I can't promise you anything." His voice broke, and she heard him swallow. "It's not fair to you." His hands tightened around her shoulders, the fingers gripping her flesh through the thin fabric of her gown.

Trixianna clasped one of his hands and moved it to her breast. She heard his sharp intake of air. Her nipple instantly hardened, as if seeking his touch. His hand trembled, then squeezed gently, cupping the weight in his palm.

He came up onto one elbow and stared at the bronzed hand that sheltered her silk-covered breast. He traced his fingertip across the rigid bud, then circled the aureole. With his thumb and forefinger he rolled the nipple between his fingers. Trixianna's stomach clenched tight.

"God, you're so beautiful," he said. He lowered his head and kissed her through the fabric, his lips seeking and tugging. His tongue prodded the sensitive nubbin.

A thrill barreled through Trixianna's body, tingling shafts that curled her toes. Heat flared in her abdomen and lower, much lower. Her body stiffened. "Oh, oh."

Chance lifted his head and stared into her eyes. He didn't speak, just sought and held her gaze. Her heart flip-flopped in response. Against her stomach, an intimate part of his anatomy nudged her, then again. This time Chance took her hand and held it against the front of his trousers, his hand holding hers tight against his body. Through the coarse fabric, he throbbed against her fingertips.

"I haven't even kissed you yet and I'm about ready to explode," he gritted out between clenched teeth. "Trixianna," he whispered. "Unbutton my trousers."

As her trembling fingers worked the buttons, he kissed her chin. His mouth grazed her earlobe, and she shivered. When his tongue slipped inside her ear, she shuddered from head to toe. He moved to her cheek, then her nose, where she heard him sigh. "I love your freckles. They're like little droplets of cinnamon and I want to lick them all." His lips trailed across her cheeks and nose as if he were doing just that.

She undid the last button. His sex came free from his trousers and thrust insistently against her taut belly. He turned his attention to her mouth while his hands molded the contours of her breasts. He seemed

244

to know where she'd be most sensitive, his hands and mouth caressing and touching, sparking a fire all over her tender flesh.

He lifted her gown over her head, and tossed it onto the floor. Then he tugged his trousers over his hips and pulled them from his feet. They ended up on the floor.

They lay facing each other; bare, hot skin against bare, hot skin, his thigh over her hip, heat pulsing between her legs. She was filled with an anticipatory wanting, while he peered intently at her. His eyes gleamed, then flashed eagerly.

"This is it, honey," he rasped through clenched teeth. "You have to tell me to stop now because we can't later."

"Huh?" Trixianna didn't have an inkling what he was talking about.

For some reason he found her confusion amusing. He gave a quick bark of laughter. "Trixianna, you're going to lose your virginity if we don't stop now. You could become pregnant."

She swallowed around the apprehensive knot in her throat. "I understand that."

"It might hurt at first."

"Oh?"

He squeezed his eyes shut a moment. Then he clasped her chin in his rough fingers and stared at her. "I've heard that, but believe me, I've got no experience with virgins."

Trixianna stared into his beloved face; his thick black brows drawn together in a worried frown, his pale, blue eyes so intense with wanting and passion. She wondered if her face mirrored his. She, too, felt desire unlike anything she'd ever known. "Do you want to?"

"Do I want to what?" he said in a hoarse whisper.

"Do you want to make love to me?" she asked. Her eyes filled with tears.

"Oh, honey," he whispered. He clasped her tight to his chest, squeezing the breath out of her. "More than anything."

"All right, then. What's next?"

Chance flopped onto his back, one arm resting over his eyes. Rising from a nest of soft black hair, his engorged shaft quivered. Trixianna sat up, unable to remove her gaze from that part of him. She shook her head. It was much too big to fit inside her. It would never work.

He groaned. "God, do you have to be so analytical? We're not about to butcher a hog here. This is supposed to be exciting, passion-filled loving; hot, heavy breathing, touching, wanting, sweating, kissing, that sort of thing."

"I do want all that, Chance, I really do, but I can see with my own eyes that it won't work."

His eyes flew open. He sought her face, then followed the line of her vision. He choked back a grunt of laughter. He reached down and worked the sheet up to his waist. Then he pulled her over onto his chest. He wrapped his arms around her waist. "Trixianna, darling, it'll work. Believe me."

"Are you certain? It seems awfully . . . well, large. Are all men . . . ?"

He exhaled a long sigh, then said in an amused voice, "It's normal for me. I can't speak for other men."

"I'm sure you're right," she assured him. "It's just

that you said it would hurt, and it looks very big and I'm just worried is all."

"Are you sure now? 'Cause there's no turning back."

"Yes, I'm sure."

"Thank God," he murmured.

He pulled the sheet from between their bodies and rolled her onto her back. Keeping his weight off her, he balanced on his hands. With his knees he nudged hers apart, and settled between her legs. Then he kissed her with a hunger that diminished all her doubts.

His mouth caressed, worshiped, adored Trixianna. Outside the window, the stars shone brighter in the night sky. Inside the small bedroom, stars blossomed and danced behind her eyes. She couldn't focus, she couldn't think, she could only feel.

Her sensitized nerve endings felt every part of Chance. His rough beard scratching against her cheek, his chest hair rubbing against her nipples, the hair along his legs rasping along her thighs. Her hands on his muscled back felt each sinew, each tendon, as he stretched over her.

He nudged his shaft between her legs. "Are you ready?" he asked, his voice reedy with unresolved passion and obvious need.

"Yes," she whispered. She was. She wanted this, needed this, had waited her whole life for this man. She would never love another as she loved Chance—desperately, the love overflowing her body and encompassing his. This was the only way she knew how to show him that love.

He thrust against her, pushing gently. Then he rose up on his elbows. His face, damp with perspiration, showed traces of strain. Furrowed brow, tight lips, flared nostrils. He rested his head against Trixianna's forehead. "My God, I don't know if I can do this."

"I love you, Chance."

He swallowed, the sound deafening in the quiet of the bedroom. Then he buried himself deep within her.

The man that blushes is not quite a brute.
                —Edward Young

Chapter Fourteen

"Don't move," Chance growled. If Trixianna so much as twitched, he'd lose control. She wasn't ready, but her avowal of love nearly pushed him over the edge. He needed to slow their lovemaking and make this good for her. He needed to make it right with himself. He needed her love.

Guilt nudged his conscience. Chance mentally pushed it aside, concentrating on the beautiful woman in bed with him. He could scarcely believe she wanted him, much less loved him. When she'd admitted it, he'd wanted to shout with joy. And he could no more deny her than he could stop breathing.

She made a whimpering sound. Chance looked down to find tears glistening on her lashes. Regret rocked him. He hadn't been easy enough with her. "Damn, I've hurt you."

"No," she whispered, her voice hitching as she

fought to control it. One fat tear rolled down her face, then another.

He licked both up with his tongue, and said, "Then why are you crying?"

She gave him a tentative smile. "I'm not crying."

He wasn't fooled. He'd hurt her. Although he'd never heard of such a thing, maybe he *was* too big for her. He felt his ears burn as a flush worked its way up the back of his neck.

"You're blushing," Trixianna observed. Her mouth tipped up at the corners in a pixielike grin.

"I am not."

"I'm shedding tears and you're blushing," she said softly. "Is this the way of things when a man beds a woman?"

"Not in my experience," Chance muttered. He was still imbedded deep within her, straining for release. His body fought for a culmination, quickening with each slight movement she made. He concentrated on her glowing face. "Have I hurt you?" he repeated. "Because if I have and you want to stop, I reckon we may have a problem here 'cause I'm not sure I can stop."

"Oh, Chance," she said, her tone one of awe. Her green eyes danced with love for him. *For him.* A lump lodged in his throat. "There's nothing wrong. I'm just so happy to be here with you . . . even if it's just this once."

"Me, too, honey, me, too," he rasped between clenched teeth. At last, he gave in to the instinctive desire to thrust.

Trixianna gasped. She held his buttocks tight in her slender grasp urging him on, seeming to understand his need. A pure and crystal-clear pleasure seized him. He reclaimed Trixianna's lips, rousing her passion as well as his own.

She moaned, squirming beneath him. He felt the beginning of tiny spasms start low in her body. She arched her hips. He flung his head back as a thrumming began in his own body. Coaxing Trixianna with whispered love words, he found himself hurtling beyond control. Trixianna cried out his name at her moment of climax. His came on the crest of hers, shouted hoarsely from deep within his chest.

They fell to the bed, entwined still, satiated and laughing.

Sometime in the dark of night, Chance reached for Trixianna. She had no idea of the time, nor did she care. His rough, calloused hand wrapped around her waist and pulled her to his side, encircling her within the warmth of his strong arms.

Not quite asleep, yet not quite awake, Trixianna waited with an expectant knot in her throat. She touched his beard-roughened cheek, her heart thudding rapidly in her breast. The night sounds—the whisper of the wind, the commonplace bark of a dog—combined to heighten her senses. With this man beside her, his heart beating rhythmically with hers, she felt secure and protected.

Next to her ear, he released a deep sigh of contentment. Gooseflesh rose up and down her arms. When his breathing deepened, she realized he was asleep.

Trixianna pulled the discarded bedcoverings up to her waist. She stopped before she covered Chance. His naked body, gilded gold by the moonlight, was hers to visually explore. He lay on his back. The gunshot wound on his shoulder looked puckered and pink, but it was healing well. A light dusting of black hair ran the length of his body, starting with a vee of hair between the nipples on his muscled chest, growing denser between his legs. The inky hair drifted down his thighs and calves. He even had little tufts of hair on the tops of his toes. She found that quite endearing.

She recalled the wonder of being held in his strong arms, the magic of his gentle touch, the spellbinding words he'd used to caress and urge her. His lovemaking was so much more than what she'd expected—wondrous and beautiful and fulfilling. She loved him so.

Trixianna folded the blanket beneath his chin, then kissed his lips. She watched his face as he slept, his lips parted, his mouth relaxed.

She thought she should be feeling sinfully wicked, wholly guilty at the very least. She didn't. Tomorrow Chance would wed Fanny, and the mayor's daughter would have him to herself the rest of her life. One night with Chance would be all Trixianna would ever have, and she wasn't about to feel bad about it.

Anger at Fanny simmered inside Trixianna, anger for not calling off the wedding when she knew she didn't love him. But perhaps that was only Trixianna's own jealousy and resentment at not being able to have Chance to herself. A woman wasn't required to love the man she married. Women married for many other reasons—security, money, children.

She wanted love for Chance. She grieved for the loveless marriage awaiting him. He was honest and loyal to a fault. He'd live with his promise to Fanny no matter what kind of marriage they'd have.

Trixianna was glad she wouldn't be around to see the day when Fanny became round with Chance's child.

Trixianna lay down, turned her head away from Chance and wept bitter, pitiful tears into her pillow.

*   *   *

Feeling as if he had a knife-wound in his heart, Chance stared down at the warm, sweet-smelling woman lying in bed. He'd hated like hell to have to leave her this morning, but he had a long day ahead of him. The last place he needed to be found on his wedding day was in bed with a lawless woman known as Mad Maggie West.

He kissed Trixianna's cool cheek and caressed the tangled web of hair that surrounded her face like a sunset-colored halo. "Goodbye, honey," he whispered. Tears burned behind his eyelids. "No matter what, I will always love you."

The lump in his throat and the acute sense of loss increased with each measured step he took away from the house.

By the time he reached his office, he'd convinced himself that he'd mastered his inner turmoil. He pushed open the door and walked inside. He leaned against the jail cell and eyed Burnsey. Passed out and snoring, as usual. Chance cleared his throat. Nothing. He rattled the bars. A slight flaring of nostrils, a fluttering of eyelids, but the man snored on.

"About that lawyer fella of yours," Chance began.

"Unh," came the reply from the semi-conscious Englishman. He rolled to his back and groaned. With one bloodshot eye on Chance, the other squeezed shut, he muttered, "What?"

"I'd hire him if I were you."

"What?" Burnsey repeated. "Who?"

"The lawyer, dammit."

Burnsey cleared his throat. "James is no solicitor," was his somewhat garbled reply. He sat up, blinking his eyes like a nearsighted owl. He stretched, yawned loudly and scratched his stubbled jaw.

"What does that mean?" asked Chance. "Is he just no good as a lawyer, or not one at all?"

"He is not one at all, my good man. James is my valet, and he excels at the position."

"Valet?" repeated Chance.

"Yes. In this country I believe you would call him my manservant."

"Dammit, Burnsey, I know what a valet is."

"Please pardon me. My mind is a bit muddled."

"Oh, yeah." Chance threw the cell door open. It flew back and clanked against the bars, sending a loud ringing throughout the small room.

Burnsey jumped as if he'd been goosed. From beneath narrowed eyes, he frowned at Chance. "Please have a care, Sheriff."

Chance pointed a finger at Burnsey. "What I'd like to know, *Mr. Burns,* is why you felt the need to lie about the man."

"Simple." Burnsey leaned back on his elbows and crossed his legs. In his red-flannel long underwear, and with a disheveled ascot tied haphazardly around his neck, he didn't quite project the image he seemed to be aiming for—that of an elegant, self-possessed, highborn lord. "As I believe you Westerners are fond of saying, I was saving Trixianna's bacon."

Chance snorted in derision. "She doesn't need her bacon saved. That woman can take care of herself."

"I am well aware of that now, but I wasn't sure of your position at first and assumed that if you thought she had a solicitor it would keep you from doing anything rash."

"So how long did you think you could carry on that little lie?"

"Long enough, Sheriff. Long enough." Burnsey rose to his feet. "Is the coffee on?"

"Yeah. You know where it is." Chance walked back to his desk and sat down. He watched Burnsey trudge over to the potbellied stove, stubbing his big toe halfway there. Hopping on the other foot, he rubbed the toe and cursed his "royally rotten aching head." Chance winced when Burnsey turned his backside toward him and gave him a glimpse of a bare, pale buttock. The man had no shame. Chance shook his head.

With shaking hands, Burnsey managed to pour himself a cup of coffee without scalding himself. Carrying the cup with both hands, he settled in a chair across the desk from Chance. He blew on the steaming brew, then tilted his head and inhaled. As he released a deep sigh, his bleary gaze seemed to be focusing on Chance. "So, Sheriff, this is the big day."

Chance nodded.

Burnsey peered at Chance over the rim of his cup. "Is Fanny ready?"

"Far as I know." Chance stared at Burnsey, scanning his face for . . . something. The man wasn't saying what was on his mind. His eyes, shot through with whiskey-induced redness, held cynical skepticism.

"She's going to make a fine wife."

"Uh-huh," agreed Chance.

Burnsey's head shot up. "Do I sense some reticence on your part, Sheriff?"

"If I knew what the word meant, I'd probably deny it. It sounds like an insult."

"It isn't." Burnsey glanced into his cup, his lips

drawn in a tight line. Then he said in a voice laced with admiration, "She's an excellent cook."

"Trixianna?" asked Chance.

"No, Fanny. She also has a keen fashion sense. She dresses exquisitely."

"I never noticed," Chance admitted.

"Oh, my, yes. Lovely shades of purple she wears. Very regal." Burnsey's brow furrowed. His eyes were glazed over . . . with thoughts of Chance's betrothed.

Chance stared. Lost in his reverie, Burnsey didn't even seem to notice Chance sitting across from him and gawking. Like a fist to the solar plexus, Chance recognized the besotted look on Burnsey's face.

The man was in love with Fanny.

As surely as the sun would set this evening and the rooster would crow in the morning, Burnsey loved Fanny Fairfax.

What a disaster.

Bursey loved Fanny.

Chance loved Trixianna.

Trixianna loved Chance.

Who did Fanny love? She didn't love *him*, Chance knew, but did she love Burnsey? And if she did, why hadn't she broken off their engagement? He glanced at his pocket watch. He had three hours to find out. "Burnsey?"

A befuddled look crossed Burnsey's features. He roused himself long enough to peer at Chance. "What?"

Chance stood up and headed for the door. "I've got business. You know your way out."

"See you later then, Sheriff."

"Don't forget to put on some clothes, Burnsey. And take a bath. You smell like the back end of a mule."

Chance pushed his Stetson low on his forehead and stepped out into a cold drizzle. His clothing was instantly soaked. He strode down the boardwalk, his head bent, his thoughts racing.

The streets were empty. All the women in town were either cooking up something special for the wedding reception, or in the church decorating it with early fall flowers. He remembered Fanny talking about roses, mums and ribbon garlands. She wanted candles placed just so about the church, and had specified where each and every one was to go. Right now the pews were being dusted and polished, and the floor swept so the menfolk could track in mud later. He knew the light drizzle wouldn't let in much light through the polished windows, but the candle glow would suffice.

Preparations for Grand Fork's biggest wedding in a month of Sundays had begun a long time ago, and right now, the process was in full swing. How was he going to stop it?

These thoughts passed through Chance's fevered brain as he hurried to the Fairfax home. His stride lengthened until he was almost running.

Thoughts of the previous night spent in Trixianna's loving embrace nearly brought him to a standstill. He should have felt more guilt and remorse about his actions, but he didn't. He couldn't. He loved her, and nothing would tarnish his memories of the night they had shared.

He slowed his step as he approached the mayor's stately red-brick home. What would he say to Fanny? No immediate words of wisdom came to mind. He considered himself a well-spoken man, seldom at a loss for words, but Fanny left him befuddled and speechless most of the time. He never knew what to say to her, and he couldn't understand her when she deigned to speak to him. Theirs was a relationship based solely on longtime acquaintance. And a union of politics.

She was soft-spoken, never raised her voice and never complained. At least not to him . . . until the other evening when he'd brought Frank home drunk and requested a simple kiss from her.

He trudged up three wide wooden stairs. Shaking the rain from his clothing, he removed his hat. He brushed back his damp hair and knocked. His heart was in his throat, his mind reeling.

Fanny's mother, Eloise, pulled the door to and peered out. She stared at him in obvious surprise. "Why, Chance, whatever are you doing here?"

"I've come to see Fanny. Is she home?" he asked, knowing full well she was. He shuffled his feet and clutched the wet brim of his hat between his thumb and forefinger.

"It's bad luck to see the bride before the wedding," Eloise reminded him. She pursed her mouth as if she were sucking on a lemon.

He felt as if that same lemon were in his own mouth. "It's important, ma'am."

"I don't know." She shook her head, then gestured him into the darkened foyer. "No sense standing there in the rain."

"Thank you, ma'am." Chance cautiously followed her inside, aware of his bedraggled, soaked appearance. He soon stood in a spreading puddle.

She gave him a disparaging glance. "I'll see what Fanny says."

"I'll wait here."

"See that you do," she stated, turning her back to him. She started up the stairway, her hand trailing over the polished mahogany banister, and disappeared down the hall. He heard the whisper of a door opening, then closing.

Releasing a long drawn-out sigh, Chance glanced around. Although he'd been in the Fairfax manse on numerous occasions, he still felt ill at ease and out of place. Too many breakables, skinny-legged tables and portraits of stuffy ancestors. The heavy drapes were always closed against even the meagerest of daylight. The house felt about as welcoming as a cemetery at midnight on a foggy night. Today was no different. He strained to hear Eloise and Fanny, but heard nothing but the steady drip, drip, drip of the rain in the eaves and the thumping of his own heart. Like a watch winding down.

He waited.

And waited.

After what seemed like hours, Fanny called to him from the top of the stairs. "Chance."

He glanced up, and started forward. He then stopped at the base of the stairs, unsure if he was to proceed.

She had her back to him, one hand on her hip, the other around the newel post at the top of the stairs. One slippered foot tapped against the carpeted floor in an impatient cadence. Dressed in a voluminous wrapper of dark purple silk, her hair tied up in rags, she gifted him with her abundant backside. An aura of brusque peevishness accompanied her voice. "What is it, Chance?"

"I, um," he began. Feeling foolish, he cleared his throat. "Aren't you going to turn around?"

"Bad luck," she declared. "Now what is it? I've got a hundred things to do."

"Just one question, Fanny, and I'll be on my way."

"All right."

"Are you still sure you want to marry me? It's not too late to back out."

Her back stiffened. Her foot increased its rhythmic pattern. Her unrestrained buttocks jiggled, reminding Chance of Trixianna's smaller hips that fit perfectly in the palms of both his hands. He glanced away, guilt gnawing at his insides. "Are you deliberately trying to humiliate me, Chance Magrane?"

"No, of course not." His voice sounded empty, meaningless, even to his own ears.

"I know I'm not pretty."

"Fanny, that's not—"

"Don't interrupt me," she ordered in a frigid voice. "This may not be the marriage you dreamt about when you were younger, but this is the marriage you're getting. I'll make you a good wife."

"Fanny, I know you will. I'm not trying to back out," he stated in a deliberately calm, restrained voice. "I just want you to know that you still can get out of this if you want."

"Well, I don't."

"All right then. I'll see you at the church."

"Fine."

"Fine." Chance turned his back. He trudged across the foyer, his booted feet squishing with each step. He stopped in front of the massive mahogany door, and stared at his face reflected in the rain-splattered oval glass, eyes narrowed, lips thinned, lines bracketing his mouth. He shook his head, then released a sigh. Twisting the brass handle, he glanced over his shoulder and up the stairs. Fanny had disappeared back into the bowels of the darkened house. Chance shuddered and swallowed hard. He shoved his Stetson onto his head and headed outside into the waiting, cold drizzle.

Trixianna awoke to a bleary day, the sun no more than a dull gray light edging above the horizon. She blinked the sleep from her eyes and reached across the bed for Chance. Nothing but a slight indentation in the mattress met her searching fingers. The scent of spearmint lingered in the bedsheets. She buried her face in the pillow and inhaled. An unfamiliar, yet thrilling, ache between Trixianna's thighs reaffirmed the wondrous night she and Chance had shared. She rolled over and plopped onto her back, staring at the ceiling. Listening to the rain drone against the window glass and drip off the trees outside, she recalled what this day would bring.

Chance's wedding.

A suffocating sensation enveloped Trixianna. Her breath felt trapped in her chest. She sat on the side of the bed, her head hanging between her knees, her heart hammering.

No regrets, she reminded herself. No grief. And most of all, no pity.

She fought the urge to seek Chance out, to cling to him and beg him not to make this terrible mistake.

But she couldn't. He didn't think this wedding was a mistake. He was being honorable, doing exactly what was expected of the upstanding, right-minded sheriff.

What would the people of Grand Fork think of their sheriff if they'd seen him in all his naked glory as she had last night?

A fierce blush seized Trixianna, heating her from head to toe. It was then she realized that she sat on the side of the bed in her own naked glory, bare as the day she'd been born.

She sat up and wrapped the sheet around her. After a few calming moments, she got out of bed, washed and dressed to begin her day of baking. No matter what else happened today, Bertram Sinclair would expect his pies. Later, when she delivered her baked goods, she would be ready to face Grand Fork with her head held high and a perfect smile pasted on her features. She wondered how many people she would fool.

As Trixianna trudged home after her delivery to Sinclair's, she found that either the rain or wedding preparations were keeping most people off the street. She hadn't had to make small talk or even polite conversation with anyone, much less Bert Sinclair. He had been in an especially foul mood. The townsfolk of Grand Fork were either skipping their dinner meal or eating at home in anticipation of the good food that would be served later at the wedding reception. Sinclair's Fine Restaurant was virtually void of human inhabitants.

Trixianna was just unlatching the gate in Chance's picket fence when she heard a voice calling her name. "Miss Lawless!"

The out-of-breath, excited voice and running feet pounding down the boardwalk brought Trixianna's head up, startling her out of her reverie. Barreling down the street toward her was a bundle of vitality in the form of a small child.

"Miss Lawless!" came the call again.

Trixianna stopped with her hand on the gate. She brought her other hand up to protect her eyes from the drizzle and see if she could recognize who was calling to her.

One of the young Perry brothers, of the window-peeping incident, skidded to a stop before her, dripping wet. His flushed face met her expectant gaze with gleaming eyes and a wide gap-toothed smile. Water dripped off the back of his straw hat and skittered off his oilskin slicker onto the walkway. "Look," he exclaimed, his finger pointing at his chest. "I come right to the door and didn't even take a peek in the window even if I was wanting to."

"Good for you." Trixianna returned his contagious smile. She took his elbow and guided him inside the gate and up the walkway. Peering beneath the brim of his hat, she asked, "Is it Michael or Thomas?"

"Michael."

Trixianna stepped onto the porch and out of the downpour. "Let's get inside where it's dry. Wouldn't you like to come in?"

"No, thank you, ma'am. Pa just sent me over to say that you got folks waitin' on you down to the train station."

Surprise made her mouth drop open. She closed it enough to reply, "I do?"

He nodded, spraying water around him like a soaked dog. "Sure 'nough. Pa says they're family. All dressed up in right nice duds, too. Pa says they's religious folks, for certain."

Trixianna hid the grin that tugged at her lips. "How would he know that?"

Michael leaned forward and said in a loud whisper,

"They look like you—that's how I know they's family. One's got red hair just like yours."

"They? How many are there?"

He held up three fingers.

"Three, hmm? But what did your Pa say about being religious?"

"He said one's a nun, a sister. What's a nun, Miss Lawless? Is she your sister?"

"A nun? In my family?" Trixianna repeated. "My family? Why, we're not even of the Catholic faith." *Could it possibly be her own family?* She and Georgette did have the same shade of red hair. It took all her willpower to keep from hooting out loud and dancing a jig around the porch. She grabbed Michael, took his face in both her hands and kissed his chilled cheek soundly.

His face was bright as a carrot, as he mumbled, "Aw, shucks." He squirmed out of her hold and backed down the stairs. His eyelids swept down to hide the frank look of regard in his hazel eyes, but not before Trixianna caught the honest, slightly young but undoubtedly male stare of admiration.

She wrapped her wool cape tightly around her and tossed the covering over her head as she scooted off the porch alongside the boy.

"Do you want to race?" he asked, excitement glimmering in his eyes.

"I surely do, young man."

Like a child, she ran with him down the street, oblivious to the rain, ignoring the mud that flew up and splattered her clothing.

At the same time that Trixianna and Michael Perry were racing through the streets of Grand Fork, Jake, the telegraph office operator, sent the other Perry brother, Thomas, off to give Chance an important telegram from the sheriff in Dena Valley. On the off chance he wasn't home, Jake sent Thomas to Chance's office first. He'd returned with the telegram. So he had sent him to the sheriff's home.

Chance was walking home in the rain when Thomas finally caught up to him. He gave the boy a few pennies and thanked him for his trouble.

Scanning the missive, Chance saw that the sheriff had been delayed, and would arrive in Grand Fork about the same time his wedding began. The timing couldn't have been worse.

So engrossed was he in reading the telegram that he passed right by the train station and the disembarking passengers.

He would have been astounded to see Georgette Lacina and her husband and their newfound friend, Sister Mary Margaret, from the Little Sisters of Mercy Convent, waiting to see Trixianna. If he'd by chance looked up, he would have been shocked to realize that there were two women in Grand Fork so unbelievably similar in appearance. In fact, he would have thought he was seeing double.

And he would have been. But if he had also peeked beneath the nun's habit and seen this woman's face and hair, he would have thought he was seeing triple.

As it was, he passed by without a glance.

Time and chance reveal all secrets.
—18th-century proverb

Chapter Fifteen

With a burst of black smoke belching from its smoke-stack and a screech of brakes, the westbound train pulled to a stop at the station in Grand Fork, Kansas. Maggie West stared out the window at the dreary, low-ered sky burdened with shower-filled clouds. The rain-slickened station platform shimmered ghostlike in the iron-gray gloom. A faint light beckoned in the solitary window of the depot. She smiled to herself. What a beautiful day it was going to be.

Beneath the disguise of her severe black nun's habit and pristine white wimple, her heart beat like angel wings in anticipation of new adventures to come and innocent people to fleece. She would be ever grateful to be rid of the hard wooden seat beneath her aching, numbed posterior. Besides, the prospect of invading Grand Fork masquerading as the devoted, God-fearing Sister Mary Margaret tickled her consider-ably.

Covered from head to toe in black, Maggie believed she had cleverly disguised her features and her own well-known russet-colored locks as well. She tried not to laugh outright. That would be unseemly, now wouldn't it? She glanced at the soggy, fog-enshrouded town. She hoped to be in town for only a short time—long enough to rob the bank and free that innocent woman who'd reputedly been arrested. She didn't feel right about anyone else taking the blame for her own misdeeds. Curious about the woman's looks, she could hardly contain her excitement about seeing her face-to-face.

"I'm just so excited," gushed Georgette Lacina to her new traveling companion as she gathered up her voluminous gray silk skirts to step off the train. Carefully, Maggie took Georgette's outstretched arm and followed her onto the wooden railroad platform.

Maggie released her into the care of her pensive husband. Georgette's cheeks were flushed and her hair, the exact shade of dried apples, flew about her head like a misbehaving halo.

Her husband, Jonathan, smiled benignly as he took her elbow and guided her around the many puddles, and out of the way of the two remaining passengers disembarking behind them.

One of the older women gave a startled gasp as the couple walked away. "Why, Trixianna, is that you?"

Georgette spun on her heel, one hand holding onto her bonnet. "No, I'm—"

"I knew you'd get away before Chance became aware of your good qualities," the woman interrupted. "He never was very wise when it came to women. Oh, well. I'm sure he and Fanny will do just fine together. It was kind of you to return for the wedding, though."

She hurried off with her companion, leaving Georgette with a befuddled expression on her face. "I'm always being mistaken for my twin sister."

Maggie West, known to law-enforcement officials throughout the Midwest as Mad Maggie, hid a smile as she watched the loving couple glance wide-eyed at each other and laugh. Heads bent together, they moved out of the rain to stand beneath the overhanging roof of the depot, obviously discussing the woman.

"Sister Mary Margaret," called Georgette.

Maggie turned, and offered a blank smile at the eager young woman. Catching her wide black skirt in one hand, she strode toward the young couple.

"I'll be right there, Mrs. Lacina," Maggie answered in a quiet and, she hoped, holy and pious tone of voice. She shaded her eyes and scanned the empty platform. "Is your dear sister expecting you? I don't see anyone waiting."

"Oh, no. We're going to surprise her."

"I'll just bet your sweet arse you are," Maggie muttered beneath her breath. "And so am I." A bit louder, she said, "I'm sure she'll be delighted to have you once again in the warm embrace of her loving arms."

Georgette sniffed, tears once again forming in her already reddened eyes. The woman had cried practically the entire trip as she'd related to Maggie, ad nauseam, all about her most unfortunate misunderstanding with her sister. Maggie, playing the role of kind-hearted nun, had had no choice but to listen to her incessant chatter all the way from Abilene to Grand Fork when what she really wanted to do was strangle the woman and toss her weepy body from the train. The longest ride in the history of mankind, Maggie would have ventured to say. She'd been mighty proud of her restraint.

The naive young couple had swallowed Maggie's own tall tale about visiting the poor, sick and indigent folks of Grand Fork as if it were sweet butter melting on warm hotcakes. What a hoot!

She was anxious to meet this sister who, as rumor had it, was locked up in the Grand Fork jail for robbing the Dena Valley bank. Chortling would probably be uncalled for under the circumstances. Instead, Maggie tucked her hands inside the folds of her sleeves, ducked her head and came to stand with the Lacinas. "What are your plans, dear hearts?"

Jonanathan spoke first. "Well, Sister Mary Margaret, we don't rightly know. Trixianna didn't say where she was staying."

"Trixianna?"

"My sister," Georgette explained.

Maggie coughed to hide the bark of laughter that crept up her throat. My God, the name sounded like a woman who worked in the local brothel, or at the very least, danced the hootchie-kootchie with a traveling minstrel show. "Perhaps the hotel?" she ventured. Her voice came out sounding as if she'd swallowed a frog.

"A sound plan, Sister," Jonathan said, bobbing his head. "If you ladies will just stay put, I'll try to find the establishment myself. No sense in you two getting wet traipsing the streets locating our Trixianna."

"That's a good idea, Jonathan," Georgette said. "Whatever would I do without you?"

"I hope you never have to find out, my dear." He

269

patted Georgette on the shoulder, then lingered as he kissed her forehead. Maggie watched as Georgette's cheeks turned a rosy pink. Young love. Wasn't it god-awful? Maggie felt like gagging. She turned her head to hide her distaste.

"Goodbye, ladies. I won't be long." He hurried away, one hand holding his hat on his head against the wind-driven rain.

They found a bench beside the depot—another damned hard wooden bench—and sat down. Maggie lowered herself, arranging her skirt in a slow, ladylike fashion that wouldn't give away her disguise. She wasn't used to sitting in skirts; or walking, or riding, or doing much of anything else in them, for that matter. They were a confounded nuisance.

The crucifix around her neck swayed, then pressed against her chest, catching her attention. It was a nice reverent touch, thought Maggie. She brought it to her lips, kissed the cold metal and moved her mouth in a resemblance of prayer. She couldn't have repeated one if her life depended on it.

Georgette turned toward her, and out of the corner of her eye, Maggie saw her open her mouth. Her eyes widened, then she clamped her lips shut. The proper Mrs. Lacina waited, her own head bowed.

"I've finished thanking the Lord for our safe arrival, Mrs. Lacina."

She nodded. "Sister Mary Margaret, where will you be staying while you're in Grand Fork?"

Maggie didn't have an answer. She hadn't planned on being there long enough to need a place to stay. "I, um, well, let me think," she hedged. "I'll be staying with the sheriff."

"How odd."

"Yes, perhaps one might think so, but I understand the sheriff in Grand Fork is a devout man and loves the Lord." Maggie didn't know the man from Adam, but she could prevaricate with the best of 'em. "He sincerely believes in the Lord's work."

"Of course he would, for it benefits his town as well as his friends and neighbors," Georgette said. "It must be wonderful work that you do, Sister. Very rewarding."

"Indeed it is."

A crack of thunder followed by a slash of bright lightning brought both their heads up. For a moment the town lit up like a Fourth of July fireworks display. Then, just as quickly, gloom settled back in. The sound of running footsteps echoed close behind the thunder. A young boy and a woman, both soaked and mud-splattered, careened around the side of the depot. The sound of their voices and exuberant laughter rang out through the downpour.

"I won, I won," the boy exclaimed, his face shining, his eyes gleaming. Water streamed off his drenched head. His hair, flattened against his skull, was the color of strong coffee. He seemed oblivious to his saturated condition.

"I concede," the woman said, her hand over her heart. Her damp cape swirled around her body, and fell off her head as she bent at the knees, obviously trying to catch her breath. "Michael, you're quite a runner."

"Trixianna!"

She looked up. "Georgette?"

A cry of joy bubbled from Georgette's lips. She leapt to her feet and despite the mud and water-soaked clothing of the other woman, threw her arms around

271

her and hugged her tight. "I'm so, so sorry for saying those horrible things to you."

"No, no, it's all right. I should be sorry."

Georgette hiccuped, fighting tears. "It was all my fault. I was a featherbrain for even thinking you and Jonathan could, that you could—" She gulped hard. "You must hate me."

One tear fell down Trixianna's cheek. "I could never hate you. I love you so much. Where is Jonathan, anyway?"

Georgette's face brightened. "He went looking for you."

"For me? In this downpour?" She turned a mischievous grin on Georgette. "He won't be having any luck now, will he?"

They stared at each other, their lips twitching with amusement. Soon they let out great peals of laughter. Both women had tears streaming down their faces, half laughing, half sobbing. They clutched each other, oblivious to the rain, their arms around each other, their faces glowing.

Maggie didn't need to be told that this was the mysterious, missing sister. She and Georgette were mirror images of each other, right down to the freckles on their noses. They had identical bright green eyes and auburn hair that refused to be tamed no matter how many pins they undoubtedly used. Right now, two fiery redheads were having a reunion the likes of which Maggie had never seen. They obviously loved each other.

But how on God's green earth this sister could be mistaken for Mad Maggie West was beyond Maggie's ken. Maggie had a beak to be proud of. These two little missies had cute little buttons in the middle of their faces, hardly worthy of being called noses. And that hair, why, it was curly as a pig's tail. Maggie's hair was lighter red, what she referred to as coral. Straight as the barrel of her Winchester rifle, it hung down to her waist. But by damn, when she put her hair up on her head, it stayed there.

This was a downright insulting how-do-you-do. The Grand Fork sheriff must be either dead from the neck up or blind as a bat. Maggie almost had a notion to throw off her disguise and come clean. Almost. Good sense, and a wish to live past her twenty-fifth birthday, prevailed. She watched the loving sisters with a skeptical eye. Trying to see the resemblance proved impossible. She and these women looked nothing alike. Absolutely, positively, nothing alike.

Trixianna, swept up in her exuberant reunion with Georgette, initially failed to see the nun sitting on the depot bench. When she finally did notice the quiet woman, she stopped dead in her tracks.

Why, Trixianna thought to herself, I must look positively irreverent. And what a sight she was making of herself. Racing young Michael Perry through the muddy streets of Grand Fork had been foolish, but such fun. Her hair had come loose from its chignon, pins flying about in every direction. But now that she'd calmed down, she realized how truly terrible she must look. She glanced down at her skirt. The muddy hem that she'd dragged through the streets looked the worse for wear. In fact, Trixianna doubted that an overnight soaking in lye soap would clean it.

She came to stand in front of the sober-garbed woman. "I do apologize, Sister. Michael and I were racing to the depot to see who was here to see me and

I completely forgot myself. I was just so anxious to see if it was Georgette and Jonathan."

Georgette came to stand beside Trixianna. She plopped down on the bench beside the nun and clasped the women's hand to her breast. "We don't ordinarily act like such wild hooligans. Truly. In case you haven't guessed already, this is my sister, Trixianna Lawless. Trixianna, this is Sister Mary Margaret, who we met on the train."

With an obliging, cheerful expression on her features, the nun disengaged her hand from Georgette's and surreptitiously wiped it against her skirt. Her lips turned up in a thin-lipped smile. "Very nice to make your acquaintance, dear. But there's no need to apologize. Your exuberance is quite refreshing."

Trixianna, still trying to understand the odd gesture the sister had made, hesitated a moment before replying. "Why, thank you." Trixanna leaned closer. "You know, you look kind of familiar to me."

The woman chuckled, then ducked her head. Then her head bobbed up again, a twinkle in her eye. "I'd say we all look familiar. Have you ever seen so many green-eyed redheaded women in all your days?"

Trixianna glanced at Georgette, who was staring at her. She turned to look at the nun, who was studying Georgette. Three heads swiveled in an effort to inspect each other at close range.

"Why, look here," Michael exclaimed, all but forgotten in the mayhem. "You all could have come from the same acorn."

Georgette giggled. Trixianna couldn't help but laugh also. When the nun hooted in a most unsisterly-like manner, all heads turned her way.

"Golly," Michael mumbled. "Did I say something funny?"

Trixianna patted the boy's head. "Why, it's just—"

"What the hell is going on here?"

Trixianna whirled at the sound of Chance's voice, and took a step toward him, a smile on her lips. Then she saw the frown on his face, and her smile faded. She backed away, confused by the odd expression in his pale blue eyes and the stiff set of his shoulders.

Where was the gentle, patient lover of the previous night? Where was the Chance she admired and loved? What had happened to make him look at her that way? As if she was something to be avoided.

Before her stood a stranger.

He wore a black oilskin coat and his Stetson was pulled low over his eyes. With his hands on his hips, he'd pushed the coat to either side of his body. Trixianna saw he was dressed for his wedding in a black suit, a black waistcoat, a crisp white shirt and a black string tie. He wore a single white mum pinned to his lapel.

He reached inside his coat and pulled out a wrinkled telegram. He shook it in her face. "I just got this from the sheriff in Dena Valley, Donald Boyle."

"What does it say?"

"It says, *Trixianna*, that Mad Maggie West is definitely headed for my town. My town, dammit, and she's loaded for bear. Would you know anything about that?"

He didn't wait for her reply. "How about you two?" He glanced at Georgette, then at Sister Margaret. His head swiveled back to Georgette. He grimaced, then turned toward Trixianna. "Who are these women and

275

why in God's name do they all look like you?"

Something cautioned Trixianna not to lose her temper. She saw the look on Georgette's face, and knew her sister was close to losing her temper. She attempted a smile. "This is my sister, Georgette Lacina, and this is Sister Mary Margaret. They both got off the train today."

"Well, hell," muttered Chance. He swept his hat off his head and ran his hand through his hair. The recently combed locks now stood up in ebony clumps. He clapped the hat back on his head. "I've got to go. I'm just going to have to lock you up."

"Not again, Chance," Trixianna pleaded.

"Again?" Georgette exclaimed. "You locked her up before?"

"He thought I was the bank robber Mad Maggie West."

"Who does he think you are now?"

"I think," said Chance. He glanced meaningfully at Trixianna and Georgette. "That I'm going to have to lock you two up."

Georgette gasped. "You can't do that."

"Can't I?" He pulled out a pair of handcuffs.

"What about the nun?" Trixianna asked.

The question stopped Chance in his tracks. "What about her?"

"You believe in her innocence because of the way she looks. But what about *my* innocence? Don't you believe in that, too?"

He stared at all three women and shook his head. "Well, all right then. Forgive me, Sister."

He attached one end of the cuffs to Georgette's wrist and the other to Sister Mary Margaret's. They both complained in loud voices—Georgette using rather unladylike language and the nun invoking the name of the Lord and several saints that Trixianna had never even heard of. Chance ignored them. He took Trixianna by the wrist. He began herding them all down the street. When Trixianna balked and dug in her heels, he asked, "Would you let your sister go to jail in your stead?"

"No, of course not."

"You going to try to shoot me again?" he asked.

Georgettte's brows shot upward. "Again?"

Trixianna glanced at her sister. "It was an accident."

"Uh-huh. Maybe you'd like to toss your knife at my personal parts . . . again."

Georgette stopped on the boardwalk and stared at her sister. Her face turned the color of a ripe tomato. Sister Margaret had no choice. She stopped also. A smile played around the corners of her mouth. "You stabbed the sheriff?"

"It was an accident, too." Trixianna looked up at Chance and gave him a disgruntled look. "Why are you bringing this up now?"

"I just want you to remember that you're not all that innocent," he whispered for her ears alone.

"All right, I'm coming."

Chance shot a glance over his shoulder. "Michael Perry, go fetch your pa and bring him directly to the jail."

"Yes, sir." Wide-eyed and mouth hanging open, he scampered away.

Trixianna whispered in Chance's ear. "Sister Margaret is a nun, you know. Are you really going to incarcerate her, too?"

"I don't care if she's the pope and she's come all the way from Rome. Just look at her."

Trixianna did. Amusement flickered in the dark green eyes that met hers. "What do you see, Miss Lawless?" the nun asked in a matter-of-fact voice.

Chance answered for Trixianna. "She looks more like you than you do."

"What?" asked Georgette and Trixianna at the same time.

"I haven't got time to argue. I'm locking all three of you up so I can get to the church on time. Then we'll sort this out when the Dena Valley sheriff gets here." He glanced, somewhat shamefaced, at Sister Mary Margaret. "If I've abused your sensibilities, Sister, I apologize right now, but an hour or so in a jail cell never killed anybody that I heard tell."

"What about *my* sensibilities?" Georgette wailed. "And what about Jonathan?"

"Who's Jonathan?"

"Her husband," Trixianna explained. "He's gone looking for me."

"Well, he'll play hell finding you, won't he?"

"What kind of attitude is that, Sheriff?" Georgette leaned across Sister Margaret and glared at Chance. "We've done nothing wrong and still you're locking us up. How will Jonathan ever find us now?"

"Listen, I've got about five minutes to get to church. I haven't got time for any of this."

"You're the one getting married?" Sister Margaret asked.

"That's right." He shoved the door of the office open, and then ushered all three women into one jail cell. He removed the handcuffs, then took the key out of the top drawer of his desk and locked them in. Shoving the key in his pocket, he stood staring at them a minute. Fine lines of concentration deepened around his eyes. A muscle jumped at his jaw. "I reckon there will be hell to pay over this, but I'm at a loss about what to do. When I look at the three of you, my head plain aches. All I got to say is, that sheriff better know which one of you is Mad Maggie West."

"I'm not her, Chance," Trixianna whispered. A smile found its way through her uncertainty. "Please believe me."

"I do," he said with quiet emphasis. His eyes, brimming with tender determination, sought hers. "More than anything."

He cleared his throat and looked away. He hesitated at the threshold of the office door, his body still. He then cast one somber glance over his shoulder at Trixianna. "I've got to go."

Chance met Harvey Perry just outside his office door. "Harvey, I'm glad you're here. I need your help."

"I gathered as much from Michael."

"You know, I'm getting married in a bit."

"Chance, every last man, woman and child in Grand Fork knows that."

"Yeah, well, I've got a problem."

Harvey leaned toward Chance. "Did you really lock up a nun?"

Chance nodded. "Along with Trixianna Lawless and her sister. The thing is they all look like the woman on the wanted poster. I didn't know what else to do."

Harvey chewed on the inside on his lip and nodded. "I see your problem."

"The Dena Valley sheriff, Donald Boyle, is supposed to get to Grand Fork this afternoon. He's seen Mad Maggie, so he knows what she looks like. I just want you to make sure he comes to the church to get me after the ceremony—before he comes here. I've got enough explaining to do as it is." He shook his head. "If Aunt Tildy finds out, she'll skin my hide."

"Is Tildy back?"

"Oh, yeah, she was on the same train as the nun and Trixianna's sister. Oh, and if you see a strange man walking the streets, he's probably the sister's husband. Send him over to the jail, too."

"Is that all, Sheriff?"

"I hope so. Thanks for the help, Harvey. I owe you for this."

"Good luck."

"Uh-huh. See you later."

Strangely enough, Sister Mary Margaret sat down on the floor after Chance left, and within minutes was sound asleep. Trixianna marveled at the woman's calm in light of their combined strange circumstances.

Trixianna and Georgette shared a bemused expression. They sat down on the straw-filled mattress. Georgette took Trixianna's hand in hers. "I'm going to have a baby," she said.

"Huh?" Trixianna thought she'd misheard her sister. Her mind was still on Chance.

"Jonathan and me, we're going to have a baby."

"Why, my goodness, that's wonderful news." Trixianna leaned over and hugged her. "That's just wonderful." She then proceeded to burst into tears.

Georgette reached into her reticule and handed Trixianna her handkerchief. "What's wrong? I thought you'd be pleased to hear you're going to be an aunt."

Trixianna wiped the tears from her face, but couldn't stop the flow. "I am."

"Then why in heaven's sake are you crying?"

"Because I love him," Trixianna wailed.

"Who?"

"Chance Magrane."

"The sheriff?"

"Yes," Trixianna replied to her disbelieving sister.

"The man you shot and stabbed?"

"Those were accidents, Georgie." Fresh tears coursed down Trixianna's cheeks. She swiped ineffectually at them. "And he's marrying Fanny Fairfax at this very moment."

"Let me get this straight, Trixianna. You're in love with the sheriff but he's marrying someone else right now. Does he know how you feel?"

"Yes."

"But he's marrying another woman? How does he feel about you?"

"I think he loves me, too."

"What?" Georgette jumped to her feet and began pacing the length of the cell, deftly stepping around the sleeping nun. "If he loves you and you love him, why would he marry another woman?"

"He made a promise. Chance is a very honorable man. He asked Fanny to marry him and he won't break that promise."

"Even when he loves you?"

"Yes."

"That's just plain crazy. You must do something."

Trixianna wiped the tears from her eyes. Determination welled up from deep inside her. "You're absolutely right, and I know just what it is." She grabbed her reticule from the cot where she'd tossed it earlier. She began shuffling through the contents. "I believe I have the key."

Georgette stopped pacing. She leaned over and peeked into Trixianna's bag. "The key to what?"

"The key to my future." She pulled the heavy key out and held it aloft. "Ah-ha."

"Is that what I think it is?"

"I believe so."

"How'd you get that?"

"I didn't take it on purpose, it was an accident. I didn't know what it was until I saw Chance use the other one—it looks just like it."

Georgette's brows drew downward over her green eyes. A slow smile turned up the corners of her mouth. "You've had a lot of *accidents* since you've been in Grand Fork, haven't you?"

"Georgie, you have no idea."

Trixianna struggled to get the key in the outside lock. When she turned it, the mechanism gave a satisfactory click and the door swung open.

Chance took the front steps slowly and entered the church. He glanced around, shaking the chill off his body. As he suspected, the ladies had the church decked out in enough flowers and candles for a king's funeral—the smell was strong even in the foyer. And that was appropriate to how he felt when he entered the vestibule. As if he was attending his own funeral. He'd noticed on the walk over that his footsteps became shorter the closer he came to the building. The cold, soaking rain hadn't even bothered him.

Rider stood just inside the front door of the church, waiting. Dressed in a stiff new suit of clothes and new boots, clean-shaven and his mustache trimmed, he looked presentable, yet obviously anxious. He shuffled from one foot to the other, his hands clasped behind his back. He'd been running his hand through his hair, and it stood up on the back of his head. When he heard the door open, he jerked his chin up, then gave a relieved sigh. "About time, brother."

"Sorry. I had business to tend to."

"More important than your own wedding?"

"I thought so."

"You don't sound too convincing. Another five minutes and your future father-in-law would have been stalking the streets with a shotgun."

Chance shrugged out of his drenched coat and removed his Stetson. He hung both on a peg near the door. A mirror hung just inside the foyer. He glanced at it and finger-combed his unruly, damp hair. The mirror reflected the face of a grim man.

Rider came to his side. He stared over Chance's shoulder, his expression skeptical. "Are you sure you want to do this? You have the look of a man about to be hanged."

"I can't say for certain, but I think it's just a case of the mulligrubs, as Burnsey would say."

Rider snorted. "Never heard of any mulligrubs, but you look bad."

Chance jerked a thumb toward the sanctuary. "Full?"

Rider nodded. "And anxiously awaiting the groom."

"How late am I?"

"Only about ten minutes. I just introduced myself to Frank Fairfax, and promised you'd be here."

"All right then, let's do it." He started toward the door.

Rider grabbed Chance's sleeve. He stared at him, his

expression serious. "It's not too late to change your mind."

Chance sighed, then shook his head. "I can't do that to Fanny."

"You sure?"

Chance shrugged. "I've got no other choice."

"All right."

Rider yanked the door open. Every head in the place turned and stared.

Chance heard several sighs of obvious relief. He swallowed hard. With Rider's hand at his back, they walked up the aisle to where Fanny waited alone.

Heat worked its way up Chance's neck. The tips of his ears burned. He spotted Annie V. and her girls filling up the entire back pew. She winked at him when he caught her eye. His collar tightened until he could scarcely breathe. He tried to smile at Fanny, but was unable to meet her eyes. Equal parts of guilt and anger formed a cold knot in his stomach. He wished he could love her as much as he loved Trixianna.

Dressed in a pale lavender satin gown that dipped just above her full bosom and skimmed her rounded hips, she looked as lovely as he'd ever seen her. A veil of white covered her hair and hung down her back, where it puddled on the floor. Chance had seen the ocean once. The veil of white reminded him of that ocean where it washed again and again upon the shore and left a swelling mound of foam.

Someone had tied Bluebeard with a very short length of rope to the front pew, a lavender silk ribbon around his neck. Unable to chew on anything, the goat looked truly perturbed.

Eloise and Frank Fairfax, sitting in the front pew just out of Bluebeard's reach, glared at Chance as he passed. He chastised himself for wanting to vent his anger on them. Instead he turned toward the minister.

"Shall we begin?" the man said.

When Chance didn't reply, Rider nudged him in the ribs and said in a forced whisper, "Chance?"

Belatedly, Chance answered, "Uh, yes. Yes, sir. Go ahead."

Rider backed up and sat down beside the Fairfaxes. They glowered at him, but he just shrugged his shoulders and grinned. Bluebeard began stalking toward Rider. The smile left his face. He frowned and scooted down the pew.

Chance stepped up alongside Fanny and stood beside her. He clasped her warm right hand in his left. She squeezed his fingers, compelling him to look down at her. When he did, he was surprised to see her turn and give a superior smile to the townspeople. This wedding was what mattered most to her, not him, certainly not his feelings.

He felt as if he was just about to be reeled in—hook, line and sinker—her very own prized possession. Bile rose in his throat and threatened to choke off his air.

Chance swallowed hard, then nodded at the preacher to begin. He started with a short invocation. Chance bowed his head, but heard none of the actual words of the prayer or any of the meaning. His head ached so bad he imagined that Rider in the front row could actually hear the pounding.

Chance realized that the minister had stopped the prayer and begun the ceremony. He lifted his head and stared out a window beyond the altar. The rain trickled down the glass and disappeared. His heart thudded in his chest. Chance didn't listen to the droning monotone until the preacher said, "If anyone knows of any good reason why these two people should not marry, speak up now or forever hold your peace."

Love is lawless.
—Latin proverb

Chapter Sixteen

The double doors of the church flew open and banged against the wall. A blast of frigid wind and icy rain followed. The candles flickered, and blew out. The flower arrangements scattered mum petals and greenery up and down the center aisle. In unison, a mighty gasp rose among the startled wedding guests.

A disturbance began in the rear pews: people standing, gaping, complaining to the small horde of unwelcome interlopers who stood soaked and bedraggled at the back of the church. The furor advanced forward so that by the time it reached Chance, who by now had turned around and was gaping himself, the noise was deafening. One old man, known among the townspeople as Crazy Ike, stood up and uttered an obscenity that brought blushes to the faces of the women nearby. When he shook his fist skyward and called down the wrath of God, babies and toddlers wailed in fright. Grown men flushed beneath their stiff go-to-church collars, and women swooned.

"Please take your seats, ladies and gentlemen," the minister said. "And you new folks—please find a seat as well. Now, where was I? Oh, yes, does anyone know why this marriage ceremony shouldn't go on as planned?"

Several voices rang out among the din and confusion.

"In the name of Her Royal Highness, Queen Victoria of England, I wholeheartedly object to this entire ridiculous matter."

"For Trixianna's sake, so do I."

"Oh, my stars."

"I reckon I object, too, then . . . for my brother's sake."

"Well, hell."

"I object also." Tildy's voice rang out from her front-row pew.

"Honey, you shouldn't be marrying that uppity woman," Annie V. hollered, loud enough to be heard from her seat in the last pew.

"This is highly irregular, Sheriff Magrane," the minister said. "Highly irregular. I've never had anyone actually 'speak up' before, and now I've got half a dozen. I'm not quite sure how to proceed."

"Well, don't look to me 'cause I sure as heck don't either."

Trixianna's hair hung in limp, wet strands down her back, her gown was ruined beyond repair, and the whole population of Grand Fork was staring at her as if she, Trixianna Lawless, was an escaped lunatic. She wanted to die.

And now she probably would. This would be the reason they would hang her. Forget robbing a bank.

Forget shooting a bank teller. Forget all those other charges as well. Interrupting the mayor's daughter's wedding was undoubtedly punishable by death in Grand Fork, Kansas.

Trixianna watched Chance at the front of the church. He cocked his head to one side and squinted, peering around the room. He stood with his hands on his hips, emphasizing the length and power of his legs and his lean, rangy body. His broad shoulders shook.

Shook? Realization caught her off guard. He was doing his darnedest not to laugh outright. Maybe things weren't as bad as she'd originally thought.

A devilish look came into his pale blue eyes when his gaze met hers. "How?" he mouthed.

She held up the telltale key.

He shook his head and tried to hide a grin. She could have sworn that he winked at her. A flash of perplexed amusement crossed his face, then disappeared as he turned to speak in a quiet whisper with the disgruntled clergyman.

"Hold everything!" Burnsey pushed aside two widows, then apologized with a tip of his hat. He barreled down the aisle toward a perplexed Chance and a chagrined Fanny, who stood at the altar. Walking cane in hand, dressed in a black frock coat, top hat and white gloves, he looked more like the groom than . . . the groom.

Chance stepped aside as Burnsey rushed to Fanny's side. Burnsey removed his hat, then bowed to the preacher. He grasped Fanny's hand in his own. In a strong voice, he declared, "I love this woman."

Eloise Fairfax, mother of the bride, apparently heard the declaration of love. She gasped, then fell into a stone-cold faint. She slid from the pew and dropped to the floor before her husband could catch her. Frank kneeled on the floor and patted her cheek in an effort to revive her. Trixianna noticed that he kept one eye on the circuslike spectacle before him, though.

Fanny flushed. Her voice quivered when she said, "But Alistair, you're a common drunkard."

"Alistair?" Chance repeated, brows raised.

Burnsey nodded. "Alistair Burns, sixth Viscount of Huxford, to be correct, sir." He turned back to Fanny, his voice soft as he said, "But I'm an extremely rich drunkard."

"You are?" squeaked Fanny. "I didn't know that. But you know it was never the money."

"Assuredly." He bent to one knee and kissed the hand he still held in his. "I promise that if you'll accept my offer of wedlock, from this day forward I'll do everything I can to stop my excesses."

Sitting next to the aisle, Annie V. plucked a handful of Trixianna's soggy skirt and yanked. Trixianna glanced down into warm, smiling eyes. Beyond Annie V. sat the other girls, with equal expressions of laughter and surprise on their worn faces.

"You go get that man right now, honey. You love him and he, by God, loves you." She pointed her finger at Chance. "Go grab yourself some happiness."

Trixianna took Georgette's hand in her own shaking fingers and pulled her along as she moved down the aisle. She loved Chance but how could she tell him in front of the whole town? She'd have to find a way.

She stopped at the front pew, her gaze on Burnsey and Fanny. Fanny's big brown eyes, intent on Burnsey's bent head, glowed like twin copper pennies in her face. She stared at him with such obvious love that it brought tears to Trixianna's eyes. She turned her gaze toward Chance, who looked confused.

"What the hell are you doing, Burnsey?" Chance demanded, "proposing here . . . and why now? Hell, half of Grand Fork is gussied up and sitting in these pews. If you wanted to marry her, what have you been waiting for?"

"Unless I'm mistaken, Sherriff, she was engaged to you when I came to town."

"And?"

Burnsey rose to his full height, a good bit shorter than Chance, and with a belligerent stare, gazed up at the man. He sniffed, then tapped his cane against Chance's calf. "It would have been quite ungentlemanly to interfere."

Chance pushed the cane away. The answer seemed to amuse him, for a teasing glint glittered in his eyes. "Ungentlemanly, huh? What about now?"

Georgette stepped forward, dragging Trixianna alongside behind her. "May I say something here?"

Everyone in the church, including Burnsey, Chance, the minister and Fanny, all turned to stare at Trixianna's sister. Georgette squeezed Trixianna's fingers, then gave her a warm smile, which she then turned on the waiting assemblage.

"You don't know me, but I guess you can tell by looking that I'm Trixianna's sister. She's explained all that has happened since she's lived here." She gazed out over the congregation. "I'd say it was quite a lot."

Several people tittered, and Trixianna heard a few loud guffaws from some of the more outspoken persons present.

"Anyway, the thing is, she's not a bank robber, or anything else the sheriff says she is. She's just the best sister anyone could ever ask for." She put her arm around Trixianna's waist and hugged her.

A lump formed in Trixianna's throat. The shadow that had entered her heart when she and Georgette had had their falling out now lifted. She held back tears of joy.

"What does this have to do with the wedding proceeding as scheduled, young lady?" asked the minister.

"I'm getting to that, sir." Georgette glanced at Chance, who returned her serious, knowing look with a contagious smile all his own. Georgette smiled back. "My sister loves the sheriff."

"And Chance loves her," added Rider. He ambled over to where a red-faced Chance stood. "Don'tcha, big brother?"

"I'm confused," confessed the minster. He scratched the top of his balding pate.

"Well, hell."

"No swearing in church, Sheriff."

Chance ran a hand through his already mussed hair. "Well, hell, Parson, if this doesn't call for some good old-fashioned cussing, I don't know what does."

The minister frowned at Chance before continuing. "Let me get this straight. The English fellow loves Fanny, and Chance loves this woman's sister. So why are Chance and Fanny the ones getting married?" He leaned down and whispered to Fanny, "Whom do you love, Miss Fairfax?"

She blushed scarlet. "I do love Alistair."

The minister lost his control. Close to shouting, he bellowed in an unpious tone of voice, "Then why in blue blazes are you marrying the sheriff?"

Fanny's eyes widened and, if possible, her blush

deepened. She stuttered, and stammered, but nothing came out except gibberish. Burnsey glared at the minister, then threw a comforting arm around Fanny's shoulder. She moved closer to him, her eyes shining with a loving, thankful glow.

"Why didn't you say something, Fanny?" Chance asked. He leaned down to peer into her face. "I thought this was what you wanted."

"It was," she said.

Burnsey slapped Chance on the shoulder. "I never meant for this to happen. We just took to each other the first time we met, didn't we, Fanny love?"

Fanny nodded.

"That's neither here nor there," Chance said. "I just can't believe that Fanny would go ahead and marry me if she loved you."

"I accepted your proposal of marriage," Fanny said.

Chance frowned. "As I recollect, *you* proposed to me."

"You did?" Burnsey beamed at his beloved. "Why, Fanny, you forward woman, you."

Fanny ducked her head. "I didn't want to humiliate Chance by backing out at the last minute."

Chance stared at her, baffled. "You would have gone through with this farce of a marriage because you didn't want to humiliate *me?*"

"Truth to tell, I felt it was my duty."

Burnsey touched Chance on the shoulder. "Let's just forget this whole unfortunate incident. If you don't mind, I'd like a word in private with Fanny. I want to tell her how I'll change my ways and become the man she wants."

"From now on, just try staying out of the saloons,

Burnsey," Chance muttered. "That seems to be where you get into trouble."

Burnsey nodded his agreement. "Yes, sir, Chance. You're absolutely right."

He walked Fanny back down the aisle, their heads bent in conversation, oblivious to the shocked stares that followed them. The door swung shut behind them as they disappeared into the foyer.

Not thirty seconds later, Harvey Perry burst through the door and ran up to Chance. "Sheriff! Come quick," he whispered in his ear. "Someone's robbing the bank!"

For an instant Chance searched Trixianna's face. Then he sprinted down the aisle and out of the church.

Mad Maggie West thought her luck couldn't get much better. Not only had the twin sister, Trixianna, had the key to the jail cell, but she hadn't even questioned why Sister Mary Margaret wasn't going to accompany them to the church. Trixianna had accepted her regrets without hesitation.

The stupid woman had believed Maggie's concocted story about resting at the hotel until the sheriff could conduct her home. Oh, my, wouldn't the sheriff be surprised when he left the church? And to sweeten the pot, almost every living soul was at that wedding.

Maggie hurried down the empty boardwalk, her hands inside the sleeves of her habit, her head bent against the rain. She stopped in front of the bank. Someone had posted a sign on the door. *Back at four, at the sheriff's wedding.*

"Excuse me, Sister."

Maggie's heart momentarily ceased to pump as she whirled to find the young man from the train standing behind her. It started up again when she realized he wasn't the law. "Yes?"

"Remember me? I'm Jonathan Lacina."

At her nod, he continued. "This sounds crazy, I know, but I've been wandering this town for almost an hour and I can't find a single living soul. All the shops are shuttered and closed. It's a regular ghost town."

"It is very quiet. But I understand there's a big wedding going on. I didn't leave your wife alone. Your sister-in-law showed up. They said they were going to the wedding. A friend of your sister-in-law's, I believe. I was exhausted, so I thought I'd try to find my own accommodations."

"I'm sorry. You must have gotten tired waiting for me to return."

"It wasn't a bother at all, young man."

"Thank you for saying that." He pointed down the street. "That looks like the church there. I'll just mosey on over unless there's something I can do for you."

"There's really no need, young man. I'm quite capable of taking care of myself."

"No offense intended, Sister."

Maggie patted his hand. "You just run off now and find that pretty little wife of yours."

He lifted his hat and smiled before turning down the boardwalk. "See you later then."

"Good-bye, Mr. Lacina." Maggie smiled, resisting the urge to swat his backside to get him moving. He was a fine-looking young man, although a bit stuffy for her taste. Still, she couldn't help but admire his attractive male body as he strode away.

A married man. Maggie, you should be ashamed of yourself.

Maggie grinned, and waited until he disappeared. Then she looked both ways down the street, and slipped inside the bank's locked doors with the help of a clever, criminal tool—a hairpin.

The vault stood open. Maggie had to stop herself from rubbing her hands together in glee. Like taking candy from a baby.

"Hey!"

Jonathan wanted to ignore the authoritative male voice and find his wife, but better sense prevailed. Georgette wasn't going anywhere.

He stopped and waited for the man to catch up. As he came nearer, Jonathan saw the star pinned to his vest. They were about the same age, but there was an enduring strength etched in the fine lines around the man's eyes and mouth. He turned weary, gray eyes on Jonathan and held out his hand. "Donald Boyle, sheriff in Dena Valley."

"Sir." Jonathan shook his gloved hand. "Jonathan Lacina."

"Do you live here?"

"No, sir."

"Would you mind telling me your business in Grand Fork?"

"Not at all. I'm here with my wife, Georgette, visiting her twin sister."

"And her name?"

"Trixianna Lawless."

He stroked his chin, regarding Jonathan carefully. "I see. When did you arrive?"

"About an hour ago. I left my wife with a nun at the train station and went on to see if I could find Trixianna myself. Funny thing about that nun, too, Sheriff, she and Georgette and Trixianna, why, they could have all been related they looked so much alike."

"Did they now?"

"I'll say. Anyway, I didn't want Georgette to have to walk all over town in this rain."

"Uh-huh."

"But so far, I haven't found any living soul, besides you, of course . . . and Sister Mary Margaret. She told me there's a wedding going on, so that was where I was headed."

"And this nun?"

"She'd stepped in the doorway of the bank, probably to get out of the rain."

"Holy Moses!" Sheriff Boyle hollered. He grabbed Jonathan's arm and swung him in the opposite direction. "You're coming with me, son. I believe we've got a bank robbery in progress."

"What the—?"

Trixianna watched with wonder as Fanny prepared to wed Burnsey. With Chance no longer the preferred groom, Fanny had decided to take Burnsey up on his offer of marriage. Immediately. After all, the church was already decorated and full of well-wishers, and the confused minister was willing. Why wait? Eloise Fairfax herself was relighting all the candles and straightening the flower arrangements.

"I just love weddings," Georgette whispered to Trixianna. They were seated in the last row of pews watching the shenanigans. "Don't you?"

"Ordinarily I do, but don't you think this one is a mite peculiar, Georgie?"

"I know, but Mr. Burnsey's declaration of love made

it so romantic. It was lovely. You don't mind if I stay and watch?"

"No, of course not, but I just can't stay. If I see Jonathan, I'll send him over. In the meantime, I'll just go pack my things. In all the confusion I think I can disappear, and we can be on the afternoon train home to Abilene."

Georgette cocked her head, then wrinkled her nose. "I understand. What about the sheriff?"

Trixianna sighed, her heart heavy in her breast. "He never said he loved me. He didn't even ask me to wait."

"But I saw the tenderness on his face when he looked at you. He cares a great deal."

"Enough to marry me?" Trixianna shook her head. "I don't think so. If he was willing to marry Fanny, and he didn't even love her, what does that say about me?" *Or about what we did together last night?* She refrained from mentioning that to Georgette, however.

"Maybe he just didn't feel it was appropriate to say anything to you considering he was already engaged. After all, what man uses normal logic anyway? He was taking Fanny to wife and that was that."

"That was that." Trixianna sighed again and turned to go. "Enjoy the wedding. I'm going home to pack."

The rain hadn't stopped. It just continued to fall from the sky in a dismal downpour. In her rush to leave the church, Trixianna had forgotten her cape. Wet, cold, and disheartened, she hardly noticed as she dashed across town toward Chance's home.

She pulled the door open, welcome warmth enveloping her near-frozen body. Angel met her with a meow, curling his body around her leg. She picked up the cat and hugged his soothing white fur against her face. "I'll bet you're hungry. I'm sorry I forgot you this morning. Other things on my mind . . ."

She poured him a saucer of milk, then sliced off a bit of leftover roast chicken and handed it to him. With tail twitching, he stalked off to find a quiet place to eat.

"I really am sorry I neglected you," she muttered as she watched him stalk away. "It's not been a very good day."

In her room, Trixianna pulled her dress off over her head and untied her petticoat, then dropped it onto the floor. She caught her reflection in the mirror. Startled by the image, she leaned closer and stared.

Spotted with dirt, her cheeks and nose looked like they had grown a dozen new freckles. Mud stained her hair, too. It hung in tired russet-and-brown ringlets down her back and into her eyes. She choked back a tired laugh. Shaking her head, she wandered back to the kitchen, dressed only in her pink silk chemise and drawers, to heat water to wash her hair. She certainly couldn't go out in public looking like this. As she pumped water into the kettle, she smiled, remembering another time when she'd been concerned about her appearance. . . .

Chance had lain flat on his back in her parlor bleeding on her braided rug from a gunshot she'd inflicted. From this less-than-advantageous position, he'd arrested her. But before she'd left the house she'd insisted on fetching her bonnet. Chance may have hauled her off to jail after she'd shot him, but she'd made sure she saw to the proprieties first. A lady didn't go out on the streets without something covering her head.

Now look at her. Racing through the muddy streets in the rain with young boys, traipsing around town in a ruined dress with hair that looked like it belonged on a ragamuffin's head. And she didn't care. She actually found it laughable.

She set the kettle on the stove, then sat down at the kitchen table and suppressed a giggle.

"What's the joke?"

At the sound of Chance's familiar voice, Trixianna jumped to her feet. He'd come in by the back porch, so he was out of sight. She heard him grunt as he tried to remove his boots. It sounded as if he was hopping from one foot to the other. One boot thudded on the floor, followed by the other. Unfortunately, she couldn't get to her room without passing him. She stood rooted to the spot.

"You'll be happy to know we just arrested the real Mad Maggie West when she tried to rob the bank. She was dressed as a nun."

"What!"

"Yup. Damn good disguise, too. Your brother-in-law even helped out by pulling a knife on her as she tried to make her escape. Kept it in his boot." His eyebrows shot up as he smiled at Trixianna. "He'd make a right jim-dandy lawman. The Dena Valley sheriff, Boyle, is taking her back right now. Your sister and brother-in-law are at the hotel. . . ."

Chance sauntered into the kitchen in his socks. He tossed his hat onto the table, then turned his gaze toward her and stared. His eyes widened when he saw how she was dressed . . . or rather, undressed.

Trixianna attempted to cover herself as she dashed around the table to escape his searching gaze. Chance had other ideas. He reached out and grabbed her arm. "Whoa there."

"Chance," she wailed. "I'm not dressed."

"I noticed," he drawled. A grin played about the corners of his twinkling blue eyes. He pulled her into his arms, then tipped her chin up with his thumb. Peering at her intently, he asked, "What are you doing?"

"Washing my hair."

He glanced at the stove and the kettle, which wasn't even beginning to boil, because she hadn't thrown any wood in. "Did you forget something?" he whispered in her ear.

Trixianna forgot her hair, her bedraggled condition, everything but the man who held her in his arms. In Chance's snug embrace her nipples hardened, pressed against his wet shirt. Her skin tingled. She shivered. "You're all wet."

He looked her in the eye, a playful glint in his expression. "So I am."

He didn't release her. His mouth twitched with amusement. "You know," he murmured. His voice lowered to a low, languid drawl. He dropped a kiss on her nose. "You look good enough to eat."

Trixianna gasped. The slow-smoldering flame she saw in his eyes heightened her awareness of his hard body against the length of her nearly naked one. She swallowed hard.

"Do you know what else I'm thinking?" he asked.

"That I'm covered in mud and smell like a pigsty?"

"No, not quite." One of his hands moved down her back, pushed her chemise up and clasped her silk-clad bottom. He pulled her up against him. His arousal pressed against her stomach. "I'm thinking that you have the fanciest drawers this side of the Mississippi . . . and how much I'd like to see you out of them."

Trixianna shoved against Chance's chest and withdrew from his arms. His eyes widened.

Desire raced through her body. Maddened at her inability to control her desire where Chance was concerned, she tossed her hair over her shoulder and marched to the stove. She had it stacked with wood and lit before Chance had drawn a breath. She turned back to him, her hands on her hips. He stood watching her, a critical squint in his eye. "You shouldn't parade around like that," he said. "Rider might walk through that door any minute."

"You listen here, *Mr. Magrane.* I am not parading around. You have no right to tell me what I can or cannot do. I'm no longer under arrest, am I?"

"Well, no, but—"

"So I can do whatever I damn well please."

He raked his fingers through his hair. "Except talk like that."

"Oh, pooh. First, I'm going to wash my hair because it's a muddy mess."

He grinned. "It is that."

"And then I'm leaving."

He frowned, his black brows drawn together. "Leaving for where?"

"Abilene, of course."

"You can't do that," he protested. He took a step forward.

She held out a hand to ward him off. "Don't come any closer."

"I'll do whatever I damn well please, Miss Lawless." He headed toward her, walking slowly. "And what I damn well please is to take you in my arms and kiss your socks off."

"I'm not wearing any."

He took a step closer. "Then I've got a good start."

"Chance, we need to talk."

"Later," he growled. "Right now what I've got to say doesn't need words."

"Wait."

"Trixianna," he coaxed, his voice as soft as butter warmed in the sun. He held his hands out palms up. His intense blue eyes seemed to stroke her with an eager, compelling force she was unable to deny. "Please."

She took a step toward him.

Unwelcome excitement surged through her. She stared at his face . . . wanting just to touch him; to trace his brows, feel the roughness of his beard, his cheekbones, the curve of his ear. God, how she loved this man.

She needed to keep her distance, though. Her love for Chance, deep and intensely overwhelming, threatened to overcome her common sense. She could see that he wanted her. If nothing else, the bulge in his trousers proved that. But did he love her? He had yet to say so. Did he trust her? She didn't know. Most important of all, did he want her for his life's partner? He hadn't said that, either.

"Did you know Fanny and Burnsey got married today?" she said.

He took another step. "I don't care."

Trixianna backed up. Her backside brushed up against the cupboard. "When I left, Bluebeard was eating all the flowers and chewing on Burnsey's cane."

"I always hated that goat."

"Chance, I—"

He paced forward and bent over Trixianna, one arm on either side of her, pinning her in front of him. He tilted his head until their noses almost touched. "I don't care about Fanny, or Burnsey, or that blasted goat. I care about you."

His nearness stole her breath away. Heat radiated off him in waves. His pale blue eyes captivated her with an eager, yet gentle, sparkle. And he smelled so wonderful—leather warmed from his skin, his own distinctive male scent, and always, always spearmint. "Me?" she said.

"You. With mud spattered on your face, dried muck all through your hair and dressed, or should I say undressed, in the most unbelievable drawers in all of God's creation."

"What are you saying, Chance?"

"You've brought fun back into my dull old life. Me, my life. Can you credit it? Chance old-reliable-always-doing-his-job Magrane. I almost married a woman I didn't love—hell, I didn't even like her all that much—because I thought I was doing the right thing, the honorable thing."

"I—"

He placed a finger to her lips. "Hush, I'm not finished, and this isn't easy. You've changed me, Trixianna. And I don't mean by shooting me, stabbing me, nearly drowning me—"

Trixianna ducked her head. He lifted it up with his finger. "I'm just teasing, honey. Honest. You are the very best part of me."

She stared into his beloved face, wanting to believe him with all her heart.

"The very best part. And you're not getting away

from me now. Even if I have to lock you back up in that jail cell."

She gave him an exasperated look.

He smiled, a slow, gentle smile. "I'm asking you to be my wife. Should I go down on one knee and declare my love for all eternity?"

"Do you?" she asked, around the lump in her throat.

A look of confusion crossed his face. "Do I what?"

"Do you love me?"

"Well, hell. Isn't that what I've been saying for the last few minutes? I know I'm nervous, but I thought I was at least making sense."

"You are making sense, Chance. I just want to hear you say it."

"Trixianna Lawless, I love you."

Joy welled up inside her and she whooped aloud as it bubbled over. She threw her arms around his neck and squeezed with all her might.

"I guess that was clear enough. Can I kiss you now?"

"I thought you'd never ask."

He gave her a beguiling grin. "You realize, though, that dressed in your drawers like that, I can't be responsible for what might happen next."

"I'll take my chances."

By many a happy accident.
—*Thomas Middleton, English dramatist*

Epilogue

One Month Later . . .

"I now pronounce you husband and wife. You may kiss the bride."

Chance took Trixianna's face in his hands. He caressed both cheeks with the pads of his thumbs. Then he smiled before placing a kiss on the tip of her nose. At her surprised expression, he leaned close and whispered for her ear only, "I fell in love with your freckles first, then the rest of you. Besides, I'd rather wait for a more private place to kiss you the way I want to."

Trixianna's face blushed a rosy hue. Chance chuckled. God, how he loved this woman. For the wedding, she'd worn her hair loose just to please him. Throughout the ceremony, it had taken all his willpower not to plunge his hands into those wild, rust-colored tresses and kiss her senseless.

Dressed in an inappropriate, but sexy as hell, low-cut green velvet dress he'd ridden to Wichita and picked out himself, she was the culmination of all his dreams. And now she was all his. He couldn't wait to get her alone.

After the near-disaster of the last wedding in Grand Fork, they'd decided on a quiet ceremony with just Rider and the minister present. Which was fine with Chance. The gown was too low-cut for anyone else's curious eyes anyway. The parson, no matter how pious, was still a man, and that was bad enough. At least Rider was family.

Chance felt a nudge in his ribs. He turned to find Rider grinning at him. "Say, big brother, are you gonna let the rest of us kiss the bride, too?"

"No," growled Chance. "Keep your hands to yourself."

Rider's eyes danced with merriment. "I promise I won't touch her."

"The answer is still no."

Rider winked at Trixianna.

Chance scowled at him, irked by the sudden stab of unreasonable jealousy.

"Fine," Rider said. "I'll just wait until your back is turned. Then it won't be a friendly peck either. I'll give her a kiss that'll curl her toes."

"You just try it and I'll toss your sorry butt in jail."

"What, again?"

Chance heard the teasing quality in Rider's voice. "Sorry. I guess I'm a little jealous."

Rider quirked a brow. "A little? Ha!" He patted Chance on the back, then leaned over to place a kiss on Trixianna's cheek. "Sweetheart, it's been a mighty big pleasure getting to know you these past few days, and I'm sure gonna miss those sweet treats of yours. A man could grow to like that."

"Why, thank you, Rider."

"One more thing, try not to torment Chance too much . . . unless he's got it coming, of course." Despite Chance's warning glance, Rider gave Trixianna a hug.

Chance grabbed his shoulder and spun him around. "You going someplace?"

"Yep. I got a few amends to make over to Drover."

Chance blew out his breath.

"All right, but be careful, and for God's sake, stay out of trouble."

Rider started down the aisle, then called over his shoulder, "Don't worry, I'm a big boy now."

"That's exactly what worries me."

Rider just laughed. "Take care, Trixianna."

"You, too, Rider."

"Don't let Chance get too fat with that cooking of yours."

Trixianna giggled. "I won't." She turned to Chance. "Where is Rider going?"

"He's going back to our hometown, Drover."

They heard Rider whistling as the outside door slammed shut.

"Watch your backside," Chance called out. Turning around to smile at his new wife, he took her hand and placed it on his arm. "What do you say, Mrs. Magrane, about you and me finding a big, warm bed and—"

"Chance!"

He glanced at the minister. The man had turned crimson. His Adam's apple bobbed as he tried to swallow his embarrassment.

"Sorry. I just can't wait to get my bride alone."

"Please, Sheriff, don't tell me about it." Huffing like a steam engine going uphill, he turned on his heel and escaped through the back door of the church.

"Alone at last," Chance murmured. He allowed his gaze to roam over Trixianna's exposed neck and the swell of her high, rounded breasts, noting for the first time that she had more freckles that he'd missed in their previous lovemaking. He memorized each and every location, and wondered where else they might be discovered on her body. His own body thrummed to life with that enticing thought.

"Chance?"

Trixianna's questioning voice brought his lust down a bit. He pulled her into the circle of his arms, then kissed her with his eyes, then his lips. With careful deliberation, he moved his mouth over hers, demanding a response. She returned the kiss with all the abandon he'd grown to love about her. When he lifted his head, they were both panting.

"Let's get the hell out of here," he croaked in a tight whisper. Thank goodness she had no idea she could bring him to his knees just by being near her. She already had him wrapped around her little finger. She just didn't know it yet.

He turned quickly and caught his boot on the hem of her skirt. She backed away, trying to free the material, and Chance lost his balance.

He threw out a hand to catch his fall, but missed the back of the pew. He fell, cracking his head on the armrest. The thud resounded in the empty building like a distant clap of thunder.

Chance lurched to the side as he tried to right himself. Then his eyes rolled back in his head. He opened his mouth, muttered, "Well, hell—" and pitched forward at Trixianna's feet like a felled oak tree.

"Oh, my stars." She knelt down beside Chance. "Here we go again."

SONYA BIRMINGHAM

Song of the Lark

When the beautiful wisp of a mountain girl walks through his front door, Stephen Wentworth knows there is some kind of mistake. The flame-haired beauty in trousers is not the nanny he envisions for his mute son Tad. But one glance from Jubilee Jones's emerald eyes, and the widower's icy heart melts and his blood warms. Can her mountain magic soften Stephen's hardened heart, or will their love be lost in the breeze, like the song of the lark?

___4393-9 $5.50 US/$6.50 CAN

Dorchester Publishing Co., Inc.
P.O. Box 6640
Wayne, PA 19087-8640

Please add $1.75 for shipping and handling for the first book and $.50 for each book thereafter. NY, NYC, and PA residents, please add appropriate sales tax. No cash, stamps, or C.O.D.s. All orders shipped within 6 weeks via postal service book rate. Canadian orders require $2.00 extra postage and must be paid in U.S. dollars through a U.S. banking facility.

Name_____
Address_____
City_____ State_____ Zip_____
I have enclosed $_____ in payment for the checked book(s).
Payment <u>must</u> accompany all orders. ☐ Please send a free catalog.
CHECK OUT OUR WEBSITE! www.dorchesterpub.com

Elaine Fox
Untamed Angel

Bestselling Author of *Hand & Heart of a Soldier*

With a name that belies his true nature, Joshua Angell was born for deception. So when sophisticated and proper Ava Moreland first sees the sexy drifter in a desolate Missouri jail, she knows he is the one to save her sister from a ruined reputation and a fatherless child. But she will need Angell to fool New York society into thinking he is the ideal husband—and only Ava can teach him how. But what start as simple lessons in etiquette and speech soon become smoldering lessons in love. And as the beautiful socialite's feelings for Angell deepen, so does her passion—and finally she knows she will never be satisfied until she, and no other, claims him as her very own...untamed angel.

___4274-6 $4.99 US/$5.99 CAN

Dorchester Publishing Co., Inc.
P.O. Box 6640
Wayne, PA 19087-8640

LEIGH GREENWOOD'S
SEVEN BRIDES
Laurel

Although Hen Randolph is the perfect choice for a sheriff in the Arizona Territory, he is no one's idea of a model husband. After the trail-weary cowboy breaks free from his six rough-and-ready brothers, he isn't about to start a family of his own. Then a beauty with a tarnished reputation catches his eye and the thought of taking a wife arouses him as never before.

But Laurel Blackthorne has been hurt too often to trust any man—least of all one she considers a ruthless, coldhearted gunslinger. Not until Hen proves that drawing quickly and shooting true aren't his only assets will she give him her heart and take her place as the newest bride to tame a Randolph's heart.

_3744-0 $5.99 US/$6.99 CAN

Jade

NORAH HESS

BESTSELLING AUTHOR OF
BLAZE

Kane Roemer heads up into the Wyoming mountains hell-bent on fulfilling his heart's desire. There the rugged horseman falls in love with a white stallion that has no equal anywhere in the West. But Kane has to use his considerable charms to gentle a beautiful spitfire who claims the animal as her own. Jade Farrow will be damned if she'll give up her beloved horse without a fight. But then a sudden blizzard traps Jade with her sworn enemy, and she discovers that the only way to true bliss is to rope, corral, and brand Kane with her unbridled passion.

___4310-6 $5.99 US/$6.99 CAN

SEVEN BRIDES
LEIGH GREENWOOD

Iris

Rough and ready as any of the Randolph boys, Monty bristles under his eldest brother's tight rein. All he wants is to light out from Texas for a new beginning. And Iris Richmond has to get her livestock to Wyoming's open ranges before rustlers wipe her out. Monty is heading that way, but the bullheaded wrangler flat out refuses to help her. Never one to take no for an answer, Iris saddles up to coax, rope, and tame the ornery cowboy she's always desired.

___4175-8 $5.99 US/$6.99 CAN

The Bestselling Author of *Tennessee Moon*

Hunter. Unforgiving and unsmiling, the arrogant lawman
is the last person Blaze Adlington wants to see when her
covered wagon pulls into Fort Bridger. The beautiful orphan
is desperately trying to make a new life for herself in the
wilds of Wyoming. But now she is face-to-face with the man
who'd hunted down her father's outlaw band.

Blaze. She is the kind of woman who sets a man's senses
ablaze, the kind who will only trample his wounded heart.
Still, his pressing need for a housekeeper to care for his
motherless little girl forces him to approach her. Then,
against all reason, he begins to hope that this is the woman
who can warm his empty home, heat his racing blood and
light up his lonely life.

__4222-3 $5.99 US/$6.99 CAN

Dorchester Publishing Co., Inc.
P.O. Box 6640
Wayne, PA 19087-8640

Please add $1.75 for shipping and handling for the first book and
$.50 for each book thereafter. NY, NYC, and PA residents,
please add appropriate sales tax. No cash, stamps, or C.O.D.s. All
orders shipped within 6 weeks via postal service book rate.
Canadian orders require $2.00 extra postage and must be paid in
U.S. dollars through a U.S. banking facility.

Name_____
Address_____
City_____State_____Zip_____
I have enclosed $_____ in payment for the checked book(s).
Payment <u>must</u> accompany all orders. ☐ Please send a free catalog.

"Norah Hess not only overwhelms you with characters who seem to be breathing right next to you, she transports you into their world!"
—*Romantic Times*

Wade Magallen leads the life of a devil-may-care bachelor until Storm Roemer tames his wild heart and calms his hotheaded ways. But a devastating secret makes him send away the most breathtaking girl in Wyoming—and with her, his one chance at happiness.

As gentle as a breeze, yet as strong willed a gale, Storm returns to Laramie after years of trying to forget Wade. One look at the handsome cowboy unleashes a torrent of longing she can't deny, no matter what obstacle stands between them. Storm only has to decide if she'll win Wade back with a love as sweet as summer rain—or a whirlwind of passion that will leave him begging for more.

_3672-X $4.99 US/$5.99 CAN